GUNBATTLE
IN DEXTER TOWN

"Give me a fair shake, Deke," Travers begged.

"Fair shake, hell! I'll give you three in the gut, you sonofabitch! I'll blow—"

"Over here first, Deke," said Lash Lashtrow from in back of Vennis.

Deke Vennis spun and fired instantly, his .44 jetting orange, but Lash had already lined home a slug that shattered Vennis's right shoulder. Snake-quick, Vennis went for his other gun, only to go reeling backward as a gunflame stabbed into his left side.

"Throw him over your saddle, Travers," said Lashtrow, whistling for his sorrel. "We gotta clear town before the King's clan gets moving."

Also in the LASHTROW Series:

RIO GRANDE RIPTIDE

CRUSADE
ON THE CHISHOLM

Roe Richmond

LEISURE BOOKS  **NEW YORK CITY**

For Henry Jurras,
a great pardner
and
a fine sports writer.

A LEISURE BOOK

Published by

Dorchester Publishing Co., Inc.
6 East 39th Street
New York, NY 10016

Printed in the United States of America

Epitaph for a town marshal and former Ranger: "He took plenty of 'em with him."

—Milton Travers
Texas, 1878

1

Salt Creek Reunion

Lashtrow drew rein on the escarpment overlooking the settlement of Salt Creek, and stroked the golden mane of the big sorrel under him. He had ridden some distance out of his way to reach this objective and see two old friends: Tonk Hiller and Anse Amidon. It occurred to Lashtrow, with a touch of sadness, that there were not many men left, outside of the Rangers, whom he would go out of his way to visit. They had died or gone away or disappointed him in various manners. Tonk Hiller, the town marshal, and Anse Amidon, the owner of Andiron Ranch, were among the remaining few who mattered.

The lamps of Salt Creek were burning orange and lemon in the mauve dusk, as Lashtrow drifted down the shale slope and jogged toward Main Street lined with false-fronted board-awninged buildings of adobe and wood. There was a light in the marshal's office, and he swung down to flip the reins over the hitch-rail and stretch the saddle cramps out of his lean rangy frame. Hesitating an instant at the door, Lashtrow was half-afraid he might find a stranger inside.

But it was Tonk Hiller's gaunt lined face behind the desk, lighting up with surprise and delight at the sight of the tall dusty Ranger. "Well for godsake, if it ain't Lash himself." He rose, a bit lopsidedly, and limped forward to shake hands, grinning and blinking. "Been quite a spell, boy."

"Too long, Tonk, too long by far." Lashtrow gripped the gnarled hand and smiled back, his own eyeballs smarting. "Good to see you, pardner."

"Got a bottle here I been saving. Cut the dust a little, hey?" Tonk Hiller hauled out a chair, and hobbled back to lift a sealed quart and two clean glasses from a desk drawer. "How's things with the old regiment in Austin? Cap McKenna still running the show? Good old Cactus Bill."

"Salty as ever. Still threatening to retire. You know when that'll be, Tonk."

"Judgment Day—maybe. How about Fox Edley and Milt Travers?"

"Same hellers as ever. All the boys sent their best, Tonk. We sure felt bad when he heard about your wife. Abbie was a great little lady."

"Well, it ain't the same without her, Lash. But Tess done a good job keeping house for me, till she went away to school." Hiller refilled the glasses, accepted a thin cheroot, and they both lit up and settled back, comfortable and happy with one another, closer than words could say.

Lashtrow sipped whiskey and nodded approval. "I was hoping to see Tess, too. She must be a beautiful young lady by now."

"She is, Lash. A great little gal. As nice and sweet and pretty as her mother. And she shoots even better than Abbie did."

"You can't say more'n that, Tonk. Nobody could. You're still a lucky man."

Hiller drew on his cigar. "Can't complain. I do, but I shouldn't. Even dragging this goddamn leg around."

"Does it bother you much now?"

Hiller smiled bleakly. "Just walking or riding. It don't hurt too much setting down here, where I am most of the time."

"Salt Creek's been quiet and peaceful?"

"Mosta the time, Lash. Till Deke Vennis went to work on Andiron."

"Deke Vennis? What's that gunslinger doing on a working ranch?"

Tonk Hiller sighed. "Claimed he wanted a chance to go straight. Anse give it to him. I told Anse he was crazy, but you know how big-hearted—and bull-headed—Anse Amidon is. So it went all right, until they caught Deke using a running iron on Andiron stock. He was altering brands, and his old crew—Fern Morales and Yaqui Tupelo and Steel Huyett—was running off the cows."

"From what I know of Deke Vennis," said Lashtrow, "he had another reason for going to work on Andiron. Anse's daughter Kate."

Hiller nodded glumly. "You're right. Anse and his wife never could tame that gal down. Kate met Vennis at a dance on some ranch, and that started it. He *is* a goodlooking bastard."

"Anse has been as unlucky with his daughter as you've been lucky with yours, Tonk. I ran into Kate once in Fort Worth, and I was about ready to yell for help. That girl goes right after whatever she wants."

"Yeah, she's a hellcat, for sure." Hiller poured another round of drinks. "You heard about Anse driving a herd up the old Chisholm Trail to Abilene?"

"I read about it in the papers," Lashtrow said. "Don't make much sense now that they're all shipping beef by rail or boats. Some Chicago meatpacking company arranged and financed the deal as a publicity stunt, the way I got it. They'll pay Amidon a big bonus and top price for his cattle, if he beats the deadline."

"That's about the size of it, Lash. I told Anse it was foolish, but he's hellbent on making the last big drive up the Chisholm. All that newspaper stuff, he'll get hit by all the outlaws and renegade Injuns in the Nations, for chrisake. But he's set on doing it regardless. Three thousand head

9

and twenty drovers. He ain't got a chance of getting through.''

Lashtrow contemplated his cigar ash. ''Anse could do it, if anybody could. But it's a helluva long shot, and he doesn't need the money. I reckon he always wanted to make one more trail drive, and this is his chance.''

''Exactly correct,'' Tonk Hiller agreed. ''But he'll just lose the whole goddamn herd and get himself and his crew wiped out. And he's even thinking of taking his wife and daughter along.''

''What did he do about Deke Vennis?''

''Fired him on the spot, of course. Should've killed the sonofabitch. Now Vennis says he's going back to Andiron and call Anse out.''

Lashtrow straightened in his chair. ''Anse can't face a gunfighter like Vennis. Where the hell's his foreman Kloster? Klos is supposed to be good with a gun.''

''They're likely all out rounding up cattle for the drive,'' Tonk Hiller said, wagging his gray-fringed balding head. ''Kloster and Pueblo and Santee and Tench, all the gunhands. I would step in myself, if I could get around better. But I wouldn't be no match for Deke Vennis. Ten-fifteen years ago, maybe, but not now.''

''Well, I was planning on hitting Andiron anyway,'' Lashtrow drawled. ''Thought you and I'd go out and talk over old times with Anse. Didn't figure there was any hurry, but if Deke Vennis is gunning for Anse, I'd better get out there right away.''

''I'll string along with you, Lash,'' said Tonk Hiller. ''Maybe not quick anymore, but I can still shoot pretty straight with a sixgun or a long gun. And Vennis is likely to have some of his boys backing him up.''

''I don't want to drag you into anything, Tonk.''

Hiller scowled into cigar smoke. ''You don't wanta try to stop me from coming either, do you, Lash?'' He took a stubby shotgun off the rack.

Lashtrow smiled fondly at him. ''I reckon not, Tonk.''

10

"My horse is right outside," Hiller said. "Let's get going."

A deputy, whom Hiller introduced as Luke, came in to relieve the marshal as they were leaving, and Luke's eyes widened at the name of Lashtrow. He kept them fastened on the big lithe wide-shouldered Ranger.

"We're going out to Andiron," said Hiller. "You seen Vennis or any of his gang around town?"

"Nary a sign of 'em, Tonk," said Luke. "But I wasn't really looking for 'em, you know."

Out front, Hiller untied his rawboned buckskin and glanced admiringly at Lashtrow's horse. "Old Sorrel's looking mighty fine. Fast and strong as ever, I allow."

They made the rounds, but neither Vennis nor any of his henchmen had been sighted in Salt Creek that day. On the way out of town they passed the large adobe-block bank building, and Tonk Hiller remarked, "Been worried some about that bank, since I heard Vennis's bunch was in this part of the country. Pretty rich bank for a small town, Lash. Lots of big spreads like Andiron around here, and draw their payrolls outa there."

"Mystery to me how Vennis has gone unhung so long," Lashtrow said. "But he never seems to get caught at anything."

Andiron was only a few miles distant, and the extensive layout looked dark and deserted on their approach. The bunkhouse, mess hall, barns, sheds and outbuildings were unlighted, with only a vague glimmer in the ranch house itself. Lashtrow feared that Vennis might have struck and gone already. But Anse Amidon himself answered their knock on the door, his square somber features brightening in recognition of them.

"Lash! And Tonk, too! Godamighty, if you ain't a welcome sight. Come on in, boys, come in." Hauling them inside, Amidon hugged and mauled them about in his powerful embrace. "Nothing ever looked better to me than you two homely mavericks. Hey, Grace! Come here and see

11

what the night wind blew in. Lashtrow and Hiller, well I'll be damned all to hell and back. Nobody ever burned more powder or drank more booze or hoorawed more towns than us three buckaroos.''

Grace Amidon was as small and demure as her husband was huge and boisterous, and her plump pleasant face glowed with pleasure as she welcomed the unexpected guests. While Anse broke out bottles and glasses and cigars, Grace went to the kitchen to rustle up some grub, in spite of their protests. Anson Amidon poured with a heavy hand, and they clicked glasses before settling down in deep leather chairs.

"Where the hell is everybody, Anse?'' asked Tonk Hiller. "This place looks deserted as a ghost town. Not even a hostler or ranch hand in sight.''

"Out on roundup,'' Amidon said. "Lash, you know about the big cattle drive I'm taking up the Chisholm? Last one in the history of the Old West. Sure wish you boys could ride with me.''

"You really figure it's worthwhile, Anse?'' inquired Lashtrow.

"Hell, yes! I been dreaming about it for years. Thought the goddamn railroads had killed it dead, till this proposition came up.''

"You get in the Indian Nations, Anse, you'll have bandits and Injuns and Comancheros and gunsharps all over you.''

Amidon shrugged his massive shoulders and refilled the glasses. "We'll fight 'em off, don't worry. I'll have twenty picked men who'll follow me barefoot through hell's lowest pit.''

"How about Deke Vennis?''

Amidon's expression changed abruptly and his eyes clouded. "That nogood sonofabitch!''

"Has he been back since you canned him?''

"Not till tonight. He come back tonight and called me out.''

"What happened, Anse?''

"Nothing. I'm going out in the morning. At sunup."

"Very dramatic, Anse," drawled Lashtrow. "Just like in a stage show."

"You can't do that," Hiller protested. "It's suicide. Deke Vennis is one of the top gunfighters in Texas."

Amidon shook his shaggy gray-flecked head. "What else can I do, for chrisake? When a man's called in this country he has to stand up. It's a matter of honor, you know that, Tonk."

"Not for a middle-aged family man," Lashtrow said. "You're not honor-bound to stand up against a young professional killer. Not by a damn sight. Now where is Vennis?"

"Over in the bunkhouse."

"Alone?"

"Don't know, but I doubt it. Most likely Huyette and Morales and Tupelo are with him. We'll know when—" Amidon stopped suddenly.

"When what, Anse? Where the hell is Kate?"

Amidon's broad ruddy face went redder. "She—she went over to talk him out of it. We couldn't stop her, Lash. We just can't control that girl. It'd take a straitjacket to hold her."

Embarrassed for him, Lashtrow and Hiller stared into their drinks, while Amidon reared his bulk out of the chair to pace the floor, cursing through gritted teeth.

"If she wasn't there, we'd go and take 'em right now," Lashtrow said.

"No, Lash, it's my business. I fight my own battles." Amidon stiffened to his full broad height. "Always have and I ain't backing down here."

"Sorry, Anse, but I'm taking over," Lashtrow said gently. "I'm a Ranger with a statewide authority. Vennis was caught rustling cattle, and I'm taking him. Don't try to argue. You boys are just ex-Rangers. I'm taking official charge."

Amidon snorted like a bull. "That's hogwash, Lash, and you know it."

"That's how it is," Lashtrow insisted quietly. "Now let's forget it and drink this fine liquor and not worry Grace any more. When Vennis steps out at sunrise, I go out and get him."

"We'll be covering you close," Tonk Hiller declared.

Lashtrow smiled his slow wry smile. "I should hope so. Don't figure I could handle all four of 'em at once. Now I need a place to wash off some of this trail dirt before Grace calls us to the table."

When Lash returned from washing up, Kate Amidon was in the room talking to her father and Hiller. She was a tall long-limbed girl with a strong curved figure and handsome high-colored face, smoky gray eyes and ripe sensuous mouth, crowned by dark curly hair.

"Lash!" she cried, running to him and wrapping her arms around him, face eagerly uplifted. He turned his head slightly to take her kiss on the cheek, and held her away at arm's length. "I couldn't talk Deke into going away. But everything's all right, Daddy, now that Lash is here. Lash and Tonk both, I mean."

"Is he alone in the bunkhouse?" Lashtrow asked.

"Yes, but I know he's expecting company before day-break. Deke didn't admit it, but I could tell. His three horrible friends will be there."

Lashtrow shook his tawny head in sorrow. "He's a murderer, a thief, he kills for money, and he came here to kill your father."

"I never would've let him do that," Kate said lightly. "But now that you're here, Lash, there's nothing to worry about."

"Not a thing," Lashtrow agreed dryly, thinking: *Except three tough gunmen and the best knife-user this side of the Rio Grande.*

2

Sunrise at Andiron

Lashtrow awoke alone in a strange bed to a sense of impending trouble and conflict, an unpleasant incident in the night and a more unpleasant issue to meet come morning. It was still dark. A breeze scented with sage and grass and sand blew in the opened window. He was at Andiron, feeling sympathy for Tonk Hiller who had lost his beloved wife, and for Anson Amidon, a strong successful rancher who could not discipline his own daughter. Age and time wore people down with relentless pressure.

Sometime during the night when the house was deep in slumber, Kate Amidon had crept into the room and tried to get into his bed. The remembered musky fragrance of her filled him with mingled desire and distaste. She was passionate and persistent, and Lashtrow had forcibly restrained and ejected her.

"You were with Deke Vennis last night," he said, holding her off. "Now you come to me. I don't know where Anse and Grace got you, girl. Get the hell outa here."

"I—I don't do anything with him but flirt around," Kate said. "He's nothing to me, Lash. You know I've always wanted you. Since that night in Fort Worth, I've been in love with you."

Lashtrow had laughed softly. "You're a liar, kid, among other things. Beat it before I get up and throw you out. You wanta wake the whole damn house?"

She had gone finally, pleading and sobbing, and Lashtrow had found it difficult to sleep after that. He had been sleeping well until her brash intrusion. He needed to be rested, keen and sharp, ready and right, when he went against Deke Vennis at sunup. For a moment he yielded to a callow petulance and complaint. *Why does it always have to be?* . . . . Then he wiped the shameful thought away in flushed disgust. When you're rated the top, you have to go on proving yourself time and again. He ought to know and accept that by now. Anse and Tonk were too old to face Vennis.

The windows were gray with pre-dawn light and he was still drowsing fitfully, when a rap on the door roused him and Tonk Hiller's voice came through: "It's about time, Lash."

"Be right with you, Tonk." Lashtrow rose, stretched his long arms and legs, washed hands and face briskly at the basin, and started dressing.

Shrugging into the bleached blue shirt, he pulled on stockings and soft buckskin pants and the hardworn halfboots, the rawhide vest with its handy pockets, and knotted the soiled crimson scarf loosely at his throat. He would wear both guns today, not for show but for utility and expedience. More than once the extra Colt had saved his life, and the lives of others. He latched the left-hand sheath onto the shell belt, buckled it on, tied down holster bottoms, and checked both of the matched .44s, easing them in and out of the leather. It was best to make these preparations in private, Lashtrow figured. There was enough tension in the Amidon family already.

Grace had breakfast on the table, appetizing in appearance and odor, but nobody was able to eat much, and Lashtrow took nothing but coffee, the last of three cups laced with brandy. Mist still shrouded the winding course of Salt Creek, but the eastern horizon was growing luminous. As yet there were no signs of life or movement at the bunkhouse and other outbuildings. Kate made a final plea to go talk

16

with Vennis, and Anse sent her back to her room with such violent authority that the girl obeyed immediately and without protest.

"I still say it's my fight, by God," growled Anse Amidon, the lines in his coppery rugged face etched deeper than ever.

"No, Anse, it's Ranger business now," Lashtrow said, soft yet firm. "You and Tonk will be busy enough covering the flanks, keeping the others off me."

"What a country," Grace deplored, with a sigh. "Men never grow up. Always like little boys showing off how brave and strong they are, getting themselves killed for nothing but senseless pride."

The sky was reddening in the east, and Lashtrow got up to walk around and limber his muscles, fixing his gray gaze on the bunkhouse from one window to another. He felt hollow, and nothing seemed quite real.

Tonk Hiller had an extra Colt in his belt, and was fussing over his favorite sawed-off double-barreled shotgun. "Wyatt Earp says this is the best town-taming weapon," he murmured. "It always worked good for me in Salt Creek. You go round to the left, Anse, and I'll swing right. If them others horn in, we'll whipsaw 'em."

Anse Amidon nodded grimly over his sixteen-shot Henry rifle. He was seething with shame at his daughter's behavior and rage against the entire world. "Lashtrow hadda come and spoil everything, goddamn it."

Grace patted his muscular shoulder. "If he hadn't, Anse, you'd be lying dead out there in your own front yard a few minutes from now."

"She's right, Anse," whispered Tonk Hiller. "Quit griping. Neither one of us is up to facing Deke Vennis."

"What if he takes Lash?"

"Nobody takes Lashtrow," said Tonk. "You oughta know that, Anson."

The sun rose over the eastern hills, a flaming ball of fire, and the bunkhouse door swung open. Deke Vennis emerged

17

with a swagger, a compact medium-sized young man moving with arrogant ease, dark curls tumbled over his handsome smiling face. Thumbs hooked in gunbelt, he stood there staring calmly at the ranch house.

"He's out there, Lash," called Tonk Hiller.

"I see him," Lash said from an inner room. "Let him wait a little."

Grace sat at the kitchen table, bowed head in her hands.

Amidon and Hiller slipped out the back door, and moved off in opposite directions along the rear of the ranch house. Deke Vennis extracted tobacco sack and papers from his gaudy striped vest to roll and light a cigarette. Lash grinned at the kid's deliberate braggadocio.

Lashtrow bit off a chew of tobacco and went out the front door, across the gallery, down three stone steps into the yard. The sun, off to his left, was no problem. In lazy strides he moved to about forty yards from the other man and halted, a high loose lounging shape, his bronze head streaked with gold. It's too theatrical to be true, he thought.

Deke Vennis must have been surprised, but he didn't reveal it. "What the hell is this anyway?" he asked mildly. "You work for Amidon?"

"No, I work for the state."

"I thought Amidon would send for help."

"He didn't send for me," Lashtrow drawled. "I just happened by."

Vennis laughed in disbelief. "Who the hell are you? *What* are you?"

"A Ranger named Lashtrow."

Vennis's mocking eyes flickered a bare trifle. "Lashtrow, huh? I shoulda known you. Everybody in Texas knows Lashtrow. Well, I didn't come to fight you."

Lashtrow smiled slowly. "No, but I came to take you in, Vennis."

"You'll play hell doing that." Vennis's laugh was scornful. "Nobody takes me in, mister."

18

"Reach for it then." One hundred twenty feet of rusty dirt separated them.

"Not at this distance."

"Reach or drop your belt."

Vennis shook his curly head. "Come in a bit closer. I ain't no goddamn target shooter."

"This is close enough," Lashtrow said. "If you're any good with a gun."

Vennis laughed. "Looks like a Mexican standoff, big man."

"Not quite. I'm drawing—and shooting. If you don't reach or drop your guns."

Deke Vennis flicked a glance over his shoulder, and three men came out of the bunkhouse and fanned out behind him. Fern Morales was squat, mustachioed and froglike to his conchaed jacket, a perpetual sneer twisting his lips. Steel Huyett was the hulking giant reputed to be deadly with his bare hands or a knife. Yaqui Tupelo looked like a dark vulture, part Injun and part Mexican with perhaps some Creole and Cajun blood mixed in. None of them had drawn, but they were ready to. An evil wicked trio in back of the smiling debonair Vennis.

"What do you say now, Ranger?" mocked Deke Vennis. "You still drawing and shooting?"

"If necessary, but I doubt it will be." Lashtrow spread his hands to either side, and Anse Amidon loomed gigantic with his Henry trained on the foursome, as Tonk Hiller limped out from the other corner of the bunkhouse, his sawed-off Greener leveled at Vennis.

"Go for your guns, you sonsabitches!" roared Anse Amidon. "Or drop 'em and get the hell off my place and never come back."

Deke Vennis coolly studied the situation, shrugged and shook his glossy dark head. "We ain't apt to draw against odds like these, for chrisake."

Lashtrow scarcely seemed to stir, yet his Colt .44s were in hand and lined on the four renegades. "For the last time,

19

drop your belts and ride out. We oughta shoot you down like rabid coyotes, but we can't operate the way you vermin do. Shuck 'em off or die where you stand."

Grumbling, snarling and swearing, the four men unbuckled and dropped their gunbelts into the dust.

"There'll be other guns and other days," Deke Vennis said.

"Shut up, you smirking bastard!" Anse Amidon shouted. "Open your filthy mouth once more and I'll blow your goddamn greasy head off!"

The outlaw horses were tethered behind the bunkhouse. Following the four with weapons ready, Lash and his friends watched them mount up.

"Dump your saddle guns too," Tonk Hiller ordered, shaking the shotgun for emphasis. "Oughta throw you polecats in jail, but don't wanta stink up the place that bad."

Four carbines slithered into the weeds, and four horsemen turned tail and galloped off across the billowing prairie, but Lashtrow knew as well as Amidon and Hiller that they had by no means seen the last of Deke Vennis and his ugly *companeros*.

"It's always a mistake to let men like them live, when you have a chance to kill 'em," Lashtrow said, with regret. "I've seen it proved out a hundred times, and still I let the bastards go. Unless they're shooting at me."

"It's hard to kill in cold blood," Tonk Hiller agreed. "Even when you know they oughta die." He gathered up the outlaw carbines.

Anse Amidon grunted and spat tobacco juice. "*My* blood wasn't cold, boys, and I still let the sonsabitches off alive. So what can you say or do? . . . I'm sure obliged to you boys anyhow."

"Hell, it was nothing, Anse," said Lashtrow.

"It was purely a pleasure, Anson," declared Tonk Hiller.

"Well, maybe we can enjoy some breakfast now," Amidon said. "I'm sure Grace kept everything warm for us."

"Then I better get back to Austin," said Lashtrow. "Or Cap'n McKenna will chew my ears off. Anse, I wish you weren't making that trail drive."

"I'm making it, Lash," said Amidon. "Come hell or high water." Around front of the bunkhouse, he and Lash picked up the discarded gunbelts. "We may need these extra weapons up on the Chisholm."

After a bountiful breakfast, Lashtrow and Hiller thanked the Amidons, who protested warmly that the gratitude lay on their side of the ledger, and exchanged goodbys and cordial best wishes. Lash was relieved that Kate had remained in her room. Grace's rosy cheeks glistened with tears.

Back in town, Lashtrow and Hiller had a few farewell drinks in the marshal's office, and Lash said: "It was great seeing you again, Tonk. Give my love to Tess when you write or see her again."

"It's always great being with you, Lash," said Hiller, with a tiny catch in his voice. "And Tess'll be tickled to get a word from you, too."

"Keep an eye out for the Vennis bunch, Tonk. They might come back to take a crack at you."

Hiller nodded his balding head. "I'll watch for the bastards, and keep the shotgun handy."

They shook hands with deep feeling, and Lashtrow walked out to mount his sorrel and start the homeward ride to Austin.

There was sadness as well as pleasure in seeing old friends after a long separation, Lashtrow reflected, as he rocked along in the saddle at a smooth steady rate. It hurt to see what the years had done to them, the changes that had been wrought. Death to Hiller's fine wife, and old Tonk more crippled than ever. Anse Amidon grown wealthy, but miserable over his wanton rebellious daughter Kate, and Grace suffering with him.

Well, they were alive, at least, while many comrades of their age and some much younger were dead and buried, gone forever. It was blind chance that put some men under and left others living. Without luck Lash himself could have been killed on occasions too numerous to recall or count. Fate was a freakish thing, and it ruled the destinies of all humankind. You could call it God, if you wished, and many folks did. But the end results were the same. When your number came up, you went down into final everlasting darkness. Lashtrow couldn't see it any other way.

There should be something more, a kind of redemption, some hope for an afterlife, but strive as he might Lashtrow could not conceive of it.

"It's a funny world, *Caballo*," he confided to the sorrel. "We don't know where we came from or why we're here or where we're going. Why was I born a man and you a horse? Why do some die at twenty and others live to ninety? Why are many born poor and few born rich? By what chance are people born white or red or brown or black or yellow? It is all a mystery, life as well as death."

Lashtrow had no single name for the sorrel, yet the often talked to him when riding alone, using a wide variety of names. Horse, Pard, Mate, Boy, Kid, Pal, Chico, Friend, Son, Brother, *Compadre, Companero,* Beauty, Big Gold, Sunshine, *Diablo,* Soldier, Comrade, and others. There was a close communion between them. The sorrel would come at his whistle, and often snorted a warning of danger before the rider sensed it. They were alike in many ways, big and rangy, strong and swift, combining power with grace, stamina with speed, and were good to look at.

"You are much horse, *Amigo*," said Lashtrow. "And I am fortunate to have you under me. You have saved my life many times, and I trust you will keep on doing so, for there are a lot of bad men who want me dead. Now let's see if you can still run a little."

The great sorrel pricked back his ears and broke into a fleet longstriding run, and Lashtrow bent his head into the rushing sunshot air with a smile that lighted his squinting gray eyes.

3

Fresh Blood Spoor

The following week a telegram arrived at Ranger Headquarters in Austin:

> BUFORD BANK ROBBED
> MARSHAL AND THREE CITIZENS
> KILLED BY OUTLAW BAND

Lashtrow, enjoying a rare off-duty day, was in his quarters in the main barrack, smoking his pipe and reading yet
another treatise on the Battle of Gettysburg, July 1-3, 1863.
It was a subject that always intrigued military tacticians and
scholars, and would continue to do so far into the future.
It had a particular and personal fascination for Lash because
his father, Lieutenant Dan Lashtrow, CSA, had died there
in the Rebel assault on Cemetery Ridge. Pickett's Charge,
famous or infamous, depending on the point of view.

Lashtrow had made his room comfortable and homelike
with pictures, books, magazines, and mementos. Milton
Travers III, blacksheep scion of an aristocratic Boston family, who had somehow wound up as a Texas Ranger, said
it was the only civilized place in the establishment, and he
spent most of his spare time there, with or without Lash,
and frequently in the company of Foxcroft Edley. This trio
had shared many legendary exploits and honors, and were
known as the Three Musketeers.

Whenever Lashtrow read about Gettysburg, he was, illogically he realized, disappointed to find no mention of his father's name. It didn't seem fair or right that Dan Lashtrow was omitted, even though he was only a young lieutenant. Historians inevitably, and no doubt of necessity, dealt exclusively with general officers and commanders of high rank. Lashtrow never ceased seeking and hoping he would one day come upon some reference to his father in accounts of that tragic slaughter, in which the Flower of the Confederacy, as Longstreet's Corps was called, was cut down and slashed to pieces by superior Union man- and fire-power.

Men who had been there in Dan Lashtrow's company told him they were in the first wave of the attack, and among the realtively few hundreds who survived long enough to climb that blazing slope and reach the stone-wall and the cannons at the crest of Cemetery Ridge. They were close by when General Armistead jumped on top of the wall waving the Confederate flag, and the Bluecoats began to break and fall back. For a few minutes of red roaring chaos it looked like a Southern victory, and Dan Lashtrow was one of the men in gray who actually crossed that stone barricade. He'd been seen shooting down one foeman and sabering another, before falling himself, riddled, they said. Then Armistead had been shot off the wall, his followers dropping in long ragged butternut windrows, and the charge was halted, torn apart, driven back down the hill over piles of Rebel dead and wounded. Blood-soaked mounds of mangled intertwined corpses.

Dan Lashtrow and some 7,000 other Confederates were dead on the field, the battle was lost, and that was the beginning of the end for the Southern cause.

The scene was as real to Lash as if he had been there. Awake and asleep, he had seen and felt it so many times it was a part of him. He had worshiped his father. Dad had taught him to ride and rope, to handle sixguns and rifles, to work cattle and catch wild mustangs, to run and swim, to fight with his fists and wrestle, to travel in the woods and climb mountains. Everything under the sun a man should know. And his kind gentle mother with her sweet sad smile had taught him to read and write and speak properly, to keep himself and his clothes clean and neat, to be courteous and polite and well-mannered in all situations. He'd sure been lucky to have parents like that, and the bringing up they gave him. And Grandma, on his mother's side, had been a source of wisdom and comfort, too.

If Dad had lived, they would have built their little Laurel Leaf ranch and brand into one of the biggest and best in the Southwest, working together to fill their range with fine horses and beef cattle. It was a long lost dream. Thinking of his folks after all these years still set Lashtrow's throat to aching and his eyes to stinging, made him feel desolate and lonely as a small boy.

Milt Travers came into the room then, with news of the Buford raid. "Cactus Bill McKenna is giving this one to us, Lash. As usual he can spare only two men for a campaign requiring a full regiment. Your day of ease and luxury is over." He glanced at the book. "I see you've been losing the Battle of Gettysburg again, you unregenerate Rebel."

Lashtrow grinned and closed the book. "Moneybag capitalists like your family won that war, by proxy." He sobered instantly and groaned. "Buford, that's just a little south of Salt Creek. That's bad, Milt."

Travers inclined his shapely brown head. "How many men did Vennis have?"

"Only three when I saw them. Probably got a dozen more by now."

Travers smiled. "That makes the odds fairly even." He was a slender graceful man with finely cut features, intense blue eyes, and a manner of easy assurance. There was an elegant charm about him, even in rough range garb, a serene unshakable poise. A wiry whiplash figure, thin and keen as a rapier. Many a border ruffian had been deceived by his mild appearance, boyish smile and cultured voice. In action he was cat-quick and smooth, with an explosive strength that belied his slight build.

"All right, let's pack our gear and saddle up," Lashtrow said.

Travers produced a silver flask. "After a toast to our mission, comrade."

"How come that's always full, when you're nipping at it night and day?" Lashtrow sampled it and added: "Full of rare old cognac, too."

"It's a magic flask handed down from generation to generation of Traverses," explained Milt. "The first Travers to carry it rode with William the Conqueror at the Battle of Hastings in the year 1066. Since then there was never a sober Travers until my honorable father, who is strictly a teetotaller. I have been doing my damnedest to make up for his delinquency. It's not easy, but it is fun."

"You do very well at it, but I've never seen you drunk."

Travers laughed merrily. "I get drunk, Lash, but it doesn't show. To horse and away now, noble knights."

Captain McKenna appeared at the stable as they were saddling up, pipe in his grim gray-mustached mouth, deep lines of worriment seaming his leathery squared-jawed face. "It's a crime to send only two men after a gang like that. I assume it's Deke Vennis's mad-dog crew. But it's a crime I'm forced to commit over and over again, goddamn it. Those hog-swilling politicians at the Capitol hate to spend a dime on law-enforcement. Too bad Fox Edley's busy in San Antone or I'd send him along, but that's the way it goes. You boys know how it is. I need a whole company, and all I can do is send two of my top men. If they don't give me more money and recruits, they're going to get my resignation slapped right across their fat doubletalking mouths. By God, I mean it!"

"Well, Cap, we always manage to scrape up some soldiers along the way," Lashtrow said soothingly. "Always a few good men willing to help."

"I know, Lash, you always do a good job of recruiting

on the fly, but it ain't like having our own men, goddamn it. We shouldn't have to depend on private citizens. Well, we do what we can. I know you two will do a helluva job, like always. Take care of yourselves, and don't buck the odds if they're too damn long. You boys are too valuable to lose."

Once out of Austin, they loped along at a strong steady pace. Milt Travers's horse was a tough fiery coyote dun, with a dark dorsal stripe down its back, the black mane, tail and points characteristic of the breed, a fit running mate for Lashtrow's sorrel. Milt liked to use the Mexican name, *bayo coyote,* and called his mount either Bayo or Coyote in speaking to or of him. They had ridden many long broken trails together, and the dun was one of very few horses that could keep up with the sorrel for any great distance. Being superbly mounted and armed gave the riders confidence on a mission like this, a reassurance they needed when they considered the topheavy odds stacked against them.

They moved northward through bright shimmering heat waves, with balls of tumbleweed rolling and dust devils spiralling up from the scorched brown plains. They chewed tobacco because it was impossible to smoke in the gusting winds, and even with a chew warping his thin tanned cheek Milt Travers retained his patrician image.

"You remember Tonk Hiller's daughter Tess?" said Lashtrow, who found himself thinking about Salt Creek, which might be the bandits next objective. "A cute perky little kid with yellow hair and big violet.eyes."

"Sure, I remember. She showed promise of growing into a real beauty."

"Tonk says she's done just that, and I don't wonder. Her mother was a lovely woman."

Travers nodded. "A blonde with character and personality. A real fine lady. Fortune smiles on the man who finds a wife like Abbie Hiller."

"Well, Tess had one of those kid crushes on me. And—"

Lashtrow broke off, feeling heat rise under his bronzed cheekbones.

"Don't be bashful, Prince Charming," jested Travers. "We all observed that. The girl couldn't see anyone but you."

"Well, she asked me—all serious and solemn—not to marry anybody till she grew up enough to be my wife."

"Ah ha! So that's why you've remained single and solitary. Waiting for little Tess Hiller to attain maturity. She must be old enough by this time, Lash."

"Hell, you know better'n that, Milt," Lashtrow protested, his cheeks hotter than ever. "I'm single because I want to be, and I intend to stay that way. Any man in this business stays single, if he's got a grain of sense. Until he's old enough to retire or ride a swivel-chair instead of a horse."

"Quite true. But I don't know about your case, Lash. You can't fight them off forever. Now that Kate Amidon always had a yen for you, too. The young ones just can't resist old stud Lashtrow." Travers swayed with laughter at Lash's discomfort.

"All right, joker, let's drop it," Lashtrow muttered. "Don't know why I brought it up in the first place."

"No harm done, Lash," said Milt Travers, handing over the silver flask. "Console yourself with a draft of this delicious beverage. You're about the shyest damn gunfighter I ever encountered."

Lashtrow laughed with him, took a good swig of the brandy, and passed back the flask. The awkwardness gone, they rode on in warm companionable silence for a space, until Travers raised his clear-toned voice in a rollicking old ballad:

"Oh pray for the Ranger, you kind-hearted stranger,
He was roamed the prairies for many a year;
He has kept the Comanches from all your ranches,
And guarded your homes o'er the far frontier."

28

"That was damn good, Milton," said Lashtrow.

"It didn't spook the horses anyway. I almost made the harvard Glee Club once in the long ago. Before that venerable institution expelled me."

"Give us another verse, songbird."

"That's the only one I know," Milt Travers confessed sadly.

The next morning when they rode into Buford, church bells for a multiple funeral were ringing dolefully over the small stricken community.

"They come in like a cavalry charge and hit the bank right off," said one of the civic leaders. "About fifteen or twenty men, all over the place. Seemed like a lot more, a regular army of 'em, some Mex and some white. Deke Vennis was recognized, along with Yaqui Tupelo and Fernando Morales and Steel Huyett. The marshal had dodgers on them four. They could've taken the bank money and rode out. We had no means of stopping them. But the dirty buzzards hadda shoot down the marshal and three other good men. No goddamn need of it. Then they took off whooping and laughing, shooting out windows along the way."

"Which way were they heading?" asked Lashtrow.

"North. Most likely for Salt Creek. There's a bigger bank up there."

"Thank you," Lashtrow said. "Sorry this had to happen. You folks have our sympathy. Nothing much we can do here, so we'll get on after 'em."

"Just two of you?" The man wagged his head in despair. "Only two Rangers, and always too late."

"It's kinda hard to be everywhere at once," Lashtrow said, and they wheeled off into the north with the bells pealing mournfully after them.

"It's no wonder that Bill McKenna gets stomach ulcers,"

Milt Travers said. "Those stupefied legislators give him a few hundred underpaid and overworked riders to cover an entire state the size of Texas. And when something goes wrong, everybody blames the poor benighted Rangers."

"To hell with them," Lashtrow said, teeth on edge. "Let's just hope we can reach Salt Creek before the bastards hit that town."

"We might make it, Lash," said Travers. "Those *bandidos* will spend a couple of days drinking and wenching before they storm another bank."

"I knew we should've killed 'em at Andiron." Lashtrow reached for Milt's flask. "Had 'em cold and dead, right under our gun muzzles, and I turned 'em loose. Knew it was wrong, but I let 'em go."

"We aren't executioners, and we aren't assassins," Travers said. "We always have to give the enemy an even break, and thereby handicap ourselves all to hell."

The golden sun lowered in the waning afternoon, the heat lessened mercifully, the winds eased to let the alkali settle, and the sage slopes turned a deep rich purple in the dimming light. Gophers and prairie dogs scurried over the buffalo grass, and jackrabbits bounced through the green chaparral and spiny mesquite. In the distance vultures circled over some ground creature that was dying or dead.

As the two riders breasted the barren grade of a ridge that would bring them within view of Salt Creek, the sun was sinking to a low reddening amber flare in the west. They were just below the crest of the ridgeline, when the racket of gunfire erupted to the north, with so many weapons blasting that it sounded like a full-scale battle. Warned by what had transpired in Buford, Tonk Hiller would have taken precautionary measures to defend his town. But ordinary townsmen were incapable of coping with a guerrilla force such as Deke Vennis commanded.

"Late again, goddamn it," grated Lashtrow, as they booted their horses to the ridgetop and gazed at the dusky smoking embattled settlement. "Let's get in there, Milt."

" 'Ours not to reason why, ours but to do and die,' " quoted Travers.

"Yeah," Lashtrow said, as they plunged down the shale-drifted descent on their sure-footed horses, pulling their carbines from the saddle sheaths. "Into the valley of death rode two crazy Rangers."

Travers's laughter was gay and reckless. "It helps to be crazy, Lash, in this line of work."

4

The Invasion of Salt Creek

Tonk Hiller was cleaning his house when word came of the Buford bank robbery and killings. For once, Tonk had been enjoying that mundane chore, because Teresa was coming home for spring vacation and the place needed a thorough scouring. He could have hired the work done, but he disliked having strange women in the home he had built for his wife Abbie. Her room was just as she had left it, a shrine behind a locked door. No one except Tonk and Tess ever entered that room.

Anse Amidon with a hand-picked crew of twenty top hands had started driving 3,000 prime beef stock up the historic Chisholm Trail. Fearing reprisal from Deke Vennis, Anse had taken Grace and Kate along with him. They were not useless supercargo. Grace had served as cook on early Andiron roundups, against all range tradition. And Kate, with all her wayward faults, was competent with horses, cows and guns, a good all-round hand. But the absence of the Andiron crew greatly decimated the defensive strength of Salt Creek.

Tonk Hiller had two regular deputies, Luke and Jason, and four part-time assistants. He promptly deputized a half-dozen more men, and alerted the whole population. Storekeepers were instructed to plant loaded guns under their counters, and saloon owners stashed extra weapons beneath their bars. A large number of citizens belted on pistols for the first time in years, and even housewives placed old rifles or shotguns in kitchen corners.

Selecting strategic points around the bank building, Tonk Hiller assigned his deputies to positions on rooftops, in windows, along nearby alleys, and in the carriage shed behind the bank. If Deke Vennis attempted a headlong rush here, his outlaw force would be mowed down and chopped to bloody bits. Providing the recruited lawmen followed orders, manned their posts efficiently, and stayed sober and awake. Ranger-trained Hiller had a natural skepticism about untested civilian militia.

Waiting for the stagecoach the next day, Tonk was as eager and excited as a youngster. Tess was coming at an unfortunate time, but he would have welcomed her under any circumstances. With Abbie gone, his entire life centered on the girl. She was the first passenger off, and Tonk handed her down and folded her into his sinewy arms. Tess made him forget his crippled hip and bald head, made him feel ten feet tall and young and handsome. The way Abbie had always made him feel in their young days.

She was a little lissome girl, but fully curved and rounded, with golden hair, brilliant violet eyes, and a clear smiling face that radiated an inner warmth and gracious glow. "Oh, Dad," she murmured. "I'm so happy to see you."

"Great to have you back, baby," Hiller mumbled, his throat too full to speak plainly. "You sure look prettier'n ever, Tessie."

Tonk Hiller gathered her luggage and they walked toward home, with Tonk trying to avoid limping too badly. Tess nodded and smiled at folks who greeted her along the way, but Tonk was oblivious to everything but his slim graceful daughter. Despite the dust and rigors of stage travel, she looked jeweled, fresh and pure.

"You still getting all A's?" he asked, with pretended severity.

"Not quite, Dad. A couple of B's at present. But I can bring them up in the final examinations."

"You'd better," he said gruffly. "A girl with a father as smart as me oughta get nothing but A grades."

Teresa laughed and hugged his arm in delight. "You're right, Daddy. How's the peace officer trade these days?"

"Been real quiet and peaceful, but there might be a spot of trouble coming. Nothing to fret over. Just a mite of nuisance maybe."

"I heard some talk in the stage stations about Deke Vennis and his wild bunch. They perpetrated more than a little nuisance in Buford, it would seem."

"Yeah, they caught Buford sleeping, Tess. But they'll find Salt Creek ready, if they head this way."

Tess exclaimed over the shining cleanness of the household, and Tonk said: "I'm glad you didn't see it a few days back, baby."

While she got unpacked and freshened up, Tonk fussed around dusting and rearranging furniture in the parlor and brought in a tray bearing a bottle of sherry, two crystal glasses and a dish of sandwiches. Tess came out of her room fairly sparkling, looking so much like her mother that Tonk's eyes tingled and his throat knotted in pain. They toasted one another, settled down in velvet easy chairs, and Tonk filled and fired his best pipe. He hadn't known such contentment since she went away.

"You keeping company with any boy yet, Tess?" He was overly casual to mask his anxiety.

Tess shook her bright head. "No one in particular. I've been out with a few, of course, but nothing serious at all."

Tonk hid his relief in a cloud of pipesmoke. "Lashtrow was here a while ago. Sent you his love."

"Dear sweet Lash! How I wish I could have seen him. It's been years, but I think of him often. How was he looking?"

"Same as ever. Lash don't age much, considering the

34

life he leads. Don't tell me you've still got that little-girl crush on him, Tessie."

Tess laughed softly. "I don't know what you'd call it, Dad. But it's like Lash has spoiled all other men for me. I compare them to him, and they're nothing, just nothing."

"Well, there ain't many men like Lashtrow around, that's for sure," Tonk Hiller declared. "But he's a little old for you, baby. And he ain't got much time for women, though I reckon he's had his share of 'em here and there."

"I suppose Kate Amidon was one of them," Tess said, in a spiteful tone, that brought a grin to her father's scarred and weathered features.

"If she was, it was prob'ly rape on her part. Kate's a man-eating terror."

"I read about the cattle drive Anse Amidon's making. That's one thing I envy Kate, the trek up the Chisholm."

Tonk Hiller shook his gray-rimmed head. "It's a killing trip, Tess. No pleasure jaunt and no place for a woman."

"Dad, you can drink whiskey if you want to," Tess said, noticing how Tonk was nursing his sherry.

"I don't mind drinking wine for a change. It tastes kinda nice." Blue dusk was at the windows, and Tonk hobbled around lighting lamps. "I got to make my rounds now, but it won't take too long."

"You want me to get supper, Daddy?"

"If you ain't too tired and you feel like cooking, baby. I got about everything in the icebox and pantry."

Tess smiled happily. "I'd love to cook you a fine big meal, Dad. I don't want to lose my touch in the kitchen. It'll be just like the old days."

Tonk Hiller beamed at her. "It'll be a lot better than I been eating lately. You enjoy yourself, Tessie. I oughta be back in an hour or so."

"Do you think Deke Vennis's gang will come here?" Tess asked, with a worried frown.

"They might, but they won't run into any picnic like they had in Buford," Tonk said. "We got this bank covered

35

from every angle, if my halfbaked deputies don't get drunk or fall asleep at their posts. See you soon, baby."

"Take good care of yourself, Daddy," said Tess anxiously. "Don't try to be a big hero if those bandits come charging in."

"Don't fret for a minute, sweet, I'll be all right." Tonk Hiller kissed her, crammed on his beat-up hat, strapped on his double-holstered gunbelt, picked up the shotgun, and limped out the door.

Out of respect for Marshal Hiller, Deke Vennis had wisely adopted new tactics for the invasion of Salt Creek. Throughout the late afternoon, his men had been infiltrating the community singly or in pairs, quietly and unobtrusively wandering about the streets and dropping into saloons and stores, a few even visiting the bank. Strangers were always coming and going in town, and these scattered well-behaved individuals and couples attracted no undue attention. They wore single guns, or had no weapons at all showing, and they were polite and deferential in the barrooms and markets, as well as on the slat sidewalks.

Deke Vennis and his three lieutenants, Morales and Tupelo and Huyett, whose pictures had appeared on "Wanted" posters throughout the Southwest, made their entrance in an old hooded wagon, laden with a veritable arsenal and drawn by two large disreputable mules, their horses having been led in by previous arrivals. They left the wagon in a corner of the livery-barn yard, behind the buildings of Front Street, and found their saddled horses tied out back of the stables.

As the gray dusk thickened to blue and lavender, men drifted through the shadows to collect additional revolvers, carbines, long guns and cartridge bandoleers from the canvas-covered wagon. They had long since spotted most of the vantage points occupied by the deputies, and discovered that a number of those sentries were killing time and boredom with bottles of Forty Rod or Joe Gideon whiskey.

"Use your knife on the ground lookouts, Steel," Vennis

36

told Huyett, ''to keep it quiet. Then we'll shoot the bastards off the roofs, or keep 'em pinned down.''

Big Huyett looked up from honing his wicked-looking bowie knife and nodded impassively, a man of few words and no discernible emotions with a bold craggy face.

Vennis eyed the dark vulpine features of Yaqui Tupelo. ''Take a few men and clean out that carriage shed behind the bank.'' He turned to the stocky sneering Morales. ''See that the wranglers bring the broncs out front of the bank. You and your men cover them and lay fire on the roof-top snipers, and the ones in upstairs windows. Everybody move fast.''

Tonk Hiller was hitching his way through the murky alley that opened opposite the bank, when he nearly stumbled over two prone bodies. There was a strong whiskey smell, and he thought at first the pair was dead drunk. Crouching closer he saw that they were dead, stabbed in the back, their shirts drenched darkly with blood. Lead seared past his head as a gun roared behind him. Whirling, awkward on his bad hip, Tonk triggered one barrel of the shotgun, blowing the dim form back and down into a ragged bundle, not knowing if it was friend or foe. Relieved, he saw that it was a stranger, one of the insurgents, but not Steel Huyette, as he had hoped. Tonk turned again to the alley mouth, hobbling over the two corpses, and saw men and horses rushing about in the streets, with gunfire exploding on all sides and overhead, flames spearing the dusk and concussions deafening his ears.

Tonk let go with the other barrel and blasted a running figure into a torn sprawled heap. Two of the bastards anyway, he thought, as he leaned the Greener on the adobe wall and pulled out both handguns. There were bandits across the street, holding horses and shooting upward at roofs and windows. Bullets were splintering wood, shattering glass and screeching off adobe surfaces. Tonk opened up on them, trying to pick targets, and burnt orange flames leaped back at him, the slugs burning close. Adobe fragments stung his cheek and something ripped his jacket, as he flattened out and went on firing, left and right, the Colts jerking on his wrists, the muzzle lights lancing bright and level.

There was so much shooting he couldn't tell if he was hitting or missing, but at least one of his targets went down. The street was a roaring inferno of flame and smoke and dust. Now raiders came boiling out of the bank, carrying money sacks in one hand and shooting with the other. Tonk Hiller's guns were emptied, "Sonofabitch," he said, scrunching around to reload, with bullets still screeching and tearing about him. He glimpsed the handsome face of Vennis in the turmoil, amazed to see the man laughing in the red chaos. "That crazy bastard," Tonk panted.

The outlaws were leaping and vaulting into their saddles now, the horses bucking, pitching and twirling under the lashing gunshots, dust swirling dense and high. Colts reloaded, Tonk Hiller cut loose once more. Two riders from the south came racing into the street, hanging low with guns ablaze, and Hiller's heart went up as he identified Lashtrow's big sorrel and the coyote dun of Milt Travers. But the robbers were already off in full thunderous flight, leaving their dead and wounded behind in the weltering dirt and smoke haze.

Scrambling upright Tonk Hiller lurched out of the alley to get a clear shot at the fleeing renegades, but lightning jetted back at him from one of the horsemen and a hammerblow smashed his chest, knocking him flat on the plank walk. Stunned, he lay there squirming, straining feebly to roll over and get up, but there was no strength left in his broken body. *O Jesus, what'll Tess do?* flashed through his reeling mind. *Poor Tessie, all alone. It ain't fair, it ain't right. I can't die, I can't die and leave her . . . . She just got home . . . .* But he could feel life seeping out of him, empty and hollow with blackness closing in, all black, and then he felt and knew nothing more. The world had ended for Tonk Hiller.

With no time for caution or finesse, Lashtrow and Travers had hurtled straight into the gun battle in front of the adobe-block bank, and found the bandits already on the run, shooting back over their shoulders. The street was littered with bodies, the townsmen were still firing after the outlaws. Sweeping on in pursuit, Lash and Milt galloped through a hail of lead from both sides, miraculously unscathed.

On the northern outskirts, the raiders were scattering in all directions, the rear guard throwing shots back at the oncoming Rangers. Lashtrow felt the hot breath of slugs on his cheeks, and a blistering tug at his left sleeve near the shoulder. A pinto reared screaming and floundered to earth directly before Lashtrow, its Mex rider flinging clear and firing upward as the sorrel hurdled the fallen horse and man. Blinded by the geysering explosion, Lash's downswinging shot missed. The desperado was writhing around to line on Lash's broad back when Milt Travers's bullet smashed him into the churned-up dirt.

Lashtrow reined about and threw down on the sprawled Mexican, but there was no need of another shot. Milt Travers had pulled up on the other side of the dead man and the dying horse. Both Rangers stared into the north, but with the enemy scattering out of view and darkness closing in rapidly, there was little point in a two-man chase. Travers glanced questioningly at Lashtrow, who shook his head.

"Not now, Milt. Got to see what happened in town, and how Tonk Hiller came out of it. We can pick up their trace later. They'll bunch up again when they see there's no immediate pursuit."

Filled with fear and a dire foreboding, they rode back toward the center of the community. Lamps bloomed behind shattered windows, and horrified faces peered from scored sills and riddled doorways. Overturned wagons and dead horses lay along Front Street, and there were sounds of women wailing and men swearing. The acrid stench of gunpowder and the pungent odor of dust burdened the darkening air. In front of the bank, dejected groups clustered about fallen bodies, and Lashtrow knew with sickening certainty and agonizing despair that Tonk Hiller was gone.

The deputy named Luke turned from the largest conclave and looked up at the two mounted Rangers, head wagging despondently and powder-grimed face streaked with tears.

"Yeah, it's Tonk, Lash," he panted sobbingly. "He's dead, goddamn it. And his daughter Tess just got home this afternoon."

"O God," Lashtrow moaned, sliding from the saddle to split the assemblage and kneel beside Tonk Hiller's still shape, with Milt Travers coming through to stand sad and stricken over them, his fine head bowed and his eyes welling acid grief.

I should've known, Tonk, I should've known that sonofabitch Vennis would come back gunning for you, Lashtrow thought achingly. And now there's Tess, God help the girl. How we going to face and tell her? . . .

"Old Tonk took plenty of 'em with him," Luke mumbled brokenly. "He was chopping them down all over, by God."

Milt Traver's sensitive lips moved almost silently: "Epitaph for a town marshal and former Ranger. 'He took plenty of 'em with him.' "

Lashtrow had just risen, when Tess Hiller came flying through ranked people, her golden head ashimmer, and flung herself down beside her father. Lashtrow gave her a few heartbreaking minutes, and then lifted the girl to her feet with gentle tender strength. She turned and buried her streaming tortured face against his chest.

"Thank God you're here, Lash!" she cried, and reached out blindly to seek Travers' hand. "And you too, Milt. Thank God you're both here. I couldn't—stand it—alone."

"You won't be alone, Tess," promised Lashtrow, trying to keep his voice even and soothing. "You're never going to be alone, baby."

5

On the Northward Track

A week later, Lashtrow and Travers were riding north on the track of the Vennis gang, and Tess Hiller was with them. They had tried in every way possible to dissuade her, but the girl had been adamant.

"I can't stay here and I can't go back to school," Tess had persisted, after the funerals in Salt Creek. "I've got to get away, and I can't go alone. There are relatives in Kansas, Dad's sister and her family. They want me to come there, and that's where I'm going. You know I can ride and handle a gun, Lash, and I won't be any bother on the trail. Dad's buckskin can keep pace with your sorrel and Milt's coyote dun. If you get sick and tired of me, you can always put me on a northbound stagecoach or train somewhere along the way."

"It's not that we'd ever tire of your company, Tess," Lashtrow had told her. "It's just that it's no route for a young girl to be traveling. If and when we catch up with Vennis's bunch, there's bound to be a lot of shooting and killing."

"I can shoot and I can kill," Tess Hiller declared solemnly. "Those men killed my father, and I want in on the settlement of that debt. Damn it all, Lash, you and Milt both know I can shoot as well as most men and a lot better than some." She smiled with bravado. "And I can cook a lot better than you two *hombres*."

41

"All right, Tess," Lashtrow had finally yielded. "I never won an argument with a lady, and it don't look like I ever will. But it'll be tough going, baby, dangerous all the way."

Tess smiled in gratification. "If I cry or complain or hold you back in any way, you can kick me out of camp."

"We'll hold you to that pledge, baby," Lashtrow had warned, with mock gravity. "No quarter given."

"No quarter asked," Tess Hiller said. "You'll be glad I'm along to brighten the way. Why, I can sing almost as well as Milton the Third."

She had not gotten over her great loss and grief this quickly, but she was putting up a brave front, as Tonk would have wanted her to.

They had found the spot where the outlaws had regrouped, after their helterskelter flight, but there was really no necessity of tracking the Vennis bunch. They were obviously heading for the Chisholm Trail, with the intention of hitting the Amidon cattle drive sooner or later.

"It's not very smart to bring a girl along on a trip like this," Lashtrow admitted to Travers. "Even a remarkable girl like Teresa. But before the shooting starts, we'll have her on a coach or train bound for her aunt's home in Kansas City."

"Well, she does light up the scene considerably," Milt Travers said. "Seeing a beauty like her astride that big buckskin is a most stimulating sight. In an aesthetic sense I mean, of course, nothing prurient."

"Not much!" Lashtrow laughed. "I know the lechery underlying that innocent guise of yours."

Lash himself marveled at the suddenness with which Tess Hiller had blossomed into full rich womanhood, and it stirred and moved him deeply. He hoped she no longer fancied herself enamored of him; surely she had outgrown that childish infatuation. Yet there were times and ways she looked at him with more ardor and warmth than he preferred. Tess would make some fortunate man a fine wife someday, but he couldn't afford to get involved. Not yet

42

anyway. No matter how lonely and barren his way of life might seem, or how beguiling, sweet and charming this young lady was. A Ranger had no place for a woman in his roving hazardous existence.

At odd moments Lashtrow realized how much he was missing, and it lent a somber cast to his angular high-boned features and deep gray-green eyes.

Tess was yet somewhat dazed and numb, sunken in desolation and bereavement. She and Tonk had been much closer than most daughters and fathers. Only time could dull the anguish of her loneliness, and it would require a lot of time. She never would cease mourning and missing Dad, but the first cruel agony of loss would diminish with the passage of days, as it must if people are to go on living.

Tess liked and admired the courtly Travers, but she was absolutely enthralled by Lashtrow. He cut a splendid figure on his great golden sorrel, even in rough trailworn range clothes. The tilt of his high bronze head, the eyes that could change from calm gray to deadly green, the way his strongly cut face lighted with his slow smile. The lithe effortless ease and grace of his motions, fluid and controlled and latent with power. The manner in which he sat a saddle, smoked cheroots or cigarettes, wore his weathered hat and gunbelt, walked and spoke and laughed. All these things marked him apart for Tess Hiller, trivial details that made him lovable in her eyes, distinctively himself.

Tess didn't talk much those first few days on the trail. Then one evening after supper at the campfire, with Milt Travers gone walking to stretch saddle-sore legs, she opened up a bit:

"Lash, you're still disturbed because I made you bring me along, aren't you? Tell it straight now."

"Not a mite, Tess. It's just hard to believe that you're the little scrawny towhead I used to bounce on my knee, that's all."

"You didn't expect to find me the same size and wearing

43

pigtails, did you? Nobody ever told you that little girls grow up?''

Lashtrow grinned shyly. "Maybe not. My education along that line has been sadly neglected."

"Perhaps you don't consider that line very important, Lash."

"Important, sure. But it don't fit into my field of work, Tess."

"It would, Lash—if you'd let it." Leaning toward him, the firelight glinting red-gold on her hair and tinting her clear face, Tess Hiller was lovely indeed, eyes glowing and lips parted in adoration and frank hunger. "I'm a woman now, all woman, and I want my man."

Lashtrow started fumbling for his pipe and tobacco, but Tess grasped his wrists, forced his arms apart, and thrust herself in against him, her firm full breasts crushed to his chest. Lash's arms tightened about her instinctively, against his will, and he lowered his mouth to meet the soft full sweetness of her red lips. He tried to remain cool, contained and brotherly, but it was impossible. Her mouth opened and worked under his, her arms clutched him with surprising strength, and her supple vibrant body writhed against him with soft scalding heat.

Locked in that fierce embrace, his blood on fire and racing madly, Lashtrow was lost, helpless, unable to resist her or restrain himself. They rolled away from the fireside into the shadows and came to rest on a bed of velvety moss and fragrant ferns beneath a sheltering oak tree. Every external thing vanished and was forgotten as the delicious flames consumed them completely, melting and fusing them into one ecstatic being, man and woman united in soaring rapture and bliss.

"I've waited so long, Lash," she said breathlessly. "I've loved and wanted you and waited all these years."

"Tess, sweet little Tess," was all he could murmur, as they rode the wild storm together into a far lofty realm of sheer delight and scintillating beauty, with galaxies of stars

44

exploding and the torrent carrying them to even greater heights, the ultimate summit of the world. . . . And then they floated down featherlike, still welded together, sinking gently from the highest innacles into a pleasant and serene valley of perfect peace and tranquility.

After a timeless interlude, they heard, as if from a vast distance, Milt Travers's pure voice raised in rowdy song as he returned toward camp:

"He punched lots of cattle,
Fought many a gun battle,
And rode the long trail
In Old Mexico and New.

But you gals who would marry
Had better not tarry,
For he'd rather drink redeye
Than pay court to you."

"That might be your song to me, Lash," said Tess Hiller.

Lashtrow smiled and shook his tawny head. "I reckon not, baby. Much as I like to drink."

Lashtrow and the girl were sitting sedately beside the low-burning fire, Lash smoking his pipe and Tess reading a book, when Travers sauntered into the ruddy light of camp, carbine in the crook of his elbow.

"Well, I didn't find any bad men or big game," Milt reported whimsically. "Neither did I see any wood nymphs or water sprites. Just a couple of sad old owls and a few nighthawks. So I guess I'll have to resort to my favorite sport, indoors or out." He pulled a bottle and three silver cups from his saddlebag. "I trust you children of the wilderness will join me in a few honest libations."

They promptly agreed, and Travers poured cognac and passed the cups. It was idyllic in the flickering firelight of the upland glade, the fragrance of woodsmoke mingling with the scent of pines, the warming lift of the brandy within them and the tiny creek rippling between grassy

45

banks nearby. It was difficult to believe that death lay behind them, and stalked somewhere ahead.

The upflare between Lash and Tess had been so sudden, natural and inevitable that it had taken on the ethereal quality of a fantasy, too exalted to seem real. Had Lashtrow been the innovator, he would have felt guilt and shame. There were twinges of it even now, but mostly he felt a strange mixture of happiness and sorrow. He relit his pipe, sipped the cognac, and leaned back on a log listening to Milt and Tess harmonize the sad old Civil War song, *Lorena*. They sang well together, and Lashtrow observed them in dreamy pleasure. They made a strikingly handsome couple, and he thought it would be an ideal match if Tess could transfer her affections to Milt. Black sheep or not, Travers would someday come into a rich inheritance up north in Boston. Tess Hiller would make him a wife of high quality, and she deserved the kind of life Milt could give her.

Lashtrow had nothing to offer a woman except himself, and a lot of worry, loneliness and grief.

The next day they reached the point where the outlaw tracks ran into the wide expanse of the old Chisholm Trail, freshly churned and trampled by the recent passage of the Andiron herd.

"Named for old Jess Chisholm," said Lashtrow, as they swung into the half-mile wide trace. "A half-breed trader who ran cattle and horses to the army, and established this route from Texas to Abilene, Kansas."

"Dad told me once this wasn't the first big trail north," Tess said.

"That's true. A man named Goodnight took the first drives up the old Sedalia route to Missouri, a thousand-mile trek through storms, stampedes, river crossings, hostile Indians and white rustlers."

"How did it all start, Lash?" inquired Travers.

Lashtrow shifted his chew and took a deep breath. "Well,

46

after the war, Texas and the rest of the South was in bad shape. People starving while thousands on thousands of unbranded maverick cattle ran wild on the plains and in the thickets. Ranches in ruin, others stolen by Carpetbaggers, no market for beef in the South after the Confederacy went under.

"A few ambitious cowmen like Oliver Loving and Charley Goodnight put crews together and began gathering and road-branding the Longhorns for drives to Northern markets. Everybody said it couldn't be done, but they pushed the herds through hell and high water and gunfire. They got twenty dollars a head in Missouri, and they kept Texas alive and growing. It was quite a story."

"You ever make one of those drives, Lash?" asked Travers.

Lashtrow nodded and spat tobacco juice. "Yeah, when I was seventeen. Signed on as a wrangler. My dad was dead in the war, Mother sick under Gram's care, and our small spread sunk to nothing. You grew up young and quick in them days. At sixteen I was drinking some, had my first girl, and knew all about the cow business. Or thought I did. A year later I was prodded into a gunfight, shot a man, and had to leave that town right sudden. Not so much the law, it was clear self-defense, but that man had enough relatives, brothers, cousins, uncles and all to make a good-sized army.

"Old D. J. Claiborne was making a drive north. He'd known my dad, and he took me on as a night wrangler to handle the cavvy and help the cook. By that time the railroad had been extended west into Kansas, so old D.J. followed the trace of Jess Chisholm's wagons up through the Nations and the Cherokee Strip to the new Railhead at Abilene. That was some trip. Set out with 6,000 head and thirty-odd riders. Got to Abilene short some five hundred steers with twenty men left, and two of those cowboys were shot dead in a saloon fight the first night in town."

Breathless and abashed, Lashtrow lapsed into silence,

47

and then added: "Never talked that much before. Sorry, folks."

Milt Travers laughed and handed Lash the flask. "Sorry, hell. That was real interesting, pardner."

But Lashtrow rode silent for miles, until they made camp that night on the shore of the sandy-bottomed Colorado River, where the red clay banks had been gouged and trampled by the crossing of the Amidon herd. Inspecting the tracks and droppings, Lashtrow broke his prolonged silence:

"About a week ahead of us yet. They'll do maybe twelve miles a day, while we make forty or so."

"You could do much better without me, couldn't you, Lash?" Tess Hiller asked, straight out and flat.

"Why no, Tess, not at all," he replied, not quite truthfully. "We're doing all right, plenty good enough."

"I don't believe it," Tess declared. "I'm holding you back. The next town we come to, I'm taking the stage or a train to Kansas."

"You can't do that, Teresa," put in Travers. "We want you riding with us. You're making this the best mission I've ever known."

The girl laughed, a bit harshly. "You're very gallant—both of you. But I know better. Please don't labor the point."

Relations between her and Lashtrow had become strained and uneasy, since the first delightful night. Tess felt that she had been bold and wanton, and Lashtrow seemed reluctant to let the affair develop into full involvement. Travers, ever the discreet gentleman, sought to ease the situation and give them all the freedom possible, by absenting himself from camp on nocturnal walks. But nothing healed the widening breach. The old free and easy camaraderie was gone.

Lashtrow returned from scouting the terrain ahead, and said: "Reckon we'll bivouac on Brush Creek tonight."

Neither Tess Hiller nor Milt Travers made any response.

"With the trail in this condition from the drive," Lashtrow mused, "it's hard to tell how far in front of us Deke Vennis's bunch is, but I saw some fairly new signs."

"They could have branched off most anywhere," Travers said.

Lashtrow bit off a fresh chew. "I doubt it, Milt. They want that trail herd, and Vennis wants to cut down Anse Amidon."

Tess spoke then: "From what I've heard, he also wants Kate Amidon."

"That, too," Lashtrow admitted.

"Well, it's nice to be wanted," Tess said, with a toss of her golden head. "Even by a man like Deke Vennis, I guess."

6

"Git Along, Little Dogies . . ."

On the Chisholm, the cattle drive wasn't going well, and
Amidon was being plagued by a multitude of minor mis-
haps. Stock strayed or took sick, wagons broke down, men
got drunk or lost, cliques and feuds developed, and Kate
was unruly as ever. Torn by anxiety and frustration, Anse
raged and cursed and bawled orders up and down the line,
from the point to the drag. Nothing and nobody seemed to
work right.

Kloster, the lanky sour-faced ramrod, was not the trail
boss Amidon had anticipated. Because of his shortcomings,
Anse himself often had to ride point with young Santee or
old Crull, while Kloster performed not too well on the swing
or the drag. Of the hands Anse had hired for their gun skills
rather than their range abilities, only Santee was a real
competent cowboy. "Thank God for Santee," mumbled
Anse frequently to his claybank bronc.

Crowleg Dooner, the half-crippled wrangler, was a fine
man with horses and handled the *remuda* efficiently, while
big Mule Mundorf did a good job on the drag. The gay
laughing kid, Frellick, turned out to be an accomplished
flanker, gifted protege of Hoss Crull. The majority of the
crew were adequate, except for the gunmen Pueblo and
Tench, who were far below par as drovers, and sullen and
disagreeable, to boot.

"There ain't no place for women on a goddamn trail

50

drive," Kloster had stated, early on. "And we got two female critters in this outfit. That's more'n enough to jinx and hoodoo any brand from hell to Halifax."

Most of the riders agreed with Kloster that the expedition was doomed by the presence of Grace and Kate Amidon, but young OK Frellick said: "We're sure as hell eating better than any spread I ever rode for. Mizz Amidon is some kinda cook, and Kate is pretty to look at."

"Shut up, you wet-eared yearling!" snarled Tench, a bloated barrel of a man with a mean squinched-up face and evil eyes. "You ain't growed up enough to offer an opinion, you skinny squirt."

"Lay off the kid, Tench," warned slim dapper Santee.

Frellick laughed at him. "Ugly as you are, Tench, you don't scare me a helluva lot."

"Cut the stupid squabbling and git back to work," advised the veteran Crull, known as Hoss, once a famous bronc buster and gunfighter.

Kloster hunched his high shoulders and twisted his coyote face into a menacing scowl. "Who made you trail boss, old man?"

"Nobody yet but somebody ought to," Crull said calmly. "It's something we sure ain't got on this drive."

And that's the way it went, with fist fights breaking out now and then, close to turning into gunfights on occasion.

Kate had promised to work with the cavvy and help gather wood for the cookfires, as well as drive the bed-and-wood wagon, but she spent most of her time drifting around on a piebald pony and flirting with the cowboys, young and old. Grace drove the grub wagon and did the cooking, and she was swiftly losing her plumpness along with her sunny disposition.

Anse Amidon was wearing himself down to bone-and-muscle gauntness, rampaging to and fro on his homely gotch-eared claybank, trying to be every place at the same time, turning the dust-stormed heat-laden air blue with his colorful profanity and hoarse exhortations.

"Trying to be a one-man trail drive," muttered Hoss Crull. "Anse ain't going to last at this rate, no matter how rawhide tough he is."

"He's a tough old rooster," Santee said, casually flipping out his sixgun and spinning it on his trigger finger. "He ain't getting much help from a lot of his handpicked waddies, who ain't worth a fiddler's damn at moving stock. But Anse Amidon will make it. He craves that big bonus."

"It ain't the money," Crull said. "It's a matter of pride. Anse was always a winner."

"Except when it come to raising a daughter," snickered Pueblo, a stone-faced, ice-eyed gunslinger, in the same category as Kloster and Tench and Santee. "I aim to have a piece of that myself, she keeps flaunting it around."

"She wouldn't spit on a goat like you," young Frellick laughed.

Pueblo eyed the boy coldly, but made no move with Santee looking on. Pueblo said, "You ain't going to live to see the Red River, sonny, if you don't put a curb on that loose tongue."

That night, the herd bedded down on the flats outside a town called Arrowhead, Frellick was riding his two-hour tour of duty at circling the herd, his bright young eyes yearning toward the lights of the village. Pueblo was making the circuit in the opposite direction, and they did not pause or speak when they met on the rounds. Frellick didn't have a reputation like the older Andiron gunsharps, but he figured he was up to facing any of them, even Kloster.

Frellick was singing the slow mournful ditties that are supposed to soothe cattle in the night. He had run through most of the old favorites—Saddle Old Spike, Hell Among the Yearlin's, The Dying Cowboy, Sally Gooden, The Streets of Laredo—and was improvising one of his own:

> "Lay me down gentle,
> Treat me with care,
> I got two bullets in me

I can't hardly bear.

My gun caught in the holster,
A sad trick of fate;
When I finally cleared leather
It was way way too-oo late."

Not bad, Frellick thought in modest pride, and then he saw the girl waiting in the lacy shadows of a huge cottonwood. It was Kate Amidon, of course, and she was waving a bottle at him. Frellick had been thirsting for hours, with the saloons of Arrowhead so near and yet so far. He was only human, and young, reckless and always ready for a fight or a frolic. Any pretty gal that challenged him was going to get called. He slanted his lively *grullo* toward the girl under the tree, and smiled at the yellow saber of a moon tilted among a swarm of silvery stars above jigsawed buttes and mesas, in the distance. The night air was keen and sweet.

"Light and drink, cowboy," invited Kate Amidon, her eyes shining palely.

Frellick slid smoothly from the saddle. "Don't mind if I do, ma'am." He tipped the bottle, palmed its neck, and handed it back. "Good stuff. I'm sure obliged."

Kate drank and laughed. "Kentucky bourbon. Dad has it shipped in. What's your first name, Frellick?"

"Never use it. Just call me Frell or OK."

"Does the OK stand for anything?"

"Orlando Kent," he confessed, hesitant and sheepish.

Kate burst into laughter. "That's some name. No wonder you don't use it. You're a goodlooking boy, Orlando Kent Frellick."

"Please, lady."

Kate extended the bottle. "Have another and sit down with me. The grass is nice and soft under here."

Frellick drank, but shook his head. "I gotta keep riding circle. If them cows should run, your dad would hang me from a wagon tongue."

"I deserve some thanks." Kate moved against him, and raised her clearcut face and full lush mouth. Frellick was kissing her, when the abrupt thud of hoofs split them apart.

It was Pueblo, towering over them on his mottled gray mustang. "What the hell you doing, boy? Get back on the circle, for chrisake." His gun was drawn and aimed down at the slim man on front.

"Don't point that thing at me, mister," Frellick said tightly.

Pueblo's smile was a toothy grimace. "I'll use it on you, if you don't mount up and get back on the job."

"Put the gun away, Pueblo," said Kate Amidon, with cool authority. "You want to start a stampede, you damn fool?"

Pueblo holstered the weapon, and Frellick swung aboard his blue roan, murmuring a goodnight to the girl. They rode side by side back toward the quiet mass of cattle.

"You going to turn me in, I reckon," Frellick said, dry-mouthed and tense. "The girl asked me over. She's the boss's daughter. What the hell?"

"You going in town when we get off?" Pueblo demanded.

"I was planning to."

Pueblo's teeth showed again. "See you in there, kid. I ain't going to turn you in. I'm going to shoot the hell outa you."

"That's all right." Frellick smiled thinly. "Just so you don't backshoot me."

"Who has to backshoot a punk kid? Just get into town."

"I'll be there."

They parted and resumed the circuit of the bedground in opposite directions, but Frellick's throat was too dry and taut for any more singing. He *knew* Pueblo was fast, and the *thought* he could match him or beat him. But Frellick couldn't be certain. He'd never really been tested.

An hour later, after the next shift of riders had relieved them, Frellick was making the rounds in Arrowhead,

54

searching for Pueblo. He hadn't been able to find Santee or Crull or Mundorf, anyone he could trust, and he felt very much alone. Crowleg Dooner was on duty and couldn't get away.

This is crazy, Frellick thought. This don't make no sense at all. But it had to come sometime. He and Pueblo had been at odds since they first met at Andiron. They had been instant and instinctive hatred between them. Well, there'd be no more suspense, no more waiting and wondering after tonight. He mused about what Kate Amidon would think. He knew he could have had her, but that was no great thing. She'd been with Deke Vennis, and some said the Ranger Lashtrow, and God knows how many others. Would she shed a tear if he got killed tonight? He doubted it . . . . But he wasn't going to die, goddamn it. He was going to blow apart that bastard Pueblo, and then Tench and Kloster and the others would show him plenty of respect.

Pueblo wasn't in the first two saloons he visited. The third place bore the grandiose name Eldorado, but it was just a crummy adobe-brick joint like the rest. Frellick shouldered through the swing-doors and saw Pueblo sitting alone at a small table facing him. He sensed there was a drawn pistol under that table, and knew the cowardly sonofabitch had tricked him. Frellick's right hand flicked to his Colt, but gunflames streaked at him from beneath the wood, the slugs ripping his legs from under him. Frellick was shocked and falling when the .45 blazed and bucked in his hand, missing he thought, as the sawdusted floor jarred him.

Pueblo was standing and shooting now, the blasts coming in swift succession, and Frellick felt the heavy jolts and rolled under the impacts. Then he was stretched full length with his face in the dirty sawdust, arms and legs scrabbling as he tried in vain to push himself up and fire another shot. The gun exploded, jumping out of his grip, and he felt everything pour out of him and knew that it was the end, he was dying, it was all over, he was dead. He wanted to laugh then, because it had all been an empty joke from start to finish, but his mouth was full of blood and sawdust, and he was drowned deep in darkness.

Santee came in after it was over, and he would have shot Pueblo dead if Kloster and Tench and big Mule Mundorf hadn't jumped and held him.

They rode back to camp with Frellick's body draped over his saddle on the *grullo*, and Anse Amidon had to be restrained from strangling Pueblo with his powerful bare hands, there by the chuckwagon fire.

"You dirty worthless guncrazy sonofabitch!" Anse raved at Pueblo. "You been wanting to kill that kid for months, you rotten bastard! The nicest kid in the whole goddamn crew, and the best swing rider I had. I'll bet you suckered him too, you never gave him an even chance."

"He came in the door and went for his gun," Pueblo said. "What could I do, for the luvva gawd? I had to shoot in self-defense. Ask anybody who saw it, anyone who was there."

"That's right, Anse," said Kloster. "The kid reached as soon as he spotted Pueblo. Everybody saw it."

"*I* didn't see it," Santee said. "And I still think Pueblo had a gun drawn and cocked under the table."

"You'll answer for that, Santee," growled Pueblo.

Amidon roared again at Pueblo: "Keep your lousy mouth shut, you two-bit gunslinging sonofabitch. Why would Frellick go gunning for you? Why, goddamn it, *why*?"

Pueblo glanced beseechingly at the foreman. Kloster said: "Because Pueblo caught him with your daughter, Anse, when he was s'posed to be riding circle on the herd."

"*What?* What the hell are you saying?" Amidon's rough red face was swollen to purple now, and he appeared ready to burst wide open. "Get that man outa here, Kloster. Get him outa my sight. Pay him off tonight and boot his ass outa my camp. I'll kill the bastard, if he ain't gone in fifteen minutes. And if I ever see him again, I'll kill him on sight!"

"We'll be shorthanded, Anse," reminded Kloster.

"Who gives a goddamn? We won't miss this useless no-good rattlesnake. Move him outa here, pronto!"

Pueblo opened his bucktoothed mouth, but Kloster and Tench hustled him away from the campfire before he could utter a word.

Anse Amidon groaned like a man in mortal agony. "Santee, have some of the boys dig a grave for the kid. I got something to say to Kate. From now on she'll ride the chuckwagon or the bed-and-wood wagon, and nothing else. She speaks to another man on this drive, and I'll horsewhip her within an inch of her life, so help me, God. I got one daughter and she can cause more trouble than all the whores in Mexico."

Santee was concentrating on shaping a cigarette, his pale blue eyes squinted almost shut. "There's some more bad news, boss. I hate like hell to have to tell you, but you oughta know. The news just come up the line and reached Arrowhead. Deke Vennis and a mongrel bunch of bandits robbed the banks in Buford and Salt Creek, and left a lot of people dead. One of them was Tonk Hiller."

Anse Amidon moaned as if mortally stricken. "O Christ on the cross. O God in the foothills." He was not cursing; it was more of a prayer. "Tonk Hiller. One of the best men and finest friend I ever knew. That's what we get for letting Vennis and them other three coyotes go when we could've—we should have—shot 'em dead." Still moaning, Anse groped for a whiskey bottle and lowered it about three inches in one gulp, before handing it to Santee. "Tonk Hiller dead. That's all I needed tonight."

Santee drank and shook his sandy head in sympathy. "I know, boss. I dreaded to tell you, but figured it had to be done."

"Sure, Santee, sure. You did right. I had to know." Anse Amidon glared wildly around, his square jaw-jutted face a crimson mask of pain and fury in the orange firelight. He grabbed the double-barreled shotgun that was propped on a bedroll. "If that Pueblo ain't gone, I'm going to blow his head off right here and now. I've gotta kill somebody or bust.''

He plunged off in the direction Kloster and the others had gone, toward the place where most of the cowboys had chosen to bed down in their blankets. Nipping at the bourbon bottle, Santee trailed warily after him.

But Pueblo had already ridden off into the night, vowing to all listeners that he would come back with Deke Vennis's gang and wipe out Amidon and the whole Andiron crew, including the two women.

At a distance, two men were digging a grave beside Frellick's tarp-wrapped body.

7

Ambuscade on Brush Creek

In late afternoon, the trail narrowed between two encroaching ridges, and some instinct of danger caused Lashtrow to halt the sorrel and lift his left hand, as Milt Travers and Tess Hiller drew up behind him. The ridge lines were scarfed with shale, tumbled with boulders, and spiked sparsely by ocotillo, yucca and stunted green sycamores. Nothing showed or stirred, but the sorrel's whicker convinced Lash that something was there in hidden waiting. Beyond the pass, Brush Creek flowed at spring-tide between banks screened thinly by willows and blackjack.

The hoof-chopped trace pitched downward to the passage, and Lashtrow had a vision of the Andiron herd surging and stomping through here to reach the water, and dirt-plastered cowboys yelling raw-throated into a hailstorm of dust.

"You hang back here, Tess, and keep under cover," Lash said finally. "Milt and I'll kinda feel our way forward a bit."

Tess Hiller nodded soberly, but after they had moved on ahead she yanked her carbine from its saddle scabbard, swung down and walked after them, leading the rawboned buckskin. Tonk had taught her to shoot, straight and fast, and if there were bushwhackers before them, the killers of her father would be among the number.

Tess was a frontier girl, for all of her education

no silk lace and lavender doll. There had been another unmentioned motive behind her desire to accompany the two Rangers northward in pursuit of the bandits.

The sun was a low ball of flame in the west, and light was fading as blue-gray shadows lengthened across the rolling prairies. The hazy gloom in the elongated cut was suddenly splintered with lurid lances of flame and crashing reports from either ridgeside. Only the fact that the enemy had fired too soon saved the Rangers from instant annihilation.

Caught in a vicious cross-whip of lead, bullets beating up dirt and streaming all around them, Lashtrow and Travers wheeled their raring mounts and unleashed their handguns, Lash to the right and Milt to the left, raking both flanks with their rapid shooting. Slugs snarled about their ears, plucked at their shirts, jarred saddle leather and singed the horses. *We got too damn careless,* Lashtrow thought disgustedly. *Too sure that Vennis was bent only on catching up to that trail herd.* This withering crossfire was too much to stand up under. They'd have to run.

"Pull out, Milt!" Lashtrow yelled. "Ride for it."

Flattened out in flight, hunched low over their horses' necks, they hammered back up the slope the way they had come, their right-hand Colts emptied, their left-hand guns practically impotent in this situation. *Nothing less than a God-given miracle can save us from this death-trap,* flitted across Lash's shaken mind, as the lead went on searching for their bent backs and scorching past the rocketing horses, to rip up spouts of dirt and rock shards. Lashtrow felt the hot suction of passing bullets.

But it proved to be something far more realistic and substantial than a prayed-for miracle. From uptrail a rifle was *spanging,* sharp and clear, scouring one ridge flank and then the other, throwing the outlaws into startled disorder and confusion. Tess Hiller, firing as calmly and steadily as if at target practice, drove the drygulchers back into shelter and nailed them down there on both sides of the defile.

A few of the bandits had mounted to make a pursuit, and Tess now lined her sixteen-shot Henry on them. A horse cartwheeled end-over-end, hurling its rider headlong into a motionless sprawl. Another man screamed and toppled, his foot snagged in the stirrup, his body furrowing a spume of dust as the bronc whirled and bolted back down the grade. That stemmed the renegade rush, at least for the moment.

"Great shooting, baby," Lashtrow shouted, as he pulled the sorrel offtrail behind a jumble of boulders, and Travers reined in after him. "You all right up there, Tess?"

She was too busy reloading her rifle to reply.

Lash and Milt refilled the cylinders of their smoking .44s, sheathing them to unlimber and cut loose with their Winchester carbines. Gunfire slashed back and forth in the purpling dusk, with bullets whining through the smoke and screeching off rock faces, the reek of cordite fouling the atmosphere. But there was little more organized shooting from the ambushers. By the time Tess Hiller's Henry chimed in again, the bandits were scattered and running, leaving three or four dead along the road.

His carbine spent, Lashtrow pulled both sixguns and called: "Cover me, Milt. I'm going down to see they keep going, and maybe take down a coupla more of the bastards." Travers disliked being left behind, but he quietly went on reloading his Winchester and stood at the ready, blue gaze probing the break between the ridges.

Back in the saddle, reins on the horn and Colts poised in both big hands, Lashtrow kneed the sorrel out into the open and put him down the slope at a smooth powerful gait. "Run 'em down, Mate," he said, bent over the horse's golden mane.

Muzzle light flared up at him from an unhorsed man, and Lashtrow drove the sorrel straight over him, the bushwhacker shrieking under the steel-shod hoofs. Twisting in the leather, Lash shot back on a downslant to put the bandit out of his misery. But the other outlaws had fled and vanished into the quick-deepening dark, except for the four who would never ride or raid again.

Lashtrow looked over the fallen, but failed to recognize any of them. There was nothing in their pockets to identify them either, but he felt positive they were from Deke Vennis's band. Whoever they might have been, they were nobody to mourn, and Lash had no compunction about confiscating the wadded bills that most likely were stolen from the banks in Buford or Salt Creek. "Travel money for poor underpaid Rangers, Soldier," he told the sorrel. "One of the few fringe benefits in this trade."

Well, the big ones, the worst ones, were still alive and ahead. A menace to whatever region they traversed, and especially to the Andiron trail crew and herd.

Loping back up the grade to rejoin his comrades, Lashtrow felt a flash of pride and satisfaction in Tess Hiller's fine performance today. The girl had really come through in combat. Hell, she had saved their lives, no damn doubt of it. She had sprung a pair of dumb damned-fool Rangers out of a fatal trap.

Lashtrow found Tess Hiller and Milt Travers celebrating quietly with drinks from one of Milt's ubiquitous bottles, and he gladly joined them. "You were something this afternoon, Tess," he said, with feeling. "That was real Ranger shooting, baby."

"I'm pleased that you approve," Tess said, in mild satire. She hadn't forgiven Lashtrow for his aloofness, but he would win her pardon tonight, while Milt was on lookout. It would be essential to stand night watches hereafter, divided into two shifts.

"She proved herself the best Ranger of us all," Milt Travers said, in his smooth cultured tones. "I shall compose a song of tribute to you, Teresa, when the spirit moves me. Meantime, may I be permitted to cite you in the French fashion."

He kissed her on both tanned powder-streaked cheeks with ineffable grace. Lash didn't mind at all, as long as it was Milt Travers.

They rode on to ford Brush Creek and make camp on the north bank, in a eucalyptus grove. After supper, Travers volunteered to stand the first watch. Left alone in the darkness beyond the aura of firelight, Lashtrow and Tess Hiller were soon blended in a crushing embrace, a rapturous flight among the fiery planets and celestial systems and jeweled constellations of outer space.

It turned out that Milt stood sentry through the night, allowing Lash and Tess to sleep in one another's arms for the first time.

In the morning, while Tess prepared breakfast, Lashtrow cussed Milt out from top to bottom, and Milt just grinned like a boy and said: "Get off my neck, Lashtrow. I can sleep all day on horseback if I feel like it. Done it before, you know. It's one of the advantages of higher education. Mind over matter, or some such nonsense."

They rode onward into the north, and passed sunbaked straggling settlements, some of which were on the railroad line, but Tessie Hiller made no more mention of taking a train or stagecoach to Kansas City.

They crossed rivers, the broad Lampasas, the narrow Leon, and the tree-shaded Brazos, in the wake of the vast Andiron herd. The trampled, ground-ravaging tracks were growing fresher, day by day. Finding no dead bodies or new graves, Lashtrow assumed that Anse Amidon was still driving his own beefs, and that Deke Vennis hadn't struck them yet.

Nearing the Trinity River, they saw the high-flung dust cloud of the drive darkening the northern sky, and Lashtrow suggested increasing their pace to overtake the cattle. Some of Vennis's bandits might have signed on as additional hands or replacements with Amidon's crew.

Outside of Arrowhead, they had come upon one fresh grave, marked with a crude wooden cross, on which some one had carved a most unusual name: ORLANDO KENT FREL-LICK. . . . "I remember him well," Tess Hiller said sadly, "Just a kid, a nice-looking boy. Used to come into Salt Creek with the other cowboys, real proud to be one of them, drinking whiskey and wearing a gun. He had hair like straw and laughing eyes and a sweet smile. Ashamed of that first name, of course. I wonder what happened to OK Frellick. . . ."

Lashtrow, for some reason, had an idea that Kate Amidon had been involved in the death of that cowboy, but he refrained from putting it into words.

Another long blistering day, and they overtook the drive at last, riding into the dense dust of the drag, where the hulking Mule Mundorf and a young *vaquero* called Ramos were pushing the aged, sick and weak of the herd forward in a smother of swirling dirt.

"How's it going, Mule?" asked Lashtrow.

Mundorf shook his sweaty dusted head and spat a disgusted stream of tobacco juice. "We ain't had nothing but bad luck since we started, Lashtrow. Nothing too big yet, just pesky niggling little things that heckle you all to hell. On schedule so far, but running shorthanded and racking ourselves to the bone. Anse more than anybody else. Nothing but that big bonus money keeps us in the leather."

"*La cola del mundo*," Ramos said, with a wide grin.

Lash nodded and smiled with him. The drag of a cattle drive could well be called the tail-end of the world. "Lost any men, Mule?"

"Just two—so far. No need of it neither. Pueblo shot the kid, Frellick, and Anse fired Pueblo. We miss OK Frell. A good boy and a good swing man. Nobody missed that sonofabitch Pueblo. Unless it's Tench and maybe Kloster."

"Nobody's tried to jump the herd?"

"Not yet. But we're expecting Deke Vennis, one of these days."

"Thanks, Mule," said Lashtrow. "Be seeing you later."

They skirted the dust-drenched drag and rode forward,

past the flankers and swing riders, on toward the point. Three thousand cows and steers on the march was a tremendous monumental sight, and even Lashtrow was stirred by it, while Tess Hiller and Milt Travers were exuberant and incredulous.

"Watch it well," Lashtrow advised them. "You'll never see anything like it again. Nobody will. This is the last big trail drive ever. They tell of driving ten thousand head, in the early days, yet lots of oldtimers claim that's an exaggeration. But I know they've driven herds of five and six thousand."

"Think of it!" cried Tess, her tone as awed as her wide violet eyes. "Twice as many cattle as this or more. What a grand spectacle."

"It's hard to envision anything larger than this," Milt Travers said. "A sight to remember forever. Wish I could paint it, or even put it in prose or poetry. It would require a genius, and I don't quite qualify."

Passing the swing on this right wing, Lashtrow paused to exchange greetings with Hoss Crull, a wizened veteran with sparse white hair above a leather-tough face etched deeply by scars and seams. "Sure happy you're here, Lash," the old man said, his bleached eyes still alert and keen. "We need some help on this one. It's damn near falling apart. Men that Anse trusted are failing him bad."

"He'll be all right as long as he's got you, Hoss," said Lashtrow.

Crull grinned and spat brown. "This old Hoss ain't what he used to be, Lash."

As they cantered on toward the point, Anse Amidon hauled his ugly hammer-headed claybank around to meet them. "It's high time, Lash. What the hell kept you? Hullo, Tessie, my dear. Just heard about Tonk the other night. Ain't got over it yet, and never will. But I'm sure glad to see you, sweetie. And Milt Travers, the Duke of Boston. How are yuh, you depraved aristocrat? A sight for these sore bloodshot eyes, all three of you. Goddamn, if this don't call for about a barrel of Kaintuck bourbon, right in the middle of this mucked-up trail. Come on up to the chuckwagon and see Grace—and Kate—and wet down your tonsils, which must be dryer than the Staked Plains by now."

As they passed the point, Santee on the far left side, waved and smiled in a casual friendly manner, but Kloster, on the near right side, kept his beaked dour visage turned away, ignoring the new arrivals. Lash had always been dubious about Kloster, and he wondered about Santee.

"Is Santee still a Kloster man, Anse?" he inquired.

"Figured he was, like Tench and Pueblo, but I ain't sure now." Amidon wagged his crisp gray head. "Santee's a damn good cowman."

"And Kloster?"

"I dunno, Lash. He was a good range boss on the home spread, I always thought. But he ain't much good out here on the trail."

"You think Vennis could have gotten to any of your men?"

"Well, he might've planted Pueblo to make trouble. Tench too, maybe. Don't know about any others."

They found Grace on the seat of the chuckwagon, thinned down, hardened and drawn with fatigue, but she was glad to see them and tried to welcome them with her old jollity. Kate, driving the wagon that carried the bedrolls, warbags and wood supply, looked grim and strangely subdued, and was not particularly pleased to see the newcomers, least of all Tess Hiller.

Anse brought out a jug of whiskey and tin cups, and they all had a couple of rounds, except Grace who declined, and Kate who was not invited. It was not exactly a gala reunion, any more than it was a well-coordinated and harmonious trail drive.

"Can you use two—I mean three—new hands, Anse?" asked Lashtrow. "Tess can handle her shift on the *remuda*.

66

Milt could work into the swing. And I'm an old point rider, or all-round cowboy, as I've bragged before."

"We can use you all right," Amidon said gruffly. "We need you bad, in fact. Your coming is a godsend to this outfit right now. With you three *compadres* in harness, we might just make Abilene, after all."

"Well, we're here to help out, Anse," drawled Lashtrow. "Our assignment is to run down the Vennis bunch, and the quickest way to get them is working this drive. Because they're sure to hit you sometime, somewhere, and we want to be here when the bastards come in after you."

Anse Amidon's laugh boomed out. "I can breathe easy, by God, for the first time since we hit the old Chisholm Trail. You've lifted a thousand pounds and ten years or more off my poor old aching back. Let's have another belt of bourbon, and get them cow critters humping the way they should."

Amidon's high spirits were contagious to everyone but his wife and daughter. Tess Hiller and the Rangers left their superfluous gear in the bed wagon, and headed back for the herd, which seemed to cover the entire plains under miles-long dust billows.

"Lash, you take the point with Santee, and I'll put Kloster where he can do less harm. Milt, you ride swing with old Hoss Crull, and he'll learn you all there is to know about it in quick order. Tess, if you ain't all wore out, I'll introduce you to Crowleg Dooner and he'll make you acquainted with the cavvy. And by the Jesus, this drive'll start to rumble like a cattle drive oughta, or I ain't the best cattleman south of Montana."

"You've only lost two men so far, Mule Mundorf told me," Lashtrow said.

"That's right, Lash, and only a few head of stock," Amidon said. "A fine boy dead, and a goddamn murdering sonofabitch fired. Had I known the truth, I woulda killed Pueblo on the spot. God forgive me for not doing it."

Lashtrow gnawed into a tobacco plug. "Murder, Anse?"

67

"Yeah, I finally got it straight. Pueblo had his pistol cocked under the table. OK Frellick come in, saw Pueblo, went for his iron, and Pueblo drilled him from under the wood. The poor kid never had a chance in hell."

"What was the trouble between them?"

"They just naturally hated each other, I reckon." Amidon seemed a trifle embarrassed and uncomfortable. "Well, I might as well tell you, since you know how Kate is. What lit the fuse was Pueblo saw Frellick with Kate, when he was s'posed be riding circle with Pueblo. The bastard wanted a showdown right there, but Kate warned him not to spook the herd. So Pueblo challenged Frell to meet him in town, and burned the kid down like I told you. A goddamn shame. Frell was a fine lad and a real cowhand."

At the head of the herd, Amidon and Lashtrow pulled up beside Kloster. Amidon said: "Lash'll take the point, Klos. You go on back and help the flankers."

Kloster's eyes glared hotly above his beak of a nose, and his almost lipless mouth turned down farther than ever. "Maybe he'd like to be trail boss, too."

"Maybe he will be," Amidon said curtly, "if you don't pitch in and take hold better'n you been doing. You been sulking ever since I canned Pueblo."

Disregarding Anse, Kloster turned his big black stallion against the sorrel, his right elbow out and hand spread-fingered. "You man enough to take my job? Make you move, then."

"I don't want your job. And I don't wanta kill you. Pull in your horns, Kloster." Lashtrow sat motionless in the leather, hands resting idly on his thighs, as the two horses jostled and shifted. Watching the man's eyes, Lash saw that he was going to draw. Lash's left fist was lashing out when Kloster's hand slapped down on his pistol grip. The hooking left smashed into Kloster's right jawbone, snapping his head and jolting him out of the saddle. He landed heavily on his shoulders, head bouncing in the packed dirt, and lay there cold and still.

"Nice clean knockout," Santee said, grinning. "Maybe you broke his goddamn neck, Lash."

"I hope not," Lashtrow said simply.

Anse Amidon, canteen in hand, got off his claybank, unbuckled and ripped Kloster's gunbelt loose, and poured water onto the stunned hatchet-face. The foreman stirred slightly, but he was still unconscious.

"I'll take the flank for now, Anse," said Lashtrow. "You don't need any more trouble, and I don't wanta shoot the ornery sonofabich for nothing. When he comes to, tell him the next time he reaches or calls me he's a dead man."

"He won't come at you again, Lash," promised Amidon. "If I have to fire him, I will. He ain't been worth a goddamn on this drive anyway. I don't know what the hell come over the sour-faced bastard, but something sure changed him."

"I've got no hard feelings," Lashtrow said. "I just soon shake hands and forget it, if Kloster's willing. But if he crosses me again, he'll have to die. You make sure he knows about that, Anse."

Anse Amidon nodded heavily. "I got a lot of things to make Kloster dead-sure about, and I'm laying 'em on the line as soon as he comes to. You go ahead, Lash. See you at supper."

Lashtrow drifted the sorrel down the line until he met the cowboys working the left-hand swing. Far across the horned heads and humping backs, he could see Milt Travers riding alongside of Hoss Crull, and he knew they'd work well together. It would be a good experience for Milt; Hoss could teach him, or any man, a great deal, and not only about cattle.

8

Cattle Drive on the Chisholm

For a stretch, after the advent of Lashtrow, Travers and
Tess Hiller, the trail drive went better and faster. Morale
was higher, and Anse Amidon regained his confidence and
enthusiasm. Kloster stayed on, but he was trail boss in name
only now. He came around to shake hands with Lash, and
then withdrew into a sour sullen shell, speaking to no one
but Tench, working just enough to get by without repri-
mands from Amidon, taking no interest in the events or
people around him.

"I was damn near ready to give it up, Lash," admitted
Anse Amidon. "These cowboys today ain't got the heart
and guts for a long trail drive. They don't wanta work that
hard nowadays. The old breed is dying out, the real cowhands are gone, except for a few like Santee and Crull and
Dooner. The new ones are just punchers, fit for punching
a few cows into a railroad stock car and calling it a day."

Lashtrow rode the point with Santee, leaving Amidon
free for general over-all supervision. Hoss Crull ran the
swing on one flank, and Milt Travers, learning quickly from
Hoss, was soon capable of taking charge of the swing on
the other side. Crowleg Dooner declared that Tess Hiller
was a marvel with horses, and cut his work in half at the
cavvy. Grace and Kate Amidon required more assistance
with the wagons and cooking, as they became tired and
wornout, but even Kate stuck to the job better than anyone

70

had anticipated. Carlos served as second cook and handyman.

They made an easy crossing of the Trinity, and drove on toward the Red and the northern boundary of Texas. Lashtrow had soon proven that he could build and string out a point, ride and swing, or bring up the drag with the best of drovers.

The slow plodding days passed in stifling heat and choking dust under brassy molten skies, with sweating dirt-smeared swearing men burning out themselves and one horse after another to keep the strungout mass of beef moving. Men and beasts alike grew mean and ugly under the blazing ordeal. There were near fights about the night fires, and stampedes came close to starting in the bed grounds. But the drive went on because Anse Amidon willed it to, and some of his loyal hands sustained that will with twelve-hour days of backbreaking, rumpsplitting, lungbursting toil in furnace heat, scourging winds and boiling dust.

And around the clock they waited for the attack of Deke Vennis's lawless force that would certainly come somewhere along the route.

Lashtrow had found pleasure and satisfaction in working as a cowboy once more. It was part of his heritage, something that his father had instilled in him, a kind of legacy. It was a better job than being a Ranger, cleaner, more decent and honorable. To be a Ranger you had to kill, for that was the only way a few men could fight the legions of evil and crime. Arrests were no good. Legal processes were too long, complex and time-consuming, a waste of money, and often the guilty were set free. A Ranger was a soldier more than a lawman. His job was to kill the enemy. After years of it, a man grew tired and sick of killing. The faces of men he had shot to death came back in his dreams.

Lashtrow was bothered also by his relationship with Tess Hiller. It didn't seem right somehow, perhaps because he had known her as a child and been a close friend of her father. He couldn't look at her, a full-grown woman now, without seeing the golden-haired little girl she had been. He felt tainted with a sense of guilt and shame, unreasonable and unfounded maybe, but none the less lacerating. It was almost incestuous, in his mind, and could never bring happiness. Like most women in love, Tess was becoming overly possessive, and that was another galling irritant. Lashtrow wished he had been strong enough to resist her initial advances.

There were opportunities to slip away from private meetings and love-making, but it could not be accomplished in secrecy. Around the campfires, absences were more conspicuous than presences. Kate Amidon's comments on their frequent disappearances were acidulous and vituperative enough to set other tongues wagging. After the shooting of Frellick, Kate had been restricted to good behavior, but now she was drinking on the sly again and sometimes seeking the company of Kloster, those two drawn together by their mutual status as rebels and outcasts. Any means of defying her father was irresistible to Kate Amidon.

Lashtrow began to plead weariness in order to elude rendezvous with Tess Hiller, a weariness that was more actual than pretense. Tess was equally tired, of course, but refused to accept Lash's excuses as valid, and accused him of wanting to break with her so he could enjoy the more experienced wiles and favors of the boss's daughter. It was such a typical and irrational feminine viewpoint, so outrageous a falsity, that Lashtrow knew no method of counteraction and remained silent. This made Tess all the more furious, and they began to drift apart and avoid one another. They were both lonesome, miserable, and bereft.

Lash resumed closer comradeship with Milt Travers, Anse Amidon, young Santee, old Hoss Crull, and big Mule Mundorf, while Tess Hiller perversely struck up a tentative precarious alliance with Kate Amidon. The two girls had always been hostile rivals, but now, with the womanly fickleness and proneness to erratic switches so incompre-

72

hensible to the masculine mind, they became friends of a sort. . . . And the drive went on.

Then the rains came in a sudden torrent, welcomed at first for the coolness, catching them in a tortuous country of weird buttes and mesas, strange stone pillars, shifting sand dunes and sharp gorges, bristly cactus and yucca, red manzanita, Spanish bayonet and scrub oak and cedar. Rain lashed the slickered riders on their bent-headed broncs, and the blinded cattle crowding together, and rain danced and splashed on the earth and stones, and soaked steaming into dirt that had been so dry and hot minutes before. Cowboys raised their faces and opened their mouths to the rainfall, howling in delight as it wet their inflamed bodies, sucking drops into alkali-crusted throats. "Come on down, rain! Let it pour."

The drenching downpour came as a blessing and relief, but became a nagging torment as it continued to whip and soak the men and animals, an endless watery scourge prolonged to be as trying and hateful as the heat had been. And in the minds of Amidon, Lashtrow and the rest, was the fear that this storm might raise the Red River to full floodtide before they ever reached it, and thus turn the fording into a nightmare.

The rain had finally slowed to a dreary drizzle and they were huddled about the evening campfires for warmth, cheer and more after-supper coffee, thinking gloomily of the river crossing that lay ahead. The Red was always bad, and after this rain it would be worse. At the chuckwagon fire, Lashtrow was perched on a wet log between Anse Amidon and Milt Travers. Behind them, Tess Hiller and Kate Amidon were moving to and fro, bringing more coffee and carrying away empty dishes and cups.

Sullen men in wet ponchos clustered moodily about other fires in the vicinity, wishing the coffee was whiskey, and the usual night watch was out riding herd on the bed grounds. Snatches of plaintive song floated in from the

73

night-riders now and then as they circled the cattle. . . . *"For you know that Wyoming will be your new home . . ."*

Amidon passed long thin cigars to Lashtrow and Travers, and they were lighting up, when some impulse caused Kate Amidon to turn her smoky gray eyes toward the chuck-wagon in the rear. Her eyes widened and her mouth opened in a soundless scream, as she saw a long pistol barrel leveled through the wheel spokes, straight at the broad massive back of her father.

Without conscious thought, Kate moved into line between that wagon wheel and Anse Amidon's back, just as flame spurted with a deafening roar. The impact hurled her toward the backs of the men on that log. Lashtrow was up and spinning around, over the windfall in time to catch her in his arms. Everybody came up and whirled, stricken, shocked and staring, expecting a full-scale assault. There was no further shooting.

Lashtrow thrust the girl's limp body into her father's grasp, and winced at the horror in Anse's face. "Take care of her. I'll get the sonofabitch."

Rounding the wagon in full stride, boots driving and churning on soggy turf and puddled muck, Lashtrow cleared his right-hand gun on the run and peered into the rain-misted darkness. Everyone else seemed frozen in place. Away from the chuckwagon, no one knew what had happened. Now somebody came running in back of Lashtrow, and he knew it was Travers.

Glimpsing a blurred movement sixty-odd feet away, Lashtrow lined and let go a shot at it, the gun kicking up in his hand. The fleeing figure turned, and orange fire torched back at the Ranger, the bullet searing past his left shoulder, shredding cloth and burning skin. The man could shoot. Behind Lash, Santee had come abreast of Travers, guns in their hands.

Lashtrow leveled down from the recoil and thumbed his hammer forward. Muzzle flame speared out, bright and loud, and showed the other man sagging abruptly on spraddled legs, his pistol exploding earthward, splashing water and mud. Lash slammed another shot home. The dark form jerked backward and fell, rolled over, and finally lay still in the mire.

Striding forward, Colt cocked and ready, Lashtrow wondered whom he would find lying there. Kloster most likely, or maybe Tench. But when he turned the body over with a one-handed wrench, it was a stranger, a man he'd never seen before. Probably one of Deke Vennis's gunhands.

"It's that bastard Pueblo," said Santee, at Lash's shoulder. "Come back to kill Anse, and Kate took the bullet instead. You got yourself a good one, Lash."

"How's the girl?" Lashtrow asked.

"Still living but she's hit badly," Milt Travers said. "I'm afraid she won't make it, Lash."

They walked back to the firelit wagons in the slow seeping rain, and found Kate Amidon lying, warm-wrapped in blankets beneath the sheltering tailgate, with Anse and Grace kneeling at either side.

"Kate, Kate, Katie," Anse Amidon was moaning. "You're going to be all right, baby."

Kate turned her dark head from side to side, her handsome face drained pale and empty, and Lashtrow knew she was dying. She said, slow and broken: "Glad it—was me. Instead of you—Dad. Only good thing—I ever done."

"No, Katie, no," Anse begged. "I love you—we love you."

"Sorry I was—such a bad—girl. Don't know why—" Kate's faint voice faltered, broke and faded. Her eyes widened, blurred, and went vacant. Her carved features were cold and dead as marble.

Lashtrow turned away from the weeping parents and the dead girl, swearing with soft savagery.

"A young gal like that," Santee mumbled. "Jesus Loving Christ. I wonder if that sonofabitch come in on his own, or Vennis sent him?"

75

"It don't matter much," Lashtrow said. "We know Vennis is hanging out there somewhere—waiting. Have to guard the wagons and camp, and double the night-riders on the bed grounds."

"And we got that goddamn Red River to cross, swollen with rain," said Santee, flipping away the cigarette he was trying to roll and chomping into a tobacco plug. "This is a drive that never shoulda been made."

"I reckon Anse knows that now," Lashtrow murmured, low and sorrowful.

The next day, bright and clear after the storm, the drive reached Fort Griffin in mid-afternoon, where Amidon had planned to purchase a quantity of supplies and provisions. Too grief-stricken and distraught to bother with routine details, Anse turned the money and list over to Lashtrow.

A regular funeral ceremony was conducted in the limestone church of the settlement, and Kate Amidon was buried in the local cemetery. A hastily engraved slate tombstone was erected, bearing the girl's name and the dates 1856—1878. Later, Anse would have an elaborate marble monument installed. He and Grace and Tess Hiller departed immediately after the graveside service, and the off-duty cowboys were left to wander about town. Most of them took advantage of the tonsorial parlors to get much-needed shaves, haircuts and baths before visiting the famous Bee Hive Saloon and other palaces of pleasure and sin.

Milt Travers helped Lash buy the long list of goods and arrange for its delivery, after their own barbershop sojourn. Darkness had come and lamplights were blooming when they finally joined their fellows in the Bee Hive. The first few beers tasted like heavenly ambrosia, as Milt termed it, brewed on the heights of Olympus.

Hoss Crull and Crowleg Dooner had met an old rodeo

friend, who was telling them how Doc Holliday and Big Nose Kate had left Fort Griffin all of a sudden last January.

". . . Doc shot Ed Bailey over a poker table, and the marshal with about six deputies arrested Holliday. There wasn't no jail, so they locked him up in a hotel room. Big Nose Kate heard some of Bailey's friends talking about stringing the Doc up. She got their horses ready and set fire to the ass-end of the hotel, held her gun on the guard at Doc's room, took his iron and give it to Doc. Away they went out the front door, whilst everybody else in town was out back fighting the fire. Some gal, that Big Nose. Doc Holliday sure knows how to pick 'em.''

"They useta fight like wildcats 'tween theirselves,'' Hoss Crull said. ''Like to kill each other time and again, but I guess it's true love.''

"Still razzoo each other,'' the rodeo veteran said. ''But don't let anybody else mix in, or he'll git tore up and stomped. Even Wyatt Earp said he wouldn't try making no peace there.''

"Holliday's s'posed to be a dentist,'' Crowleg Dooner said. ''But he's pulled a helluva lot more guns than he has teeth.''

"Real gambling man, Doc is,'' said Hoss Crull. ''Saw him once up in Dodge bet ten thousand on the turn of a card, cold as ice.''

Crowleg Dooner drained his whiskey glass. ''Funny they call her Big Nose Kate. She ain't a badlooking woman, and she's built like a brick shithouse. Imagine setting fire to a goddamn hotel to spring Doc loose? That's the kinda woman to have, by God!''

Hoss Crull chuckled. ''I had me one like that once, up in Cheyenne. Turned a firehose loose on a marshal when he come after me. Knocked him loose of his gun and hell-west-and-crooked. Then she give me a touch of it to sober me up, she claimed.''

"Odd critters, women. Ain't quite human.'' Crowleg

Dooner sagely refilled his glass, and other empties along the bar. "But what'd we do without 'em, huh?"

"Well, they say sheep ain't bad," Santee said. "If you can stand getting that near to a sheep."

Lashtrow and Travers, on whiskey now, were rocking with laughter, and Mule Mundorf's guffaw rattled the backbar bottles. They were all trying to forget Kate and the Amidons, for the moment, along with Tonk Hiller and OK Frellick and other dead comrades.

Hoss Crull looked at Santee and shook his silvery head, as if in despair. "This younger generation is sure a sorry lot. They don't hardly deserve to grow up, but maybe it'll learn 'em a lesson. If they live that long."

9

Red River Crossing

On reconnaisance for Amidon, well forward of the herd, Lashtrow reached Doan's Crossing at the Red River, and found it running high and full, swollen by rains, yellow with mud from washed-out banks and cluttered with driftwood and debris. It didn't look good, at all.

He was glad to see Doan's Store still there, because he needed ammunition, tobacco, new underwear and shirts. There were a lot of people around, with horses tied at the hitch-racks and all kinds of vehicles scattered about the yard. Mostly men in Eastern suits or expensive hunting clothes, with a few elegantly gowned and hatted ladies. Lashtrow puzzled over this, until he realized these were newsmen from the big city papers and magazines, along with representatives from the Chicago meat-packing companies of Swift or Armour, and some photographers to picture The Last Trail Drive. That was the main attraction and news.

Lashtrow entered the crowded store and bought some .44-40 cartridges that fitted both his handguns and carbine, some underclothes, a couple of gay checkered shirts, and tobacco for cigarettes, pipe and chewing. Also two bottles of good whiskey and a box of thin cheroots. The cash taken off the dead bandits at Brush Creek came in handy. He was beiseged by questions and invitations to pose for photographs. Noncommittal, Lash admitted no connection with the trail herd, and forked his silver-rimmed Ranger star out of a vest pocket to justify his presence and silence.

On the way out he was hailed by a portly man in a gray derby with a drooping mustache, whom he recognized as Elmo C. Z. Judson, whose pen name was Ned Buntline.

"Lashtrow! The great Ranger shootist. You must have a story for me this time, Lash. Is it true that Anse Amidon's daughter was shot to death by a cowboy Anse had fired, and that you ran down and killed the villainous brute? As I mentioned before, Lashtrow, I could make you a national hero like Cody, Hickok, the James brothers, the Earps and Daltons, Wes Hardin, Clay Allison, Bat Masterson and the rest, if you'd give me half a chance."

Lashtrow smiled, slow and grave. "No story, Ned, and no thanks."

"Let me get a picture or two, and I'll write the story. You're making history, Lashtrow. You're a legend, a living legend. It'll make a beautiful book, man. You owe it to the public."

"I'm too busy to be a legend, Ned," drawled Lashtrow. "Got to hit the saddle right now. *Adios, amigo.*" He broke away with gentle firmness, left the store, mounted the sorrel, and rode out, uncomfortably aware of all the eyes gazing after him. He was sweating and his lean cheeks burned under the bronze. Buntline had been haunting him at odd intervals over the years. Most of his "heroes" are outlaws, or dead—or both, Lash thought wryly. Or suicidal glory-seekers like George Armstrong Custer, who had been destroyed with his command two years ago, up on the Little Bighorn in Wyoming. . . . Now Lash framed the report he would give to Anse.

The strings of horses used by Frellick and Pueblo had been reassigned to Lashtrow and Travers, and used in alternation as was the custom, resting their own mounts for the most part. The *remuda* consisted of trained cow and cutting horses. But at this crossing, the Rangers reverted to their own, because they were both strong swimmers.

80

Anse Amidon had isolated himself on the bed wagon; today marked his first return to active command. The herd held back, Anse had ridden up to survey the flooding stream with Lash, Milt and Hoss Crull.

"Never saw the Red much worse," Anse grumbled. "Have to raft the wagons over first. Break out the axes and start chopping down trees."

Toiling like beavers, the men cut down cottonwoods, bound the timbers together, lashed the wagons on top of the crude rafts, and rigged lines with block-and-tackle to ferry the unwieldy craft across the surging current. Grace rode on the chuckwagon, Tess Hiller in the other vehicle. It was a rough stormy voyage, but they made it.

At the head of the herd, a quarter-mile back and restless from the smell of water, Amidon lifted his voice: "They'll run like hell when we turn 'em loose. Lash and Santee at the point. Crull and Travers with your regular swing men flanking. Kloster and Mundorf pushing the drag. Once in the drink it's every man on the downstream side to hold the line and keep 'em going. All right, boys. Let's throw 'em across that goddamn river!"

Lashtrow lured out the big lead steer, Santee strung the other pointers forward, the swing riders moved into it, and soon the whole herd was in motion and gaining speed at every bounce, the drag men prodding from the rear. Dust spewed up in torrents over the bobbing horned heads and humping backs. It was like a thundering stampede when they struck the shoreline.

Leading the way, Lash on the sorrel hit the shallows with sheeted spray fanning out in high glistening arcs, the lead steer at his heels. The other leaders crashed into the water, splashing and snorting, and then it was like the shattering roar of ocean surf, as the stock poured down the bank into the stream. A veritable avalanche of cattle in a maelstrom of water and foam, the momentum carrying them halfway across. Lashtrow and other riders veered left to the downstream side.

At midriver the overwhelming force of the current began to press and bend the swimming steers into a deepening loop, as Lash and Travers and their followers fought and flailed to hold the line of snorting horned heads and heaving backs. Ashore with the first wave, meeting Santee there, they choused the dripping animals to the holding ground and turned back into the embroiled river. The hoarse shouted curses of cowboys were lost in the bawling of cattle and the roar of the stream.

The Red was choked full of swimming cows, a solid heaving mass from shore to shore, sagging downstream in the middle where riders were fighting to hold the loop intact, lashing out with wet riatas and quirts and floppy hats, screaming their throats hoarse and raw. On the other bank spectators were clustered around Doan's Store and out-buildings, some with binoculars and spyglasses, others with cameras or notebooks, watching it like a game instead of a life-and-death conflict.

As Lashtrow put the sorrel back into the water, panic broke out in midstream, and one segment of the herd convulsed into chaos, the animals milling, thrashing about, climbing on one another, butting and kicking and bellowing.

"Break it up!" Lashtrow yelled. "Drive in there. Go in and bust 'em." He sent the sorrel slithering toward the embroiled pack, and saw Milt Travers, Hoss Crull, Tench and others go slashing and screaming in, flogging away at the brute heads with quirts and rope-ends and gun barrels. Lash himself drove into the swirling mass, and something gave way as the sorrel reared high and trampled a crazed cow under his forelegs.

As a log jam breaks when the key timber is ripped loose, so this weltering jam of cattle seemed to burst, flatten out and flow again cross-current toward the north beach. A few head were lost downriver, but the main herd was moving in the right direction once more.

Bringing the sorrel around to search for Travers, Lash

suddenly sensed danger at his back. Twisting in the soaked leather, he saw the ugly squinched features and mad eyes of Tench, burly right arm cocked to strike with the loaded butt of a quirt. The weapon swished down, as Lash strove to pull aside. It missed his head but caught his right shoulder with crushing force, nearly driving him from the saddle.

Lashtrow hung there, stunned and helpless, and Tench was ready to chop him again, when Milt Travers threw his coyote dun against the bulky man and hooked a long lean-muscled arm around Tench's bull neck. Grappling and wrenching, they swayed straining back and forth on their plunging horses, white water seething about them, but the gorilla-like Tench could not break the whiplike Travers' hold. And then, abruptly, they were gone, their wallowing horses riderless. Gone without a trace, two interlocked men swept off and underwater and out of sight.

Righting himself in the wet leather, his right shoulder clamped in a vise of anguish as the numbness washed away, Lashtrow stared incredulously at the two empty-saddled horses. Tench's mustang was plowing toward shore, but Milt's *bayo coyote* was swimming with the current, as if seeking his rider down the river.

Reining the sorrel downstream in cold intensive fury, riding with the floodtide, Lashtrow searched the surface of the Red River. Once he thought he glimpsed Travers's head, but it was only a gleam of sunshine on the rippling water. There were floating half-drowned steers, but no sign of the two men. Travers and Tench must have drowned, caught in an undertown, locked in each other's arms. But he refused to concede that.

Lashtrow had forgotten about the herd, the crossing, the Amidons, Tess, everything but Milton Travers III. "He can't be dead, goddamn it," he gritted. "He can't be gone—like this. We'll find him, Pard. Damned right we'll find him."

The coyote dun was still swimming down ahead, and Lash thought: Bayo won't give up, and neither will we,

Brother. But we better get outa this goddamn river before we get waterlogged and sink."

He kneed the sorrel toward the near northern bank, and they clambered out on the sloped gravel bench, chilled and shivering, close to exhaustion. Then Lashtrow remembered that he had to go back for his guns and gear and some dry clothing, but he had no intention of giving up the hunt for Milt Travers.

Back at the bed wagon, Lash made a quick change and gathered his equipment, while the brawling splashing roar of the drive continued.

Anse Amidon was understanding. "I know you've got to go, Lash. I just hope you'll find him okay."

Mule Mundorf, Ramos and Kloster had now pushed the drag ashore, completing the crossing. They glanced at Lash's bleak face, and turned away. There were no words for such a time, and Lashtrow's features were bone-hard and gaunt, the strong nose, cheekbones and jaws standing out more than ever, the gray-green eyes glacial.

"Hate to leave you shorthanded, Anse," said Lashtrow. "Be back—soon as I can." The pain in his shoulder made him faint and sick.

"It's all right, Lash. We'll get along. We got 'em across the Red."

Lassiter nodded his dripping bronze head. "Tell Grace and Tess goodby for me."

"They'd rather hear it from you, pardner."

"Not today, Anse. But I'm sure glad Tess is with you folks."

"All the way to Abilene. Like she was our own daughter, Lash."

Lashtrow smiled, slow and somber. "That's where Vennis'll hit, I figure."

Amidon chewed on his stogie. "It was Tench, huh? Just like Pueblo."

"Yeah. And you better keep an eye on Kloster. Looks

like Vennis is in no hurry, on account he had men on your payroll.''

Amidon rolled his gray head. ''I ain't near so smart as I thought, Lash.''

''It's just that you're honest, Anse,'' said Lashtrow. ''And the world ain't. Being honest hobbles a man considerable. But you just keep on driving.''

Amidon lifted his brawny shoulders. ''It's about all a man can do. You bring Milton the Third back with you now, Lash.''

''Yeah, that's the ticket, Anson,'' said Lashtrow. ''We'll see you up in the Indian Territory. Keep a bottle burning for us by the cookfire.''

He rotated his aching right shoulder with experimental caution. Lash hoped he wouldn't have to use his right arm too much or soon.

Dried out and warmed up, guns and gear intact and saddlebags filled, Lashtrow turned his sorrel down the Red River to search for Milt Travers—or his body.

10

Out of a Watery Grave

Milton Travers awoke cold, wet and shivering on a sandy flotsam-littered riverbank, surprised to find himself alive. His head ached, lungs and stomach felt full of water, body chilled to the bone, but he was alive and breathing when he had expected to be drowned and dead. Risen, like Lazarus.

Groping instinctively for his gunbelt, Milt discovered it gone. He was clad only in shirts, pants and boots, all soaked. He recalled then stripping for the river crossing, leaving guns, saddlebags and bedroll in the bed wagon. Then the long breathless underwater struggle with Tench, taking cruel punishment but keeping his stranglehold locked on that bull neck until Tench was drowned, lifeless. Milt himself must have been unconscious when he floated to the surface. By some magic, the *bayo coyote* was there. Milt had caught onto something, bridle, saddle horn or tail, and been towed ashore. The dice had come seven for him that time.

He looked weakly around, and there was the horse patiently cropping grass above the beach. Milt had the dun, if nothing else. He felt helpless, lost without his guns. Then he remembered the moneybelt. He always had money, and more than usual now with his share of what Lash had taken from the dead bank robbers at Brush Creek. He could buy guns, ammunition, food, clothes, anything he needed, once he reached a town.

"I'm what the British call a remittance man," he had told the boys in the barracks. "The family sends me a monthly allotment to keep me away from home." That wasn't actually the case, but it made a good story, added to the mystique of Milton Travers III. A Ranger legend, unlike the Lashtrow one, but even more picaresque and colorful.

Slowly, painfully, Travers rolled over and sat up, stretching and massaging his numb arms and legs. Nothing seemed broken or out of joint. That goddamn Tench had been strong as a bull buffalo. Milt longed for a hot bath and dry clothing. After a few minutes he clambered groggily to his feet and paced slowly about, feeling faint and weak, his legs shaky.

The eastern horizon was rosy with coming day, and he prayed for the sun to rise quickly and climb high enough to warm him. Moving around was helping a little, stirring the blood into circulation. The coyote dun trotted down to muzzle his shoulder. Travers grinned with sudden remembrance. "My brain must be number than my body." He reached for the small special pocket in the saddlebow, and extracted the silver flask. "Blessed lifesaving brandy." He drank deeply and no longer felt so alone and lost and naked. "Where there's booze there's hope, Bayo," he told the horse.

After a few minutes and a few more nips, Travers was strong enough to mount and start riding. Fort Griffin was probably the nearest town of any size or substance. Estimating its location, he started in that direction. He had no urgent desire to return at once to the trail drive. The work there was altogether too gruelling and monotonous for his liking. The sun came up in a crimson blaze, the morning grew hot as it climbed into cloudless blue, and Travers had no hat to protect him from the glare. The heat intensified, the sun smote and dazzled him, and Travers seemed to be circling aimlessly in an immense open wasteland.

There was no Fort Griffin, no other towns, not even a ranch or homestead. He should have stayed on the river, and gone back to Doan's to buy the hat he needed. Could have retrieved his guns and other equipment when he overtook the drive. Now he was lost in a burnt-out barren country so vast it diminished a lone rider to pinpoint insignificance. Praise God there was water in the saddle canteen or he would have perished. The sun was almost overhead now, and Travers was half-blinded and burning up. He couldn't even locate the wide trampled trace of the Chisholm. Turning north in desperation, he thought if he could reach the Red River again he'd be safe. But that river too seemed to have vanished from the face of the earth, along with all other realities. Reeling in the saddle, he let the coyote dun pick its own way.

They forded a river, but it didn't seem large enough to be the Red. At least it offered water to the horse, and a refill of the canteen. Milt wanted to plunge into the stream himself, but he was so weak he feared he would drown. There was nothing around him but sunblasted reddish earth studded with rocks and desert vegetation, while faraway buttes and mesas, fantastically shaped, glimmered in the heat-wavering distance.

Hallucinations came and went in his stunned brain. He saw the family home on Beacon Hill, the graceful Colonial beauty of Louisburg Square, the summer house at Newport, the cottage on the Cape. But the people were all strangers, nobody he knew, and they looked right through him, as if he weren't there. He couldn't find his family or relatives, or the girls and friends he had known. He saw the gold-domed Capitol over the green sweep of the Common, the Old North Church, Harvard Square the calm blue-flowing Charles, the ships in the harbor. But no one he recognized, nobody who knew him, the familiar scenes peopled with hostile strangers. In his dream he was crying, ''Mother, where are you, Mother?''

Travers came to with a violent jerk, grasping the horn

to save falling from the leather. There were buzzards wheeling in the bright blue sky ahead, circling and dipping lower, and he wondered if they were waiting for him. He reached automatically for his carbine, but the boot was empty. His right hand went to his holster, but nothing was there. His eyes and head ached from the pitiless glare of the sun, and his flesh was on fire.

The Andiron crew would have given him up as dead, drowned along with Tench.

Must be up in the Indian Nations, now called Oklahoma. A raw wild country, largely unsettled, occupied mainly by Indian fugitives from the reservations, and by outlawed bad men from neighboring states or territories, roving renegade bands, red and brown and white. *And I don't even have a gun*, Travers thought dismally.

Rounding the base of a redstone butte, Travers came into view of stark horror on the sunburnt plain. A massacred wagon train, a small one, with four charred wrecked carts and scalped and mutilated human bodies strewn about the blackened ruins. Already half out of his mind, this site of carnage nearly drove Milt over the brink into an abyss of madness. Vultures were at work on the red ghastly remains.

The coyote dun shied and snorted, and Milt Travers' first impulse was to flee, shocked and soul-sick in the saddle. His duty was to inspect the scene. He scanned all four points of the compass, but the raiders were long gone. Gritting his teeth, Travers urged the dun forward. Something might be learned here. He had studied Indians, learning much from Lashtrow, and was curious as to which tribe had committed this atrocity.

Buzzards flapped away at his approach, and Travers cursed them along with the Injuns, delving back into his memory of Indian lore. The arrows, a broken lance and tomahawk, bespoke Osages. Two torn red headbands and certain modes of scalping and torture indicated the Apache. The evidence didn't jibe, any more than those two tribes did.

Milt Travers couldn't force himself close enough for clinical details. He had to nip at his flask to prevent vomiting. But amidst the debris from the wagons, he saw the sun glinting on a couple of steel barrels. Dismounting, slow and careful in his fatigue and nausea, he forked out a Spencer carbine and an old pistol, both loaded and apparently undamaged. "Manna from heaven," he murmured, but he couldn't imagine Indians leaving any such weapons behind. And the profusion of hoofprints were made by shod horses, he observed, as he started tracking them northward, the sixgun under his belt, the carbine in his right fist lying across the pommel.

Travers felt much better with the guns, even after that macabre spectacle behind him. But there was something definitely wrong with the whole picture. Injuns invariably stripped their victims of clothing, jewelry and trinkets. The dead back there had been left clothed. He had noticed buckskin jackets and silver belt buckles on some of the men. And a woman's body with bracelets and a locket on a gold chain.

It was difficult to believe that anyone except mescal-drunk savages could perpetrate such an outrage, yet some white renegades were as bad or worse than the most merciless redskins. He recalled hearing that Yaqui Tupelo, one of Vennis's tophands, had a depraved lust for torture.

Milt Travers stayed on their trace because it led in the right direction and must roughly parallel the Chisholm Trail. He was clear-headed one moment and giddy the next. Only the flask of cognac kept him going, into a raw broken land of angular mesas and choppy hills.

He drowsed off once, and when he came awake again they were in an arid expanse of alkali flats and sand dunes, splashed vividly in spots by brilliant staghorn cactus and golden gilia. Pitahaya columns loomed above squat greasewood shrubs, and giant saguaro cactus spread spiny candelabrae over chaparral, sage and catclaw. In the shade of a tilted yellow butte, Travers paused to rest, drink sparingly from the canteen, and swab out the dun's nostrils and mouth.

"Bayo, I don't know if this is real, or just a bad dream," he said.

Travers's head and face burned from exposure, and his vision played tricks on him. He should have taken a hat from the massacre site, but he hadn't the heart or stomach for it.

Now they were climbing, climbing long dry washes and barren open slopes, and as they gained altitude the hills were clothed with scrub cedar and oak and jackpine. The timber gradually thickened and brought the welcome shade of taller trees, ash and laurel and pine, like a benediction after the cruel blinding heat of the afternoon sun. Cramped and sore from the hot leather, Milt Travers stepped down and led the coyote dun in a slow easy walk. He knew he might be walking straight into an ambush, but it didn't seem to matter in his dazed condition. Nothing did. He simply wanted to fall on his face and sleep forever. He almost wished he had drowned back there in the cool rushing depths of the Red River. Maybe *had* drowned, and this was Hell he was wandering through.

Travers was sure he was seeing things when the Indians suddenly appeared all around him and closed in fast. He marveled that they weren't shooting, and they didn't strike him down with hatchets or knives or warclubs. They were Osages and they seemed almost friendly. There was no sense in trying to resist. The Spencer was in the saddle boot, the old pistol remained under his belt. Travers looked around for Gray Eagle, the chief he had met once with Lashtrow. Milt wished he could speak their language. Well, some of them no doubt knew a little English.

"Where is Gray Eagle?" he inquired, conversationally.

"Gray Eagle home in tepee." The big brawny Osage gently took the gun from Milt's belt. "Who you?"

Automatically, Travers reached for the badge he carried in a convenient vest pocket, and remembered he had no vest. "Ranger," he said, desperately striving to recall Lash-trow's Indian name. It came back to him, and he smiled. "Friend of Lone Wolf."

The big buck nodded. He was naked to the waist, with a magnificent muscled torso, a statue in red bronze. "Know Lone Wolf. Don't know you."

"Gray Eagle knows me."

"Gray Eagle no more war chief. Me, Fire Hawk, war chief now."

"That's fine." Travers was thinking: This is ridiculous enough to be part of Buffalo Bill's Wild West Show. Ned Buntline should be here . . . . He held out his hand, and was surprised and pleased when Fire Hawk grasped and shook it. The chief could have crushed Milt's hand to a pulp.

"You not with White Eyes who dress like Indians? Kill and scalp own people. We get blame."

"No, oh no," Travers said, vehemently. "I follow those men up here."

Fire Hawk shook his black head. "Alone? Why you do that?"

He's got me there, Milt Travers thought whimsically. Why *did* I do it? Damned if I know. Seemed like a good idea at the time. . . . He gave an expressive Injun-like shrug. He felt absurd standing there, surrounded by a score of redskin warriors staring at him and his horse. They seemed to admire the *bayo coyote* far more than its slender ragged rider.

"You must be brave man," Fire Hawk said, rather dubiously.

"Friend of Lone Wolf," was the best response Milt could come up with.

"We know Lone Wolf brave, great fighter, kill many bad people."

Travers nodded. "All of that and more. You take me to Gray Eagle?" He was leaning against the dun, hanging onto the saddle horn to keep from falling down. It wouldn't do for a brave Ranger to faint in front of these Osages, but Milt was on the verge of it.

"Yes, we go to old chief now."

Their camp must be nearby, because the Indians were on foot, and Milt Traverse was thankful for that.

"You tired, you ride," Fire Hawk said.

"Much obliged, Fire Hawk." He climbed into the saddle with considerable effort. "I've come a long way."

He risked a good drink from the flask, trusting his new comrades would assume it was water or some special medicine. Leaning forward, he murmured: "Bayo, we're sure lucky as all hell that we ran into real Injuns and not the fake ones."

The Osage village was in a pleasant upland valley, watered by a swift-flowing creek, cleaner than some Indian settlements Travers had seen, with many dogs sniffing and scrounging about. Fire Hawk led him to a large wickiup, set apart from the others, the entrance ornamented with bright insignia denoting a chief. A slow-moving blanket-swathed old man, withered brown features still regal under a proud headdress, shuffled out and peered closely at the Ranger. Gray Eagle, respected and revered by all.

"Yes, I know," he said at last, with dignity. "You come once with my friend Lone Wolf. We called you Light Lance. Welcome to my lodge." He dismissed the others, except for Fire Hawk, and ordered squaws to bring food and drink. The calm stolid old man was a rock of strength and security.

Settled down in the dim smoke-saturated tepee, Travers told of the Rangers' pursuit of the Vennis gang, the cattle drive, and the massacre that had brought him up here. Gray Eagle was interested, Fire Hawk bored.

"They must be the same ones who hide in these hills, darken and paint themselves, wear the clothes of Indians, and make bloody war on the White Eyes, kill and steal and burn. They even torture and scalp, to make it look the work of Osages, who are people of peace—unless attacked."

"Could be, Chief," agreed Travers. "And they plan to

take the big trail herd on the Chisholm, that is guarded by Lone Wolf.''

Gray Eagle brooded over the long pipe he was smoking. "We have been hunting those men, Light Lance. We will send warriors to help Lone Wolf. He has been a good friend. Fire Hawk will lead. You will show way.''

Milt Travers nodded, thinking with irony: I'm a great choice to show anybody the way, having been lost myself ever since I left the Red River. But any moron in this area should be able to find the Chisholm Trail, for godsake. A good night's sleep should normalize me—I hope.

And with these Osage braves, we'll have a strong enough force to hit and wipe out those rotten renegades.

Fire Hawk had been silent during the powwow, still dieferential to old Gray Eagle, but obviously not too happy over sharing the command with Travers. Outside the usual Indian dog were barking and yapping about.

Milt was too exhausted to worry over that, or to eat much of the food. All he wanted was to sleep in the safety of Gray Eagle's lodge.

94

11

Red Men and White

Clad in a fine new suit of buckskin, a gift from Gray Eagle, Milt Travers found himself in a most unlikely position at the head of an Osage war party, beside the big young chieftan, Fire Hawk. They had been scouring the hills for three days, without encountering any Apaches, real or disguised, and Milt knew it was time to diverge toward the plains and the Chisholm Trail. He now had an old Confederate Army cap to cover his head.

Glancing back along the column, Travers had to grin. The bareback riders were a strange, motley crew, ragtag and bobtailed, dressed in everything from breech clouts and warpaint to store pants, Levis, old army coats and blouses. But they all carried Henry or Spencer rifles, and many had pistols, along with native lances, hatchets and knives. A few even had bows and arrows and warclubs. They were picked warriors, rawhide-tough fighting bucks of the Osage tribe.

Milt Travers had finally made friends with Fire Hawk, and come to know and like some of the others. High Bear was large and jolly for an Injun, and White Antelope was slick, swift and graceful. Crooked Nose, wiry and vicious, was rated second only to Fire Hawk as a warrior. Running Pony was skilled as a scout, Small Rib as a hunter, and Long Spear was the handsomest buck in the tribe.

Travers studied them all, and quizzed Fire Hawk about

them, realizing the importance of knowing his personnel when it came to combat. In buckskins and deeply bronzed himself, Milt might have passed for an Indian, except for his clear blue eyes and sunbleached brown hair.

"Running Pony say bad whites, like Apaches, camp on high ground," Fire Hawk reported. "We try once more before we go down to plains."

Sighting a rude isolated log cabin in a stand of pines, Travers turned to the chief. "Somebody lives there?"

"Red Bush, old friend of Osages."

The cabin door opened and a broad husky man emerged carrying a long Sharps .58 buffalo gun, glaring from the depths of red whiskers with squinted hazel eyes. He wore an old campaign hat on his fiery head, fringed buckskin britches and a faded blue army shirt.

"Howdy, Fire Hawk. Thought for a minute it was Apaches. What kinda war medicine you boys making?" His eyes switched to the Ranger on the coyote dun. "A new chief—and a white one? Reckon I've seen everything now!"

Milt Travers, gratified at finding a white man in this wilderness, stepped down, introduced himself, and explained their mission.

Red Bush grinned and spat tobacco juice through his beard. "Mind if I deal myself in? Got a notion where them varmints are holed up. Wait'll I throw a rig on my old cayuse, and I'll string along. Ain't had any fun for quite a spell."

When Red Bush was saddled and ready, he wore a double-holstered shell belt with the two well-kept .44s, and had swapped the buffalo gun for a Palmer carbine. His leather was oiled and polished, like his weapons, and he bore himself with quiet stolid assurance. A good man to have along, Travers decided. Younger than he looked with all that facial hair.

As they rode on, Red Bush talked like a man long starved for conversation. "Useta hunt buffalo. Then I scouted some for the army and got to know Injuns pretty good. Finally figured I'd rather live with good Injuns than bad whites. Had me an Osage squaw for a time, a real beauty, but the goddamn Apaches killed her. At least it looked like Apache work. So I just stayed on, hunting, fishing, trapping a little, loafing a lot. Always was a lazy bastard. But I'm about ready to go back to civilization, so-called. Man gets sick of talking to himself and his horse and a few stray Injuns. Like to get some kinda job, hooraw a town, drink up a saloon, visit the calico queens down the line."

"The Rangers could use a man like you, Red Bush," said Travers.

"Might give it a go. I was town marshal once in Ellsworth. Cleaned up the place pretty good for 'em. Then they said I was shooting too many men, giving the town a bad name, driving away business." He laughed and shook his red head. "Real name's Bouchard. Called me Rusty."

"Rusty Bouchard." The name was familiar, probably from the days Ellsworth was a trail town. "You knew Bill and Ben Thompson then?"

"Sure did. They ran a saloon in the Grand Central Hotel. Many a night the three of us stood off a pack of cowboys up the trail from Texas. A coupla times I hadda run in Bill and Ben, too. Hickok and Masterson was around also, and the Clements brothers and Pat Garrett. Some kinda times them was."

"Must have been something, with those characters around."

"Sure was. Funny thing about 'em. One week a man might be wearing a badge, and the next week he might be holding up a stagecoach. Switched sides pretty often, some of them gunslingers. . . . Hey, I apologize for running off at the mouth so much. Don't generally talk so damn long at a stretch."

"No apology necessary," Travers assured him. "I understand perfectly. Only been on my own a few days, but I can see how it'd be—"

97

Rusty Bouchard eyed him speculatively. "If it wasn't so unlikely, I'd swear you have a Boston accent."

Travers grinned. "My only excuse is I was born there. But how'd you recognize it so quickly?"

"I'm from Bristol, Connecticut myself." Bouchard laughed merrily. "Two old New England boys meeting up in the Indian Nations. One a them small world coincidents, huh?" They shook hands again, laughing so hard the Osages stared at them in bewilderment. "A Boston boy in the goddamn Texas Rangers. I think I will join up, for sure."

"You're very welcome and much needed," Milt Travers said. "You'll like my partner Lashtrow. He's with the Amidon trail herd down there on the Chisholm."

"I've heard about Lashtrow, of course," Bouchard said. "And I'd sure like to see three thousand head moving up the old Chisholm again."

"You'll see them. This is our last day in the hills. Then we head for a rendezvous with the drive, and hope we get there before, Vennis's bunch does."

"You figure they're the sonsabitches been making up like Apaches and carrying on worse than Cochise's bloodiest braves ever done?"

"Everything points to it," Travers declared. "Only outfit I know low enough to resort to such tactics."

"Well, I hope we run head-on into the degenerate scum," Rusty Bouchard said, with a snarl deep in his throat.

They made camp that night on a bald boulder-scattered hilltop that rose above the surrounding forest. They had crossed no sign of the enemy, and Travers feared the outlaws were already on the march against the trail herd. Horses picketed and outguards stationed, they ate cold jerky, hardtack, parched corn, with some venison, fish and biscuits Red Bush had packed along. Apaches would not attack at night, as a general rule, but white renegades would, so no fires were built.

Milt Travers lay in his blankets, head on saddle, smoking one of Bouchard's stogies and thinking of various things.

Had his fantasies about home been an ill omen, presage to disaster or death? Lashtrow must believe him dead already. Lash would have made a thorough search and found no trace. But Lash never readily accepted the death of a friend. As long as no body was found, Lash would cling to the barest hope that Milt was still alive. In the bedroll nearby, Bouchard was placidly chewing tobacco and thinking his own thoughts. With an instinctive liking between them, they had become friends almost at once. It was one of those rare kindred meetings. Milt felt as sure of Red Bush, as if they had campaigned together for years. The man's solid presence was comforting and reassuring.

First instincts had proven reliable in most of Milt Travers' experience. He had seldom been forced to alter his initial impression of a man. With women, however, it was more precarious and puzzling. Women were so erratic, flighty and unpredictable, his opinions of them underwent many changes. Which was one reason he had never married, he supposed.

Night hawks wailed as they hunted the woodlands, and owls hooted eerily from the treetops. In the distance, a timber wolf howled mournfully, and coyotes barked and yipped. Or those sounds could be Apaches calling to one another, Travers reflected wryly. The sky was full of stars, tinted blue, green or red or silver, seeming close and bright, and a golden half-moon hung over the highest peaks.

With an effort, Travers relaxed in slow degrees, closed his mind to thoughts and memories, and finally slept.

He awoke to a touch on the shoulder. Bouchard was sitting up in his blankets, listening intently. The sounds of night creatures seemed nearer and somehow different. The cold penetrated to the bone marrow.

"There's Apaches out there, Milt," said Bouchard. "I mean the real Apache, no white fakers. I been listening, I know."

99

Travers threw off his blanket and reached for his guns, a chill frisking up his spine to freeze his scalp tight.

"No rush," Bouchard said quietly. "They won't come till the first light."

12

Ghost of Ill-Fame

Dexter had been a booming trail town when the Chisholm was at its height. Now it looked like a squalid derelict crumbling to ruin on the scorched brown plains, a ghost town. But there was yet life of a kind beneath the decrepit surface—it was a meeting place and refuge for lawless drifters and wanted criminals from Texas, Arizona, Old and New Mexico, Kansas and Missouri. The scum and trash of the Southwest floated in and out of this decaying settlement, a cesspool for the sewage of a widespread area.

It was inevitable that Deke Vennis's band would hole up in Dexter, after plundering the banks of Buford and Salt Creek, for this ghost of a town had plenty to offer men on the run. Booze and women and gambling, without a vestige of law and order, an ideal oasis for bandits of every creed and color.

Yet there were controlling forces in this hideout. The notorious King Fischer furnished the liquor, gambling and grub. The equally infamous Dixie Belle supplied the women. Both ruled their domains with iron wills and hands, backed by their own private gunmen, who were formidable enough to keep the wildest toughest of the renegade visitors in line. There were killings, of course. Hard-drinking men who wore guns were bound to fight occasionally over cards or dice or women. There were rumors of acres of unmarked graves outside of Dexter. But on the whole, Dexter was as peaceful as any remote frontier community.

Dexter even had its own doctor, and a good one when tolerably sober or not more than half-drunk. Sad Sam Merriwether, barred from practice in Denver, St. Louis and other cities, had set up an office in Dexter, and developed a thriving practice on gunshot and knife wounds and abortions, augmented by less exotic cases. Sad Sam was an excellent general practitioner and surgeon. A lank dour skull-faced man, always immaculate, he had a dry caustic wit but never smiled. They said the drunker Sam was, the neater he dressed. Most hardened outlaws hesitated to cross King Fischer or Dixie Belle, but Doc Meriwether had no fear of them—or anyone else. His adobe office-hospital-home was as scrupulously clean as the doctor himself. He scarcely ever drank in public, yet he was never entirely sober.

Deke Vennis and his three lieutenants had taken over an abandoned shell of a mudbrick store and made themselves quite comfortable there, while the rest of their troops were scattered around the settlement. Deke had re-established himself as a favorite of Dixie Belle, who seldom serviced any customers herself, although she was still young and attractive. Deke Vennis was handsome, devil-may-care and had a way with women; Belle hadn't resisted his gallant advances for long. His *companeros* were growing impatient over wasting so much time hanging around Dexter. They were fed up with King Fischer's saloon, Dixie Belle's whorehouse, and their own primitive untidy quarters. And with one another.

"How much longer you going lay round with that—that woman?" Fernando Morales looked up from waxing his mustache, black eyes and perpetual sneer fixed on Vennis. "Sure, you knew her in New Orleans, but Jesus, man."

"Yuh," grunted Yaqui Tupelo, cleaning his sixguns. "Shoulda hit Amidon when he was crossing the Red River, goddamn it."

102

"Yeah, that woulda been real smart," Vennis said. "With all them newspapermen and picture-takers looking on from Doan's. Sometimes you dumb bastards are so stupid you turn my stomach."

Morales' sneer widened. "You ain't so smart either, screwing your life away with that—that—"

"Watch your mouth, Fern," warned Deke Vennis, riffling the deck of cards in his supple hands. "You been doing your share in that hog ranch."

Tupelo laughed and drank from a brown bottle. "We have to pay for ours."

"You got enough money, for chrisake," Vennis reminded. "More'n you ever had in your lives. I want Amidon worse'n you do, but there's plenty of time. We can hit 'em anytime, anywhere. We'll outnumber 'em three-to-one, when Yaqui's Apaches get down from the hills."

"We won't have Pueblo and Tench working inside." Tupelo spat on the dirty strewn floor.

"They didn't amount to nothing anyway," Morales scoffed. "Pueblo killed a punk kid and a gal, before Lashtrow blew him down. Tench didn't do a goddamn thing except get himself killed."

Vennis smiled over the cigarette he was shaping. "When we hit 'em, I want that Lashtrow for myself."

"We had him and that other Ranger at Brush Creek, if some of our half-assed *peons* coulda held their fire a minute. And that Hiller girl hadn't been there to save 'em." Morales went on twirling his mustache ends, squatting on a crate like a huge toad. "She shot the shit outa us."

Vennis laughed. "That Hiller girl's quite a piece. I want her for myself, too, when we go in."

Steel Huyette, whetting his bowie as usual, remained silent, but slanted a look of disgust at Vennis. He wants everything himself, Huyett was thinking. All the money and women and credit, he wants to hog it all.

"What if the Osages get in it on Amidon's side?" Morales said, combing his long black hair now. "We won't have no three-to-one odds."

"They ain't going to get nowhere." Tupelo grinned like a buzzard. "I got some real Apaches up in the hills, going to wipe out them Osages."

Deke Vennis rose and stretched his sinewy acrobat's body. "We'll take that herd, Osages or not. Nothing to fret about, for chrisake. I crave a little action about this time of day, if you boys don't mind."

"You mean the King's Palace?" Huyett said, starting up hopefully. He did like to gamble, and King Fischer's emporium was open day and night.

"No, Steel. I mean Dixie's Red Lantern," said Vennis, with a grin.

Huyett sank back onto his broken bench, Tupelo barked a laugh, and Morales grimaced and spat. "Thought I'd seen horny studs before, but you—you beat hell outa them all, Deke."

"When you're hung like I am," bragged Vennis, "it'd be a shame not to use it and give the gals a real treat."

"How was that Kate Amidon?" asked Tupelo.

"Not bad for an amachoor. But I gotta hunch Tess Hiller's a lot better."

"What the hell's this Dixie Belle got that's so wonderful?" Fern Morales wanted to know.

Deke Vennis laughed, unperturbed. "She's got everything, Fernando, and she sure uses it all. She does things I never even dreamed of before, honest t'gawd. She wasn't *numero uno* in New Orleans for nothing."

He swung through the unhinged door into brilliant sunshine, and set off along the dusty rubbled street in his graceful arrogant stride, flat-crowned hat tilted rakishly on his dark curly head, hands brushing the lowslung bonehandled Colts tied down on his thighs.

I'll never forgive them sonsabitches for taking my other set of guns off me, Duke Vennis was thinking. Hiller's dead, and I'll take Amidon and Lashtrow in due time. Especially that big bastard Lashtrow. I want him dead more'n I ever wanted anything. Even more than the delightfully perverse pleasures offered by Dixie Belle. Maybe I'll have her bring in another girl this afternoon, just for something different.

He was passing the Palace when one of his riders named Beede ambled out with a raised hand. "Got some news, boss. Them two women from the trail drive just went into Doc Merriwether's. Old lady Amidon looked mighty sick. The other young one looked good enough to eat any day."

In the background Rammel was lolling on an awning post, with the languid aristocratic air that was beginning to annoy and irk Vennis.

"Musta been some men with 'em?" Vennis said, half-questioning.

"Only one. A little white-haired bowlegged old-timer with a big chaw."

"Hoss Crull."

"That's him, boss," Beede said. "The boys say he used to be a champeen bronc rider and hell with a gun. King Fischer knows him from way back, and the King put out a warning, loud and clear. Anybody harms old Hoss has to answer to him. Same with the ladies."

"I'd never throw down on Hoss—unless he pulled first," Vennis said. "Though he's still quick enough to hold his own, I reckon. And good women are safe as a church in Dexter, everybody knows that." He thought: But I'd sure like to get next to that Tess Hiller. Maybe on their way back to the herd. . . . "Thanks, Beede. Have a coupla drinks on me." He flipped the boy a silver dollar, and turned back the way he had come, all desire for Dixie Belle suddenly dead within him.

Here was an unexpected opportunity to strike at Lashtrow. Tess Hiller was said to be in love with him, Lashtrow's girl all the way.

It's apt to be dark by the time they head for camp, Deke Vennis mused. We could jump 'em outside of town, grab the girl, be sure not to hurt Mrs. Amidon or Hoss Crull. Then Lashtrow'll come hell-for-leather after Tess Hiller, and I can cut the big sonofabitch down.

Beyond his headquarters on the street in front of the doctor's large well-kept adobe, Vennis saw the buckboard in which they had brought Mrs. Amidon, no doubt, and two saddled horses, the buckskin that belonged to Tess and the blue roan Crull rode.

He turned abruptly into a weedgrown alley to circle behind the rundown ramshackle buildings of the street. If Hoss Crull should spot him, he'd come ashooting, Vennis knew. And if he had to shoot Hoss, self-defense or not, King Fischer would turn loose his wolves and run them all out of town, or shoot them dead on the spot.

Couldn't afford to cross King, when he had all their loot cached away.

It was time they got out of Dexter anyhow, Deke Vennis concluded. Cooped up like that, they were getting cabin fever, wearing on each others' nerves. This was the best chance he'd ever have to get hold of Tess Hiller. Just thinking of her started a rising heat in Deke's groin.

Lashtrow had made a long hard search for Milt Travers without any success. He had found the body of Tench, bloated and uglier than ever in death, but not a sign of Milt. Returning to the trail drive, he had plunged into the work like a man bent on self-destruction, scarcely speaking to anyone for days, unless it was essential to the task at hand. Lash would not yet concede that Milton Travers III was dead. Until he saw the body, he wouldn't admit it was a fact.

Tess Hiller had taken charge of the bed wagon, after Kate's death, and then moved on to the chuckwagon when Grace Amidon became too ill to continue. A young cowboy named Lyle Myatt became night wrangler and driver of the bed-and-wood cart. Andiron was short-handed and overworked in all departments. Kloster, freed from the influence of Pueblo and Tench, came back to life and began to pull his own weight and more.

Anse Amidon, like Lashtrow, sought to lose himself in work, but Grace couldn't seem to recover from the loss of her daughter. Kate had been a headache, a problem and trial, but she had also been the light of the world to Anse and Grace. The heartbreak of her death turned Anse into a slaving demon, and Grace into a sinking invalid.

Relations between Lashtrow and Tess Hiller were easier and friendlier, but the sweet fire and intimacy were gone, at least temporarily. With Travers missing, Lash felt like a hollow shell of a man, going through the motions of living. He could function effectively, but there was no meaning or satisfaction in it. Food, drink and tobacco were tasteless to him. Life had lost its tang and savor, its very essence.

The death of Tonk Hiller had hit Lashtrow with shocking force. The loss of Milt Travers was a final crushing blow. Every time a close comrade went under, part of you died with him. Lash had seen so many go, there wasn't much of himself left alive.

After getting the herd bedded down, Lashtrow rode in to leave his last bronc of the day at the cavvy. "How's it going, Lyle?" he asked the kid wrangler.

"Too damn peaceable," Lyle Myatt complained. "I seen Apaches on the skyline for days now, but nothing ever happens."

"It will in time. Just be patient, like the Apache. Cherish these moments of peace."

"That's okay for you, Lash. You seen all the action there is. I ain't seen none, to speak of."

"It'll come, Lyle," promised Lashtrow, with a slow grave smile.

Walking into the ruddy circle of the cookfire by the chuckwagon, Lash observed that both Grace Amidon and Tess Hiller were absent. Carlos had taken over the cooking, and the riders were comparing his culinary efforts most unfavorably to those of Grace and Tess.

"Eat it or leave it," Carlos said, untroubled. "You've ate so much tobacco and drunk so much rotgut booze you ain't got no taste left nohow."

Lashtrow filled his tin plate with beans and beef, his tin cup with steaming coffee, and sat down beside Amidon. "Where's the women, Anse?" He'd been worried, watching Grace decline from day to day.

"Went to the doctor's in Dexter. Grace was feeling so bad, I made her go. Tess and Hoss took her in the buckboard."

Lash's gray eyes widened. "You know the kinda town that is, Anse?"

"Pretty damn likely. But it's got the only doctor for miles around, and they claim he's a good one."

"Yeah, Doc Merriwether is a good man. But that town's an awful sink-hole. All the hardcases in the country hang out there, when the law's after 'em."

Amidon regarded him with exasperation. "I *know* that, goddamn it, just as well as you do. But Grace had to get to a doctor. She's been failing fast, Lash. I also know that King Fischer runs that town. He may cater to the lowest riffraff in the whole Southwest, but by Jesus they behave in Dexter. King keeps the peace better'n most marshals I ever seen. A respectable woman's safer there than she is in most Texas towns."

"Granted, Anse," drawled Lashtrow. "But what worries me is that Deke Vennis might be holed up there."

"Even Deke Vennis ain't going to run over the King. The King's handled tougher ones than Vennis'll ever be. And he's got a lot of respect for old Hoss Crull, too. Fischer'd burn anybody who looked crosswise at Hoss."

Lashtrow nodded his bronze head. "That's right, Anse. But the Vennis bunch could hit 'em, *outside* of town. The King can't cover the whole range."

Amidon drained his cup and spat. "Christ, what godaw-

108

ful coffee! Yeah, you got something there, Lash. I allowed they'd be back before dark. I better ride in there myself.''

"Let me go, Anse," said Lashtrow, pouring out the dregs of his coffee and lighting a thin cigar. "You're more needed here."

"Maybe oughta send a crew in."

"You can't spare the men. And a big crew might cause some kinda ruckus."

Crowleg Dooner spoke up: "I'll go with Lash. The two of us oughta be sufficient, with Hoss already in there. You need the rest on watch, Anse."

Amidon pondered and inclined his large gray head. "All right, you two go ahead then. Don't figure on any trouble. We hear a lot of guns going off, we'll come tearing in like hell wouldn't have us. I pray to God old Sad Sam can do Grace some good. She's a sick woman. Klos was right, after all. A cattle drive ain't no place for women. But I was afraid if I left 'em home, that bastard Vennis would move in on 'em."

"Grace'll make it all right," Lashtrow soothed. "Sad Sam Merriwether is a medical genius, from all I've heard."

As they walked toward the *remuda* to saddle up again, Lash slowing his steps to match Dooner's dragging limp, Crowleg said: "An old-timer come by today, down from the hills in Indian Territory. Said he saw two white men riding with an Osage war party. At first he thought there was only one white man, a red-bearded hermit he knew by sight. The Injuns call him Red Bush. Then he saw there was another, a slim clean-looking boy with light hair and blue eyes."

Lashtrow's eyes and features brightened. "It could be. . ."

"Don't want to get your hopes up too high, Lash," said Crowleg Dooner. "But it sounded pretty good. Then the old man said that boy was riding a coyote dun, and—"

"It must be, by God," murmured Lashtrow, smiling happily. "It must be Milt. I never believed he was dead.

I always felt he was alive—somewhere. He's with Gray Eagle's Osages. It's gotta be him, Crow."

"I reckoned so myself, Lash," agreed Dooner, with a tobacco-warped grin. "But I was kinda scared to put it in words, you know—"

"It's our boy, Crow. It's Milt Travers." Lashtrow laid a long arm around Dooner's bony shoulders. "And I'll bet a month's pay he's bringing those Osage warriors down to help us fight off the Vennis gang."

"We could sure use some help like that," Crowfoot Dooner said, beaming.

Lashtrow whistled up his sorrel, while Dooner roped his favorite *bayo tigre,* a smoky dun with striped legs and shoulders. After bridling and saddling the horses, they swung aloft and trotted out on a northeasterly course toward Dexter, soon raising to a canter and then a gallop. Silver-rimmed clouds obscured the moon and blotted out many stars, yet the undulating landscape was oddly luminous beneath a pale haze. It was a relief to get away from camp and the herd for a space.

"They don't exactly welcome lawmen in this town," Lashtrow said. "We won't be leaning on the bar in King Fischer's Palace this evening."

Dooner grinned slyly. "Might sashay over to Dixie Belle's Red Lantern and have a look at the stock."

"Pretty well wornout and beat up, I imagine, if Deke Vennis is around."

"They say that Dixie Belle does tricks that ain't been invented yet."

Lashtrow laughed. "If I know Vennis, he's an authority on that subject by this time. He's a heller with the female species."

"With the sixguns too, they say," Dooner remarked. "But you backed him down at Andiron, Lash."

"Not exactly, Crow. Too many others involved. I hope it's just man-to-man next time." Lashtrow sighed and spat tobacco juice. "But I'll take the cocky little bastard any way I can get him." ———>

"The Frellick kid that Pueblo murdered. He had the makings, Lash. He woulda killed Pueblo in a fair fight. That was a goddamn crime. I liked that boy, OK Frellick. He woulda made a good Ranger, Lash."

Lashtrow shook his head sadly. "It's a pity to lose a good one that way and that young. His first time out prob'ly, and he gets cold-decked by a yellah dog. It's fate, Crow."

"Yeah, it sure is," Dooner said glumly. "Some call it God, some call it Luck, but it's Fate, pure and simple, that throws the dice or deals the cards."

Lashtrow pulled a bottle from his saddlebags. "If we can't drink in Dexter, we'll drink on the road in." They drank and passed the bottle back and forth, as they jogged across the grassy plain, the night air cool and fresh on their sunburnt faces.

"Man's best friend," Crowleg Dooner said solemnly, stroking the bottle with a loving rope-scarred hand. "At least next to his mother and father, his horse and guns, his brothers and *compadres*."

Lashtrow pulled up and lifted his left hand, head cocked and listening. Ahead were the sounds of horsemen, a large cavalcade, carrying clearly in the night stillness, which was abruptly sundered by three crashing gunshots. Lash and Crowleg threw their horses forward into full reaching strides and drew their .44s, driving toward the top of a shallow scrub-wooded draw. A veritable stampede of hoofbeats followed the shooting, fading swiftly away to the east. Lashtrow was chilled to the bone.

The moon cleared a cloudbank as they reached the crest, flooding the little depression with silvery light, and they saw at the bottom the horse-drawn buckboard motionless, the seat empty, with Hoss Crull's *grullo* standing beside it, and a stubby dark form sprawled in the dirt near the horse's forelegs. The hammering hoofs of the company in flight receded in the east, and were soon beyond hearing. Lash felt cold and sick.

Lash and Crowleg hurtled down the slight grade and hauled up, horses rearing, beside the wagon. Grace Amidon, face clutched in tense hands, slouched half upright on a pallet in the back of the buckboard. Hoss Crull was stirring, swearing and scrambling to his feet at roadside. But Tess Hiller and her buckskin were gone.

Flinging themselves from the leather, Crowleg Dooner limped over to embrace Crull, and Lashtrow climbed into the wagon to comfort Grace.

"I'm not hurt," she sobbed. "Never touched me. Gunwhipped Hoss and took Tess away. Oh, dear God, I was feeling so much better—then this happened."

"Goddamn sonsabitches," Hoss Crull panted, raising his blood-laced face and holding onto his gashed bleeding white head. "About twenty of 'em. Come outa the brush and ringed us in. Never had no chance, but I hadda try. . . . Got off one shot. Then some bastard bent a gun over my head, and I went down and out."

"They hurt Tess?" asked Lashtrow.

"Naw, just grabbed her. She was trying to fight 'em, too. Got off two blasts with that Henry of hers, but they was all over her. Mighta winged one of 'em, I ain't sure." Hoss Crull patted his aching head tenderly. "They didn't try to hurt us or kill us, I'll give 'em that. They woulda wiped us out like nothing. They just wanted Tess. Deke Vennis wanted the gal, that's all."

"Doc Merriwether helped me a lot," Grace Amidon said, tears streaming down her gaunted cheeks. "I felt so good—till they jumped us. Poor little Tess. God knows what they'll do to her."

"They won't do a thing to her," Lashtrow said, with soft intensity. "Because I won't give 'em time to. I'm going after 'em right away."

"Jesus, Lash, what can you do? Against twenty or more

112

of the crummy bastards? Not even you, Lash—'' Hoss Crull groaned in loud despair.

"I gotta try, Hoss," said Lashtrow. "You know what Vennis'll do, if he gets time enough."

"I'll go with you, Lash," said Crowleg Dooner, teeth bared and grating.

Lashtrow shook his head. "Not this trip, Crow. You gotta get Grace and Hoss back to camp, and stick with the herd. Anse needs every man he's got left. You know that. We all know it. . . . I think you're going to get well again, Grace."

"Oh, I know I am, Lash. That doc's a wonder. He gave me enough medicine to last all the way up to Abilene. I'll be fine. I'll handle the chuckwagon and do the cooking again, so Carlos can work the cows."

"But the odds," Hoss Crull moaned. "Them goddamn odds are too heavy for any man alive."

Lashtrow smiled thinly. "All I gotta do is get Vennis under my gun. He'll give up the girl, and he'll keep his men off me. To save his own worthless goddamn life."

"How the hell you going to get to Vennis, with all that gun rabble round him?" demanded Crowleg Dooner.

"I don't know," Lashtrow confessed. "But I gotta try, find some way. He won't want all those saddlebums around when he gets to working on Tess. That's the best angle I can see from here. Now, I better hit the trail, folks."

"God bless you and keep you, Lash," said Grace, tearfully earnest. "You come back to us—with Tess Hiller."

"Sure, I'll come back with Tessie. And I'm liable to bring Milt Travers and a bunch of Osage bucks along, too. You explain that to 'em, Crow."

Crowleg Dooner nodded firmly. "You'll make out, Lash. I know you will."

"I wish to Christ we could ride with you, pardner," Hoss Crull said, his voice choked and shaky.

"So do I, Hoss," said Lashtrow, and then attempted a

113

bit of levity. "But this is a job for the old Lone Wolf himself. That's what the Osages call me, you know."

Hoss Crull mopped his bloody face with a bandanna and forced a laugh. "I didn't know that, son. But my money's riding on Lone Wolf. And I never pick nothing but winners."

"I won't spoil your record, Hoss," promised Lashtrow, that smile creasing his lean cheeks and crinkling his gray eyes. "Be seeing you-all."

"You're goddamn right," Crowleg Dooner said huskily. "We'll be looking for you, Lash boy."

But inside he was thinking, bitterly, that the odds were about ten-thousand-to-one, against their ever seeing Lashtrow alive again.

Riding off into the night by himself, Lash thought: I've ridden and fought many a mission alone, but I never felt so goddamn lonesome and lost and hollow and hopeless as I do right now.

13

Apaches on the Warpath

The Apaches moved up to attack the naked craggy hilltop at daybreak. Hunkered down in a cradle of rocks at the rim, blankets draped over shivering shoulders, Milt Travers and Rusty Bouchard watched them come up through the brush and trees like flitting phantoms in the morning mists.

"Keep your hands warm, Milt," said Bouchard, his own hands thrust down inside the front of his buckskin pants, and Travers followed his example. The warmth of his abdomen was most welcome.

It was cold and raw on that barren summit. Travers had cleaned and oiled the Spencer carbine and old Walker Colt he had picked up at the scene of the massacre, but he wished he had his own familiar weapons. His magic flask had been empty, for once, until Bouchard filled it with potent home-made corn liquor, which they had been drinking for breakfast, to ward off the chill.

"It's better to fight on an empty stomach," Bouchard said cheerily. "You catch one in the gut, it don't do so much damage. But another bolt of this white lightning won't harm us none." He withdrew a hand to pass a bottle to Travers.

Milt drank from it. "Who-ooo! If that doesn't wake a man up, he's dead."

Bouchard tipped up the bottle and smacked his bearded lips. "Damn good corn, if I do say so myself."

The Apaches came on up the steep slopes like spectral shadows in the white shifting fog. There seemed to be hundreds of them, but Bouchard estimated there were maybe fifty. Even that number was double the size of the Osage party, and the Apaches were much fiercer and more savage, fearless, cruel and ruthless in battle.

"If we wasn't ready, they'd overrun this hill in ten minutes," Bouchard said. "And we'd never know what hit us. But we can stop 'em, chop the hell outa the red bastards." He shrugged off the blanket, picked up his Palmer carbine, and jacked a shell into the chamber, as Travers followed suit with the Spencer, longing for his own Winchester.

The first raiders were climbing on foot, but now there were riders scattered among them and more horsemen behind. They would strike the horse herd to start, but Osage riflemen were waiting under cover about the rope corral. The Apaches gave Travers a queasy nauseous sensation, a freezing fear, as if they were not quite human, or perhaps were superhuman animals, born and bred to combat. He had a compulsion to yawn and to urinate; he yielded to the former, his lean jaws cracking widely. He wondered if the Osages would hold. If they broke and ran, it would be all over.

"They're close enough now, Red," said Travers.

"Wait'll they hit the cavvy," Bouchard said. "Then we'll all open up."

The horses were picketed off to the right, on the east rim. The invaders would swoop in there, expecting to knife a couple of sleepy sentries and run off the Osage ponies, in short order. But the Apaches never reached the rope corral. Osage rifle fire scythed them down, volley after crashing volley bursting the dawn stillness, and the battle was on.

Action came as a relief and release, after the cold prolonged wait, and Milt Travers exulted in the trigger squeeze, the kick of the butt against his right shoulder, the downslanting muzzle flashes and flames, and the levering of the carbine. The Apaches were shooting back up the grade, their lead ricocheting off boulders at the crest, but they had to retreat under withering blasts from above, dragging their dead and wounded with them. Milt and Red Bush kept hammering away, pouring it on.

The initial assault had been a disaster, leaving the Apaches shocked and dazed by the fury of the unexpected and total Osage resistance.

Travers and Bouchard rose to reload and survey the summit. The horse herd was intact, and not a single enemy had reached the hilltop alive. Fire Hawk and his warriors were howling and chanting in triumph, but Bouchard signaled across to the young chieftan to hold it down and keep his braves in readiness. "Too early to celebrate," he muttered.

"They aren't crazy enough to try it again, are they?" Milt Travers asked, in surprise.

"They'll come up again," Bouchard said somberly. "Once more anyway. They still outnumber us."

The Apaches did come again, a full-scale mounted attack this time, and as horsemen they had no equals. The gray air was torn by Apache screams as they came storming up the slope on the west side. They cut down and overran the outposts there, and came shooting, slashing, shrieking like friends with the bloodlust up, across the broad rock-studded hilltop. Gunflares leaped to and fro like lightning; thunder filled the air.

Crouching behind boulders, Travers and Bouchard fired as fast as they could trigger and lever, until their carbines were spent, and then went to their handguns, blazing away at the incoming maniacs. Ponies and braves went down, rolling and thrashing in welters of dirt and powdersmoke, as the attackers lashed in and out among the rocks. Dust spumed high and stone splinters hailed over ducking heads. Stricken horses trumpeted in anguish. Injuns screamed insults and the two white men cursed steadily. Red-roaring chaos jarred and shook the earth.

One painted madman drove his pinto straight at Travers,

fire jetting from his Henry, the bullet searing Milt's elbow as he dove aside. Bouchard's .44 clicked empty. Milt rolled and fired upward, blowing the brave off the paint's back. The Apache started up with a hatchet, but Bouchard's knife pinned him to the churned soil. Fire Hawk, empty rifle clubbed, smashed another Apache from his horse with a crushed skull. The flaming inferno was over in a few minutes, the charge ripped apart by Osage gunblasts, the Apaches fading out to the perimeter, starting to circle, then dropping from the rim and out of sight.

They left their dead behind this, ponies and bucks alike, and there were a few Osages down, too. Sweating hard, blackened with dirt and powder-grime, Travers and Bouchard gulped corn whiskey and reloaded their pieces. Small Rib came back from scouting the circuit. "They still down there. More than ever, looks like. All around this hill. They got us in trap."

"They can't carry this hill," Rusty Bouchard said. "But they can keep us penned up here—maybe."

"We've got to break out and get back to the trail herd," Milt Travers said. "We may be too late already."

"We can bust through 'em," Bouchard said. "After we rest and eat something and get the horses ready. Couldn't stay on this hill anyhow. After the sun gets up a ways, it'll stink like a slaughter pen, with all them dead men and horses laying round and the buzzards swarming."

They found Long Spear dead, his handsome face crushed into red ruin, within a cluster of three Apache corpses. Lying nearby, Running Pony was alive yet, but gutshot and begging for someone to kill him. With three slugs in his belly, Running Pony was beyond help.

Rusty Bouchard looked at Fire Hawk, then at Milt Travers. They both shook their heads. "All right, by God, I'll do it." Bouchard placed a pistol in Runny Pony's hand, and they all turned away. There was a muffled explosion, and Running Pony had escaped from his unbearable pain.

There were two more Osage dead, for a total of four.

118

Actually a light loss after such a vicious conflict. The Apaches had suffered much heavier losses. At least ten of them lay dead on the summit, and no one could tell how many they had dragged away after the first onslaught. A few Osages were slightly wounded, but in general they had been very fortunate.

"Yeah, you can say we was lucky, and I reckon it's true," Bouchard said, biting off a chew of tobacco. "But it sure wasn't lucky for Long Spear and Running Pony and them other two boys. There really ain't no such thing as a light loss in combat. It's a goddamn heavy for them that go under, and for their families and friends."

Milt Travers nodded sadly. "I was thinking the same way, Rusty. But I couldn't put it in words."

The Osages were burying their own dead, while others went around taking the scalps of the fallen Apaches. "We come back and take our dead home later," Fire Hawk said. He was thinking: If we don't die too, down on the plains, fighting this war for the White Eyes.

High Bear had built a cookfire to heat up some stew. "Men who ride and fight need a hot meal," he said. "Can't make it on parched corn and jerky beef."

"When the sun gets high enough to clear this hill and hit them Apaches down there right in the eyes," Bouchard said thoughtfully, "we'll go down that western slope like hellfire on a rampage, and ram right through them sonsabitches."

"Yeah, they're spread pretty thin," Travers said. "And they won't be expecting us."

"That's right, Milt. They never expect Osages to charge. We'll go through 'em like a bolt of lightning outa the blue."

They discussed the plan with Fire Hawk, and he was all for it. "Sure, we go. This hill stink already. Soon the sun fry us like fish in pan. That's good. Kill more Apache on way out."

"Don't stop to take scalps though," Travers said, with his winning grin.

Fire Hawk nearly smiled back. "Never mind scalps. Count coups just the same. Get name as big as Gray Eagle in Osage lodges, huh. Red Bush?"

"I'll see that you do, Fire Hawk," promised Bouchard, teeth flashing whitely in his russet beard. "Make you more famous than old Geronimo, Crazy Horse, Sitting Bull and Cochise. How you like that?"

"Me like," Fire Hawk said candidly.

It was about ten o'clock when the sun reached the proper height for their purpose. Milt Travers took a final look over the rimrock on the west. There seemed to be fewer Apaches stirring in the woods below. Some must have pulled out, perhaps to go after reinforcements. And when they looked up to face the attack, they would be looking straight into the glare of sunshine. Travers walked back and mounted his dun at the head of the triple column, flanked by Fire Hawk and Rusty Bouchard.

"Some of them are gone, only a thin line left," Milt said crisply. "We should break through and run away from them, without much trouble. They aren't ready to fight, and they won't be ready to ride after us. That sun's going to hit them full in the eyes and half-blind them. All right, Chief, let's ride."

The three front men put their horses forward, and twenty-one mounted warriors surged after them, the last trio with four spare ponies on lead. They went over the rim and down the slope in a thunderous howling torrent, an avalanche of horses and men, and their handguns began to flame and roar, as startled and sun-dazzled Apaches appeared at the edge of the woods below. In a storming hammering dust cloud they swept down the hillside, muzzle flashes stabbing out ahead of them, and Milt Travers knew the rare fierce exultance that comes in a charge of cavalry.

The enemy was shooting back now, but the shots were scattered, blind and hurried, and dirt mushroomed under the flying hoofs or spouted on either side. Apaches toppled and fell screaming and threshing in the brush, while others

120

broke and fled for cover or scrambled to reach their ponies. Treetops loomed closer, until Travers could see distinctly the individual leaves and boughs.

The grade was leveling off, and enemy gunshots were hot and near, the air vibrant with humming lead, the earth shuddering under the racing beat of hoofs. Travers felt the sun's heat on his shoulders, the kick of the old Walker Colt in his right hand, and the searching drone of death about his ears. Then he was in forest shade, with enemy guns blaring all around him. Milt blinked sweat from his stinging eyes and used the spurs.

The coyote dun ran down and trampled one dodging brown body under steelshod hoofs. Travers nailed another with a .44 slug from the big Walker. Behind him came Bouchard and Fire Hawk and the Osages, firing at a gallop, clubbing with gun barrels and slashing with hatchets, and a few hurling lances at flitting forms in the brush, rocks and trees. Sheathing the empty sixgun, Milt pulled out the carbine.

Then Travers was free and clear, all the way through the Apache lines, and the rest of the column came pouring through after him, leaving the racket and turmoil behind in the smoking dust. Onward they hurtled, away from the stunned and stricken Apaches. There would be no immediate pursuit, if any at all. The enemy had been hit too suddenly and too hard, ripped and smashed and riddled, to recover and reorganize for some time.

Turning in the saddle, Travers was relieved to see the coppery whiskers of Rusty Bouchard, and the proud stern profile of Fire Hawk. The ugly Crooked Nose, big High Bear, and the graceful White Antelope had made it, too. Travers reined aside to make a complete tally, and was delighted to see that they had come through that enemy cordon without losing a man.

"Thank God, Bayo," he murmured to the dun. "That's better, far better than I dared to hope for. Now it's on to the old Chisholm Trail and the Amidon herd. Let's hope our luck lasts and we get there in time.''

For a mile or so, Bouchard hung back to act as rear guard, and when he overtook the cavalcade again he reported no sign whatever of an Apache pursuit. ''They've had enough for one day, I reckon. They don't wanta see any more of us Osages for a good long spell. We really put it to the bastards today, boys.''

Coming down from the mountains, they descended along winding stone corridors beneath sheer cliffs, rock ledges, and eroded escarpments, down talus slopes into a more open country sparsely timbered with tall pines, silvery aspens and sturdy oaks. The heat was wicked, even at this altitude. The men rode sweat-soaked in scalding leather, and the horses were lathered and frothing soapy white.

In the foothills, east of the plains and the Chisholm, an errant breeze brought the racket of gunfire, rising and falling in volume, out of the north. It sounded as if a lot of weapons were involved.

''All they do in this goddamn country is fight,'' Rusty Bouchard grumbled, as they instinctively spurred their broncs in the direction of the shooting. ''Your guns don't even get a chance to cool off, for chrisake.''

From a low wooded ridge overlooking a shallow valley and rippling stream, they saw a wide arc of horsemen concentrating their fire on a crumbling weathered old dugout, built of adobe and logs into a hillside and facing the creek. Beyond the dugout and the riders was a sorry collection of open sheds and frame shacks that seemed about to collapse and tumble into the water. There were apparently two guns responding from the dugout, but the range was too long for either side.

''Them ain't Injuns,'' said Bouchard, squinting his hazel-brown gaze.

''No, they're a helluva lot worse,'' Milt Travers said. ''It looks like Deke Vennis's gang to me.'' Blue eyes slitted intently, he thought he could identify the squat froglike shape of Fern Morales and the bird-of-prey aspect of Yaqui Tupelo. He sought further but couldn't locate the hulking form of Steel Huyett, or the compact arrogant silhouette of Vennis.

"That's the bunch we're s'posed to keep off Amidon's back?" Bouchard inquired. "Well, if it is, why not start right here?"

Travis nodded his fine sunny head. "I don't know who they have pinned down in that dugout, but whoever it is deserves help against those murderous sonsofbitches."

"Yeah, Milt," Bouchard spat an amber stream. "And now I see a coupla the buzzards circling round to come in from the back and prob'ly stomp through that sod roof. We better get in there damn quick."

Travers glanced at the big chieftan. "Hawk, those are the killers we're after. Your braves ready to fight some more?"

"Fight anytime," Fire Hawk said. "No use waste time. Get it done, we get home soon."

"All right, let's go," Milt Travers said, and booted his *bayo coyote* forward to lead the Osages in their second all-out charge of a long grilling strife-shattered day.

"This'll be the last one, by God," Rusty Bouchard grumbled into his copper beard, as they galloped down the long valley in a storm of dust. "Horses have had it, the men have had it, and I've had more'n enough. Hope them bandit bastards run instead a fight."

Osage war cries rent the air over the drumming hoofbeats, and Rusty grinned. "Think they can lick the world now they've killed a few Apaches. Well, more power to 'em."

Milt Travers too was hoping the outlaws wouldn't make a stand. We must look like a lot bigger force than we are, he thought. That may be enough to rout the bastards into flight. We'll never chase 'em down today, if they do break and run for it, but at least we'll be on their trace tomorrow.

14

Lone Wolf on the Trace

Lashtrow trailed the outlaws all night. With the sorrel fresh and eager, he forced the pace until he came within hearing of the horsemen in front of him, and then eased off and drifted in their wake, alert for any rear guard that might have dropped behind the main body to cover the back trail. The bandits were in no hurry, and evidently expected no prompt pursuit, natural enough in the circumstances.

In a way it was fortunate that Tess Hiller was in the hands of Deke Vennis, rather than any ordinary run-of-the-mill desperado. There would be no quick crude attempt at forcible rape, in this case. Vennis had too much conceit and pride to stoop to such methods. He was egocentric enough to be convinced that he could seduce Tess, or any other woman, without using force. He'd charm her into submission. For Vennis, rape would be the last resort. Lashtrow was certain of this, and his understanding of Deke, and he derived comfort in it. Tess was in no immediate danger of being violated. Thank God that Vennis fancied himself so great a lover.

When the outlaws halted to settle down in the early-morning hours, Lashtrow left the sorrel ground-tied, unhooked his spurs, and crept in through the woodland to scout their camp and ascertain that Vennis made no premature advances. They didn't even bother to post outguards, and Lash got in close enough to observe that Vennis was treating Tess like a lady guest by the campfire, and not like a captive. Lash could have shot Vennis and the other leaders, but that would have been sheerest folly. Oddly enough, Deke Vennis was insurance that Tess wouldn't be harmed. Temporarily, at least.

Withdrawing, noiseless as an Indian in the woods, Lashtrow made his own dry camp at a safe distance, and caught a few hours of sleep.

The next forenoon, early, Lash picked up the trace once more and stayed on it hour after burning hour, careful to keep well behind and out of sight, maintaining a lookout for rear guards that never appeared. He was buoyed by the fresh hope that Milt Travers was alive yet, and with the friendly Osages of old Gray Eagle's tribe.

Now and then, when the terrain was rough and broken enough, Lashtrow moved in closer to survey the enemy company. Most of the time Deke Vennis rode beside Tess Hiller, a little apart from the column, but not removed far enough for Lash to swoop in and drill Vennis and snatch the girl. An attempt like that would have been foolhardy and suicidal. He had to be patient, wait for the right break. He could visualize how Vennis was courting and wooing Tess, with all the grace, wit and gallantry at this command. No denying he was a handsome roguish devil.

And Tess was undoubtedly impressed by him, to some extent, for Deke Vennis did have a gay reckless flair and glitter that many women found irresistible.

I haven't handled Tess very well myself, Lash had to admit. I always have trouble with the women I like the most, for some reason. With others, light, superficial and transitory, I get along fine, smooth and serene, always in control. But with the girls I care the most for, the ones who matter deeply, I run into difficulty, usually of my own making. Maybe I'm too selfish, unwilling to give all of myself, afraid of permanent meaningful entanglements. Don't know what it is, but I always do something wrong, and wind up hurting both of us.

125

By mid-afternoon they were in the foothills, approaching a long shallow valley watered by a winding stream, fringed with brush and trees. Far ahead a clump of rickety huts and shacks leaned on the river bank, and Lashtrow figured it was one of their remote hideouts. The break might come here. It had to, because Vennis was certain to strengthen his play for Tess Hiller, once they were settled in this spot. Pulling up on a rocky mesa top, Lashtrow dismounted, drank from his canteen, and dug the field-glasses out of his saddlebags to study the layout.

There was a sagging pole corral near the shanties, and about two hundred yards or more away from the buildings and creek a dugout was built into the sidehill, adobe and timber front with a shaggy sod roof. As the riders swung down to unbridle and unsaddle, a pair of Indians emerged from one of the shacks to welcome them. A flat-bed wagon loaded with barrels stood by the corral. Deke Vennis was handing Tess down from her buckskin with cavalier grace and courtesy.

"If those barrels are full of whiskey, Pard," said Lashtrow, "our friend Deke may get too drunk tonight to carry out his seduction act. The Injuns look drunk already, and the other boys are whooping-happy over something. Well, we better swing around and get on that hilltop behind the dugout."

Their broncs corraled, the men were unloading barrels from the wagon and lugging them into the largest shack. Then Lashtrow's heart sank coldly, as he saw Deke Vennis and Tess Hiller walking away from the buildings toward the dugout. "The sonofabitch is going to start his play early, Boy," said Lashtrow. "But I don't think he'll force things too much—yet. He wants her to see what a gentleman he is, the slippery bastard. But Tess won't likely forget that Deke's outfit killed her father. She just might shoot Vennis herself, with one of his own guns, if he pushes too far."

Back in his hot wet saddle, Lashtrow started the circuitous ride that would bring him to the wooded hillcrest behind the dugout. From that vantage point he could survey the whole spread below.

To the rear of the mesa, at a bend in the creek, Lash watered the sorrel, refilled his canteen, and thought with pleasure of the whiskey in his saddlebags. "We may be on short rations, Beauty, but we don't lack for good drinking liquor," he told the horse. "It's a shame that you can't drink whiskey with me."

The sun was low and crimson behind them, as they reached the hilltop, and shadows were spreading in the valley, gray to blue and lavender to purple. The sounds of drunken revelry rose from the shacks beside the stream, faint at this distance but unmistakable. The *bandidos* were holding a big fiesta of their own. The water shone dimly through willows.

Removing bridle and saddle in a smooth grassy glade, Lashtrow laughed as he watched the sorrel roll and tumble about like a great golden cat at play. After a few nips from the bottle, he returned to peer thoughtfully down into the valley. The mountain backdrop brought thoughts of Milt.

Deke Vennis came out of the dugout alone, with a look of angry frustration about him, and stalked toward the other buildings. He must have tied the girl up, to leave her behind like that, and Lashtrow thought it was going to be a whole helluva lot easier to rescue Tess than he had anticipated. Then he saw the giant frame of Steel Huyett striding in this direction, and knew that Deke had sent him to stand watch over Tess.

Cold-blooded killer though he was, Huyett might be the best choice in that evil lot. Then Lash recalled hearing that Huyett didn't drink, and had little or no interest in women. That made him practically a perfect choice for this kind of duty. Apparently Vennis had decided to get drunk with the boys, and logically assigned Huyett to guard the dugout.

Well, if I can't take one man, I shouldn't be here, Lashtrow reflected, moving back to prepare the sorrel for the venture. He slipped in the bit, adjusted the bridle, threw

127

on blanket and saddle, and cinched up the double-rigging. "Gotta be ready to travel, Horse, and carry two riders this trip. Hell, you've done it before, and with a lot heavier extra than this little girl we're after."

They don't think there's anybody within fifty miles of them, Lashtrow realized. And why should they? The outlaws had no way of knowing that Crowleg and I arrived a few minutes after they captured Tess Hiller. They might get drunk enough so I can go in and get Tess's buckskin, after I take care of Huyett.

But I can't use a gun on Huyett, unless it's just the barrel. Got to keep it quiet. Drunk as they are, someone would hear a gunshot at two hundred yards. Have to take Huyett without shooting. And the way he can use a knife, it could be rough, unless I knock him out with one belt. Well, I'll handle the big bastard somehow. We'll get Vennis and the rest later. Right now all that counts is getting Tess out of here. . . . He patted the sorrel's head. "When it's full dark we'll go down, Brother."

Night had come and Lash led the sorrel cautiously down the gradual slope. Lantern light flickered yellow from the riverside huts, and a pale illumination showed in front of the dugout. A jungle roar of laughter, shouts, curses and song rolled across the valley floor. The bandits were throwing a wingding of a jamboree, which hell itself wouldn't want. If Lash only had a small crew with him, they could wrap up the whole caboodle of coyotes here and now. But he'd better forget that and concentrate on Steel Huyett, remembering that Steel had knifed in the back at least two of Tonk Hiller's special deputies in Salt Creek.

"Everybody pays in the end, Steel," murmured Lashtrow, mouth and throat dry with tension. "And your time has come."

He left the sorrel behind a huge boulder, hesitated, and lifted the Winchester carbine from its boot. You never could tell when a long gun would come in handy, maybe in this case to reach Huyett's skull quicker. Treading softly he rounded the front corner of the dugout. Only one entrance, and nothing but slits in the wall to see through. And maybe get your head blown off, if you tried to look inside. Well, the hell with it.

Lashtrow was at the front door, under a low-burning lantern, when it burst open and slammed him reeling backward. Steel Huyett, on his way to answer a call of nature, was as surprised as the Ranger. Lash recovered instantly, carbine lined from the hip, and could have shot Huyett, but he didn't want to arouse the camp. Huyett had his pistol drawn by then, and they faced one another over the leveled barrels. Through the doorway Lashtrow glimpsed the primitive shadowy interior with Tess Hiller lying bound on a rude bunk against the back wall. She was conscious, watching.

"Drop the gun and back inside," Lashtrow ordered.

Steel Huyett shook his high tousled head. "You shoot, I shoot. And the whole pack'll be on your neck. You ain't gotta chance."

"Cut the girl loose and we'll be gone."

"Can't do that."

"Tell 'em I surprised and gunwhipped you, Steel," said Lashtrow. "You don't want Vennis raping a nice girl like Tess Hiller. You know Vennis."

Huyett nodded. "I know he's woman-crazy, dirty and no good. But he's the boss."

"You ready to die for him?"

"You can't shoot me, without getting yourself killed."

"If they did get me, it wouldn't help you any. They'd leave us both for the buzzards. Use your head. Save a good decent woman."

"I can't, goddamn it. I'd like to, but I can't."

"There must be some way to settle this," Lashtrow said wearily. "We can't stand here all night."

Steel Huyett grinned like an outsized kid. "We could use knives. No noise that way. You any good with a knife?"

"Not much. Don't like to use 'em in a fight. How about bare hands?"

"I like the knife better. Quick, clean, you don't get all beat up."

Lashtrow considered all the angles. It seemed about the only way out. Time was wasting, and Deke Vennis might decide to come over here any minute now. "All right, with knives then."

Steel Huyett grinned gleefully, holstered his pistol, undid and dropped the shell belt, and pulled his big bowie. Lashtrow laid the carbine aside, untied the thigh strings, unbuckled and let the double gunbelt fall. His own knife looked short, thin and frail in contrast to the other.

They crouched and circled warily, feinting, thrusting, parrying, dodging, lunging in and out. Huyett looked happy and confident. He faked and came in with a lightning underhanded stroke, but Lashtrow's left hand caught and locked on that powerful right wrist. Lash's blade flashed at Huyett's waistline, but Steel's enormous left paw fastened onto the Ranger's wrist, and they were manacled together in a stark stalemate, bucking and heaving in erratic circles.

It became a test of pure strength then, with both men straining from the ankles up, exerting every ounce of pressure in their bodies. Slowly they turned and weaved, swaying to and fro, their arms rigid with muscle as they trampled up dust. Sweat sprang out and poured all over them. Their eyes bulged and the breath sawed in and out of their clenched teeth.

Huyett's confidence waned as he became aware of the power in Lashtrow's long lithe frame. Huyett had expected it to be easy. By this time his knife should have been buried to the hilt in Lash's guts. Instead Huyett began to feel the first chilling encroachment of doubt and dread.

Few men had been strong enough to hold Huyett's knife-hand for any length of time, while his own bone-crushing grip had soon paralyzed the striking hand of opponents, rendering them helpless victims. But Lash's left hand was a relentless iron trap, and his right wrist was like springing steel. Huyett jerked a knee up at the groin, but Lash twisted and took it on the hip.

Huyett began to labor and flounder as they revolved slowly and lurched back and forth. Sweat streamed from them both, and their breathing was a ragged painful sound in the darkness. Lashtrow was nearly spent, summoning up will power to keep him going. He had to make his move soon.

Lashtrow relaxed and fell back suddenly, hauling Huyett off balance and after him. Wrenching explosively, Lash ripped his right hand free and brought the blade slashing up into Huyett's belly. Doubled up in a gut-torn spasm, Huyett tore loose and lashed out with the bowie, but Lashtrow leaped backward and the stroke fell short.

Retching and moaning, Steel Huyett lunged again and fell to his knees, left hand clawing at his stomach, blood welling out between his fingers. Lashtrow stood back, the crimsoned blade hanging loose in his hand, hesitant about striking again at a dying man. That moment of hesitation proved fatal.

Swaying on his knees, Huyett screamed with the last bit of energy left in him, screamed before Lash strode forward and put his shoulder into a final arcing thrust, driving his knife through the ribs into the heart. With a gushing sigh, Huyett reared upright and tottered there, blood spurting over Lashtrow's hand. Lash withdrew the blade, and Huyett pitched headlong into the reddening dirt, the bowie knife still clasped in his huge grimy right hand. I waited too goddamn long, Lash thought, disgusted.

Panting hard, deathly tired, and sick to the very pit of his stomach, Lashtrow turned away to pick up the guns and belts, and stagger into the dugout, hearing doors slam open and hoarse shouts rise from the huddle of shacks by the river. Men came running across the flats, with guns beginning to flash and boom, as Lash closed and barred the door, cut Tess Hiller loose and handed her his carbine. Blowing out the single lamp, Lash stumbled weakly to another slit, and opened fire with the Winchester.

"Give 'em hell, baby," Lashtrow said, grinning and gulping air.

Their swift accurate shooting soon stopped the initial drunken rush of the outlaws, dispersing them into scattered flight. The main force returned to shanty down and the whiskey barrels, leaving a small and relatively sober group of riflemen to keep Lashtrow and the girl penned up in the dugout. Cordite bit through the musty smell of the place.

"Are you all right, Tess?" asked Lashtrow. "Did they—hurt you—or anything?" He was still panting for breath, his eyes smarting from sweat and gunpowder.

"I'm fine, Lash. They didn't hurt me at all. Deke Vennis tried to—to make love to me. But he was nice about it. He didn't get far. But in time, of course. . . Lord, but I was glad to see you, Lash! I couldn't believe my eyes. . . . Did Huyett cut you?"

"Not a scratch. But he damn near wore me out. Strong, that man was strong."

"You were crazy to fight him with knives."

"I couldn't shoot him, on account of the noise. He wouldn't fight any other way."

"So, you beat him at his own game. Is there anything you *can't* do?"

"Plenty! For one thing, I'm to blame for us being trapped in here."

Tess laughed. "How on earth do you figure that?"

"O Jesus, I'll never learn." Lashtrow groaned. "He was dying, on his knees, and I didn't want to stab him again. That's when he let out that screech, and brought out the wolfpack."

"It shows you have heart and sensitivity," Tess Hiller declared.

Lashtrow shook his tawny head. "No place to be sensitive, for godsake. If I'd finished him right off, we'd be outa here and riding for the Chisholm. And those drunken dogs wouldn't even know we were gone."

"Is Grace Amidon going to be all right? That Doctor Merriwether seemed to help her a great deal."

"Yeah, I think she's going to be a lot better, Tess."

"Was Hoss Crull hurt bad?"

"No, just a rap on the head. Old Hoss is used to them. And we got some good news, Tessie. An old-timer rode by and told Crowleg he saw a young white man riding with some Osages. The description fitted Milt, and he was riding a coyote dun."

"Oh, that's marvelous!" she cried. "Just wonderful. You had faith, Lash, and that faith is being rewarded, you see."

Lashtrow grinned wryly. "It won't get us outa this hole in the ground."

"It might, who knows? We'll both keep faith and see, Lash."

Tess Hiller laid the carbine on the plank table, and moved into Lash's arms, her face buried against his dirty sweat-soaked shirt. "Hold me, Lash. Just hold me, darling."

"I'll hold you, sweet." Lashtrow tilted her golden head back, and lowered his mouth to hers. The kiss lasted a long interval, and all the magic and wonder came flooding back to them.

Breathless and shaken, they finally drew apart, and Lash-trow said: "Some good whiskey out in my saddlebags, and it might as well be in China."

"Deke left some here, if I can find it." Tess fumbled along a shelf and came back with a bottle and glasses.

"So, he plied you with liquor," Lashtrow teased, as they clicked rims and drank. "And now you call him Deke. I don't know about you, baby."

"You're the only man who *does* know about me." Tess flushed and bent her head. "And all you do is try and get rid of me."

"Never!" denied Lashtrow. "Didn't I come after you

like a bat outa hell? You think I wouldn't have followed
you to *la cola del mundo*?''

Tess laughed softly. ''Where—or what—is that?''

''The tail end of the world,'' Lashtrow said gravely, and
took her in his arms again, their bodies blending, their lips
fusing in sweet fire.

Later, Lashtrow got up to have another drink and peer
out a rifle slit. The sky was clear, the moon bright, the stars
glittering like jewels, and the bandit sharpshooters were out
there watching the dugout door.

''If they get a bullet in here, it'll be pure luck,'' he said.
''But they can just sit out there until we starve or die of
thirst.'' He glanced up at the timbered roof. ''If it was just
sod, we could've broken through. But it's solid wood under
those sods. A real tight trap, Tess.''

''If they try to rush us, we'll mow them down like hay,''
Tess said, from the bunk.

''Yeah, we got a good clear field of fire. But they aren't
that brave—or that crazy. They'll just wait.''

''This is the first time we've been alone together in a
house. You realize that, sweetie?''

Lashtrow laughed with irony. ''We sure picked a helluva
house.''

''Oh, it wouldn't be too bad, if those outlaws weren't
out there. We could swim in the river and everything. You'd
hunt and I'd cook, and we'd have a grand life here.''

''Don't be so damn cheerful.'' Lash poured another whiskey. ''We're in a very bad fix here, little lady. I never been
a pessimist, but I don't see any way out of this one. . . . Jesus,
why didn't I cut his throat before he could scream? He was
dead anyway, for chrisake.''

''Your language is atrocious, Lashtrow,'' she protested,
in mock horror.

''I'm a Ranger. What do you expect?''

''I'll forgive you, darling, if you'll come back to bed.''

15

West to the Cimarron

In the morning the outlaws, except for the sentinels, slept late and got up sick, groggy and stunned with blinding hangovers. Bedrolls and blankets were strewn in and around the shacks and sheds. The place stank of whiskey, tequila, tobacco smoke, and sweaty unwashed bodies. Coffee was about all anyone wanted for breakfast, and they laced it with liquor to make it palatable.

Deke Vennis was in such a state of fury that men avoided him whenever possible. "How the hell do you know it's Lashtrow in there?" he demanded of Rammel, in from sentry duty. He was a slim blond boy with a merry grin.

"Because that big goddamn sorrel of his is running wild up on the hill," Rammel said. "I tried to catch him, no chance. Beede took a few shots at him, but it's like the horse is bulletproof. He just fades outa sight."

"Who else but Lashtrow could kill Huyett in a knife fight?" demanded Fern Morales.

"Aw, don't gimme that shit," Vennis said. "Lashtrow ain't that almighty, for chrisake. How could he of got here that quick?"

"Maybe that horse's got wings," Yaqui Tupelo suggested slyly.

Vennis glared at him. "You ain't funny, Tupelo. Use your head instead of your mouth. How we going to roust 'em outa that dugout?"

"Fire arrows on that sod roof," Morales said. "Yaqui, have your Injuns fix up some fire arrows."

"They ain't Injuns, they're Mexicans," Tupelo said. "They ain't got no bows and arrows."

"Get 'em outa them Indian suits then," snarled Vennis. "And just where the hell are them faking Apaches of yours, Tupelo?"

"Mosta them up in the hills, helping the real Apaches wipe out the goddamn Osages. Some of 'em scouting that trail herd on the Chisholm, like you wanted, Deke."

"To hell with the fake Apaches," said Vennis. "We're heading for that Andiron herd, with or without your faking Injuns. We wasted too much time already."

Morales tweaked his mustache. "It was you wanted to come on this honeymoon trip, Deke, remember?"

"You ain't funny either, Morales." Vennis stood up and started unbuttoning his fancy checked shirt. "I'm going to take a bath in the creek. You stinking bastards oughta do likewise. This place smells like a goat and sheep pen, with a few pigs throwed in."

Vennis hiked off toward the stream, followed by Beede, Rammel and several others. Tupelo and Morales shrugged and remained sitting on their broken boxes by the bottle-littered board table, smoking and drinking.

It was well past noon when the swimmers returned from the creek, and started dressing in clean clothes from their warbags. Vennis yelled at the men sitting or lying around the shanties: "Get off your dead asses, for chrisake! Saddle up and get out there and lay some fire on that goddamn dugout!"

"It's a waste of ammunition, Deke. You know how tight that dugout is." Morales shook his oily blue-black head. "Can't get in close enough to hit them slits in the wall. Them people in there can shoot."

"Balls on a heifer!" Vennis shouted. "We're going to shoot up the joint anyway. Make 'em sweat a little inside. When you saddle up, throw on your bedrolls and bags and gear, ready to move out. And don't try to pack all the booze here either. Take a bottle or two apiece, but don't be god-damn hogs about it. Move it now, boys, let's go.''

Deke Vennis missed the silent solid presence of Steel Huyett. Maybe the big man never had nothing to say, but you could always depend on him.

In the dugout, Tess Hiller had prepared a scanty breakfast of coffee, biscuits and bacon in the ancient Dutch oven. After eating, Lashtrow lit one of his battered cheroots and they settled down for some more waiting, taking looks outside at frequent intervals to make sure the sentries weren't trying to move into closer range. They were envious indeed when they saw some of the outlaws head for a swim in the small river. It was suffocatingly hot in the close confines of the almost airless structure. Along toward noon they drank a little whiskey, which helped pass the time but didn't make them any cooler.

"They're all coming out, mounted," Lashtrow reported from his rifle slit. "I doubt they'll try a rush in that open field. If they do, we'll rip them to shreds. If they don't, we'll just fire enough to hold them at a distance. No sense wasting shells.''

Tess nodded her golden head calmly, and levered up a cartridge in the Winchester. "This is a fine carbine, but I still like my old Henry.''

"I used to appreciate those sixteen shots in my Henry," said Lashtrow. "Always used it till they issued these new ones.''

The shooting started in the afternoon glare, bullets chunk-ing and chopping into the front wall, cracking off adobe in spots, and they turned sufficient fire to prevent the enemy from closing in. The whole shooting match turned out to be as futile as Fernando Morales had predicted. A waste of ammunition on both sides, but sparingly by the defense.

"I reckon eventually somebody'll smarten up and sneak around back to set the roof on fire," Lashtrow said gloom-ily.

"I reckon so, pardner," Tess Hiller agreed. "Then our little love nest will get a mite too hot to linger in."

"If we have to surrender, they won't shoot you, at least. But I might as well go out ablazing with both guns, like in a Wild West show."

"I think I'll go out your way, too," Tess said. "You've heard of the fate worse than death, haven't you, darling?"

Lashtrow smiled at her. "You're quite a gal. We'll see when the time comes, baby. . . ."

Meanwhile Deke Vennis had recognized the uselessness of this long-range target practice, and had gone back to camp with Rammel to prepare some fire bombs. Carrying rag-wrapped torches and bottles of kerosene, they were riding toward the hillside north of the dugout, to swing an arc that would take them safely to the rear of the crude hovel. Then, almost at their leisure, they could light the firebrands and hurl them onto the dry sunbleached sod roof, which should ignite instantly.

"Jesus H. Christ!" Rammel said suddenly, staring and pointing to the south end of the valley, where a vast dust-cloud was blooming over what appeared to be an endless horde of charging Indians. "All the Injuns in goddamn Nations!" Ram drew his .44, green eyes slanted at Vennis.

Deke Vennis, as shocked as Rammel, paused in feverish debate for a moment. The dugout was still too far away, the Indians were coming too fast, and Vennis preferred survival to an act of vengeance.

"The hell with it," he said, flinging away torches and kerosene bottle. "Let's get outa here." Rammel sighed in relief and sheathed his Colt.

Wheeling their broncs, they galloped back toward their starting point, with Vennis signaling retreat to riders who were already falling back to the buildings beside the creek. They met in a disorganized milling mass, fear frozen on every face and some of the mustangs bucking and pitching.

"Aintcha going to stand and fight?" screamed Yaqui Tupelo.

"Fight a whole goddamn Injun army?" Vennis shouted. "Why fight them? Amidon and his trail herd's what we're after, for chrisake. Hit for the Cimarron River. We'll catch the bastards somewhere along there. Move out!"

Without firing a shot, the bandits fled northward in a frenzied pack.

Rammel was thinking, in some surprise, as he rocked along: I would've shot Vennis before I let him burn out that dugout. I truly think I would.

Before the valley bent westward, Deke Vennis pulled up to take a backward look, and saw that the charge had come to a halt before the dugout. As the dust settled, he saw that there weren't so many Indians, after all. Not more than twenty-five or thirty, and they had looked like three hundred coming in that storm of dust. But it didn't matter anyhow. There was no point in fighting poor goddamn Injuns. No percentage at all.

What mattered to Vennis was that Lashtrow had got out alive, and that he himself had gotten nowhere with Tess Hiller. But what the hell? He'd get to both of them later. He wished Steel Huyett was with him, though.

Yaqui Tupelo reined in beside him. "Hell, there's only about twenty Osages in that bunch."

"So what, you sonofabitch?" flared Deke Vennis. "Where are your fake Apaches and real Apaches? They was going to wipe out the Osages. Looks like they got burnt down themselves, don't it?"

"*Quien sabe?*" Tupelo shrugged, his vulture face blank. "Who knows about Injuns? Or white men either?"

Back at the dugout, Lashtrow and Tess Hiller had watched their saviors storming down the valley, with a great upwelling of relief, thanksgiving, and joy. Stepping out to welcome the rescue party, trying to ignore the hulking body of Steel Huyett, their spirits soared higher yet as they saw Milt Travers, elegant even in battle-grimed buckskins, slide gracefully from the saddle on the *bayo coyote* at the head

139

of the column and walk toward them with that boyish smile on his patrician face.

"About time you showed up, son," Lashtrow drawled casually, as their hands met and gripped hard.

"I see you're still getting into all kinds of trouble," Travers replied, in kind. "How'd you ever live this long, without my firm guiding hand?"

He turned to embrace Tess, who raised her laughing mouth to his lips. "I warned you, Teresa, that you'd have nothing but grief and misery with this man Lashtrow."

"Oh, Milt, Milton," she murmured. "I've never been happier to see anyone. Not even Dad—or Lash. We knew you'd come back, Milt. We never gave up on you."

Travers laughed. "The bad penny, prodigal son, and all that. Now I'd like you to meet two comrades. Rusty Bouchard—the Indians call him Red Bush, for obvious reasons. And Fire Hawk, war chief of the Osages. Later I'll introduce the rest of the tribe."

Lashtrow shook hands with Bouchard and Fire Hawk, excused himself, and walked to the side of the dugout, emitting a penetrating whistle as he faced the hillside. In a few minutes the sorrel trotted out of the woods and cantered down the slope to muzzle Lash's shoulder.

"Now that we're all back together," Lashtrow said, "let's take a swim in yonder creek. We've been roasting all day in this little furnace."

"Sorry I can't join you gentlemen," Tess said. "But I'll find a place upstream for my private bath."

The Osages made bivouac at the outlaws headquarters, indulging freely in the whiskey left there, and everyone went swimming, the men below the shacks and Tess upstream behind a row of cottonwoods. Afterward, glowing and refreshed, there was more drinking while the horses were attended to, and Tess and High Bear collaborated in preparing some kind of supper.

Both men and horses needed a night's restful sleep, and this was ideal for the purpose. There was much to be talked about and brought up to date, many stories to be exchanged. Tess had been delighted to find that, in their rush to escape, the bandits had left her buckskin in the corral with some other stray horses.

After the meal, Fire Hawk withdrew to his braves, and Bouchard fitted to perfection in the small group of whites. Lash and Tess liked him as quickly and instinctively as Milt Travers had. In the morning they would press on in a northwesterly direction toward the plains, the Chisholm Trail and the Cimarron.

"I don't wonder those outlaws ran," Tess Hiller said, as they sat around a recently cleaned table with drinks and smokes. "It looked as if the entire Osage Nation was coming down that valley."

"Sure glad we didn't have to fight again," Rusty Bouchard said. "Been fighting since the break of day, and running like hell when he wasn't in battle."

"The longest day in my life—I guess," Milt Travers said. "Although come to think of it, I've had an unprecedented number of long long days. Brought on by myself, in most cases."

Lashtrow grinned. "Our day in that dugout wasn't real short."

"Even with Tess at your side?" chided Travers. "I wouldn't count that a long day."

Bouchard chuckled. "I was staked out on an anthill one time. That was a fairly long day."

"How about long nights when you can't sleep a wink?" asked Lashtrow.

Travers laughed. "As long as the liquor holds out, I never have those kinda nights, Lash."

"I meant nights when there wasn't a drop within miles."

Travers shuddered. "I couldn't endure anything like that."

"That does it, baby," drawled Lashtrow, a flush under his high bronzed cheekbones. "Off to bed with you. And with all of us, I reckon. There's a long hard campaign coming up.''

"That's right, Lash," said Travers, meditatively. "This is like a happy ending to a story that's scarcely begun yet."

"It's too bad we couldn't push on after them bastards this afternoon," Bouchard said, rubbing his red beard. "But our horses was spent, and we we was near to falling outa the saddle. That last charge took all we had and a bit more. We was done in, Lash."

'I know, Rusty. Their horses were rested and fresh. You couldn't have caught 'em. Starting tomorrow we'll pick up ground and keep close enough. They're kinda disorganized, fulla dissension—as well as booze. We'll run 'em down.''

Tess Hiller said: "We haven't thanked you and the Osages properly for saving our lives. Please convey our thanks to Fire Hawk and his warriors.''

Bouchard inclined his russet head. "It was our pleasure, Miss Hiller. And Injuns understand without too many words, but I'll tell 'em.''

"This party's getting too serious for a wayward lad like me.'' Milt Travers politely cuffed a yawn, turning it into a smile. "I'm going to hit the soogans, as we plainsmen say. Goodnight, all.''

In a short time they were all in their blankets and sleeping, save for the Osages who stood watch in shifts through the night. Fire Hawk was far superior to Deke Vennis, as a military commander.

On the Chisholm Trail, short-handed and short of rations, the Andiron crew drove the plodding cattle on day after scorching day. They had crossed the Washita and the Canadian Rivers, and were pushing west and north for the Cimarron, impelled by the iron will of Anse Amidon and the loyalty of his cowhands.

Grace Admidon, thriving on the medicine of Sad Sam Merriwether, had recuperated enough to handle the chuckwagon, with the assistance of Carlos. Young Lyle Myatt drove the supply wagon by day, and wrangled the cavvy at night. Kloster, an entirely new and different man now, was once more ramrodding the outfit and riding a masterful point with the swashbuckling Santee. Hoss Crull on one flank and Crowleg Dooner on the other, worked their swing riders into raw, saddle-galled exhaustion. Big Mule Mundorf and Ramos prodded the drag, until it was nearly crowding the swing. Sudalter controlled the *remuda* during the day. And everyone was putting out one hundred percent.

And every day on one distant wing or the other, a few Apaches appeared on their paint ponies, limned against the horizon, silent, implacable, never making a hostile gesture or coming closer, just keeping slow pace with the herd.

"I'd feel better if they'd come in asking for grub or a cow or two," Anse Amidon said to Kloster, at the point. "Even if we can't spare food or cows. They used to do that, and it was a cheap easy way to get rid of 'em." He saw Santee turn two strays back on the left-side point.

The tall solemn Kloster nodded, his thin lips straight across now instead of down-turned at the corners. "A trail herd, strung out from here to hell-and-gone, is made to order for them red buzzards. Scattered like we are, they could hit us one or two at a time, pick us off one by one, maybe wipe us out and run off the whole herd. But it looks to me like they ain't got a leader."

"Maybe Deke Vennis is the leader they're waiting for." Amidon spat brown, with the breeze.

"Maybe so. I hear he's been working with Injuns. Some of his gang even masquerading like Injuns. People was blaming the Osages for all the raids and massacres, but we know the Osages ain't like that. Not under Gray Eagle, they wasn't."

"They been dogging us for weeks, but they ain't shown in any force yet, Klos."

Kloster rubbed his chin. "They got one somewhere. Likely built on Vennis's bunch. That Vennis sure needs killing, Anse. I hope Lashtrow gets another crack at the sonofabitch. Maybe he has by now.''

"Klos, what the hell ailed you at the start of this drive?''

Kloster shook his high narrow head. "Dunno, Anse. Sick in the head or something. Listened too much to Pueblo and Tench. They was no good, and I was too dumb to see it.'' His horse straightened out some lead steers.

"Yeah, I was too—for awhile. Jesus, I hated to lose that Frellick boy. He was a great kid. Woulda made a real top hand. Prob'ly a gunhand, too. I woulda liked a son like him, Klos.''

Kloster nodded and spat viciously. "I shoulda shot Pueblo myself, goddamn him! Instead I felt him sneak-shoot OK Frellick. I ain't slept good since, Anse. Can't get it outa my mind. And Kate, too. Christ forgive me!''

"You think Milt Travers is dead?''

"Must be, else Lash woulda found him.''

"Hope Lash gets back before long. And brings Tess Hiller with him,'' Amidon said, with a worried scowl. "I been thinking they might hit us at the Cimarron.'' Kloster's horse nudged two straying steers back into line.

"Maybe,'' conceded Kloster. "We sure need Lashtrow anyway.''

"You hold any grudge against Lash?''

"Nary a mite, Anse. He shoulda plugged me, instead a just knocking my stupid head off. Christ, how that man can hit! I been belted before, but nothing like that.''

"Good, good,'' Amidon said. "You and Lash oughta work fine together.''

"I allow that we will, the time ever comes.''

"Well, I best get on and see how my old lady's doing, Klos.''

"You got some old lady there, Anse. One in a million.''

Amidon smiled in pleasure. "You have the boys ready for the Cimarron crossing, Klos.''

"I got the boys ready all the time—for anything,'' Kloster said.

On the chuckwagon seat, Grace Amidon turned her head to watch the Apaches silhouetted against the brassy blue skyline in the distance, sinister even at long range. She had come to hate them, as she hated snakes and lizards. She wondered if the end was coming for Anson and her and all of them. It didn't seem to matter so much, now that Kate was dead and buried. Grace was feeling better in body, but ill and empty in mind. Tess Hiller and Lashtrow were still missing. Probably as dead as Travers, by now. Nothing was the same, never would be again.

Anson's pride and ambition had pushed them into this hopeless project, yet she didn't hold it against him. She was glad to be there with Anse, where she belonged, come what might.

On the flanks of the shuffling herd, riders scanned the horizon with variable emotions and reactions. Old Hoss Crull snarled and spat tobacco juice and wished he could get the Injuns under his guns. Crowleg Dooner, in constant pain from his bad leg, cursed the endless waiting and craved action, along with the return of Lashtrow. Young Santee at the point, laughed and gestured mockingly with a rope-scarred fist. "Come on in, you filthy red mongrels. Come in and get it, you dirty scum!"

Out with the cavvy by night, slim boyish Lyle Myatt felt his insides freeze and shrivel, as a faint flutter of panic thrummed in his chest and throat. They'll hit the *remuda* first. Injuns want horses more than cows. Always dreamed of riding up the Chisholm to Kansas, hitting old Abilene like a hurricane, punching the stock into the pens, bellying up to the bar in the Alamo Saloon, bedding some beauty in the Devil's Addition, maybe throwing my gun on a crooked gambler. Now I got a sad sorry notion I ain't going to make it, with them goddamn Injuns out there like ghosts and ghouls. Could be I'll never see Abilene, never mind getting back home to Texas. . . . He sang to fight off the fear: *"The old cow charged with her head way down, A-rollin' her eyes and a-pawin' the ground. . . ."*

Another day, deep in the dust of the drag, big Mule Mundorf eyed the faraway savages with cool monumental indifference. Ramos, irritable and fretful, sidled his bronc toward his partner. "Maybe they come pretty soon, huh, Mule? Maybe they wait for the Cimarron crossing, you think?"

Mundorf shrugged massively. "If they come, they come, Ramos. If they don't, they don't. No sense in fretting, boy. It's all wrote up in the book, and we ain't going to change it none."

"Yah-h, you big dumb gringo ox!" Ramos said, grinning. "I ain't scared neither. I'll live to spit on your grave, Mulehead."

Mundorf smiled broadly. "Maybe so, Mex. If you do, see that you spit tobacco juice. Something with flavor in it, son."

The drive rumbled on in its storm of dust, a surging sea of beef, and the greenery of the Cimarron showed in the sun-blazoned northwest. A sudden premonition came to Anse Amidon, clutching at his throat, sinking his stomach into an icy void:

The sonsabitches'll strike at the Cimarron, as sure as I'm setting on this hammer-headed gotch-eared old claybank of mine. I can feel it, in my blood and bones and brain.

Then he thought of Kate with her sheen of dark hair and her smoky gray eyes, and his throat knotted in anguish, his eyes filled with burning tears. I was always rough on that sweet girl, he thought. And she took the bullet that was meant for me. She gave her life to save mine.

16

Nest of Vipers

In a secluded basin, not far from where the Chisholm Trail crossed the Cimarron River, Deke Vennis had set up a command post in a deserted adobe ranch house. His followers were quartered in ruined outbuildings and sheds, the horses held in a brush corral reinforced by ropes. An old well supplied water. It was an ideal hideout.

Fernando Morales and Yaqui Tupelo were lolling on their bedrolls in the front room of the main house, smoking and drinking tequila. A drooping door in the rear opened, and Deke Vennis came out dragging a girl by the wrist, his curly hair awry and disgust twisting his handsome features. The girl was weeping and one side of her pretty face was scarlet and bruised, her dress torn and tattered.

"She's no goddamn good," Vennis said. "Get her outa here."

"You animal," sobbed the girl. "There's some things—I won't do. Can't do. Not if—you kill me."

"Dixie Belle musta spoiled you, Deke," said Morales, lips curling under his upturned mustache. "Normal women ain't good enough no more."

Yaqui Tupelo's natural snarl increased. "You and your goddamn women will get us all killed someday."

"Get her out, I said."

"What the hell we do with her?" Morales asked.

"Send her home with one of the boys." Vennis flung

her toward them, and she fell to her knees, head bowed and shapely form shaking with sobs.

Tupelo got unhurriedly to his feet, wagging his vulture-like head. "You *are* a bastard, Deke. Getting worse all the time." He helped the girl upright, roughly gentle. "Stop crying, Dolly. You're going to be all right."

Deke Vennis grabbed a whiskey bottle off the broken-down table and took a large swig. He strapped on the shell belt with the two bone-handled guns and gulped again from the bottle. The other two men avoided looking at him.

Tupelo took the girl outside, and returned after a few minutes. "Rammel's taking her back. He's a good kid. And them Jayhawkers are here, ready to enlist."

"How many are they?"

"Seven."

Deke Vennis laughed. "That ain't much like fifty of your faking Injuns, is it, Yaqui? But if we waited for them, hell would be froze over solid. Seven oughta be enough though. Bring 'em in."

Tupelo went to the doorway, signaled, and seven big bewhiskered men filed into the debris-strewn room. They wore derby hats and frock coats or dusters, which marked them as Missouri or Kansas hardcases.

"You know what you're getting into?" Vennis asked, scrutinizing them with care. "It ain't going to be no pink tea party, but it oughta get us three thousand head of prime beef."

The black derbies nodded an inch or so.

"You got any names?"

The first man said, "Green," and the others spoke in turn: "White," "Brown," "Black—"

"All right, *all right*!" Deke Vennis made a violent chopping motion. "Never mind. Names don't matter. Just bear in mind I'm running this outfit, and you take orders from me. Or from Morales and Tupelo, here. You know who I am?"

"Sure, Deke Vennis," said the one who called himself Green. "We heared tell of you, way up in Kansas City."

Vennis stared hard at him, but the bearded face was completely sober. "All right, set down someplace and have a drink." He handed over a couple of bottles, and the newcomers hunkered down against the adobe-brick wall. The duster of one Missourian fell away as he upended a bottle, revealing a shoulder-holstered pistol in addition to the regular pair of belt guns. Another wore crossed bandoleers under his loose frock coat.

"We'll hit 'em from behind and both sides," Vennis said. "Stampede the herd and pick off the riders. The cattle will stop running at the Cimarron, and we'll gather 'em up there."

"How many hands they got?" Brown inquired.

"Less than twenty now."

"Be a lot more if Lashtrow gets there with them Osages," said Morales.

"We'll still have the odds on 'em, two-to-one or better," Vennis said. "Plus the advantage of surprise."

"You using Apaches, too?" White asked. "Seen some around camp here."

Vennis laughed. "They ain't real Apaches. Just rigged up that way to work on the drovers' nerves, showing themselves every day at a distance."

"Smart notion," approved Green. "Wear them cowboys to a frazzle."

"Well, you men take care of your horses, make yourselves at home, and get rested up," Vennis said, with his charming smile. "We got plenty of grub and whiskey, and good water in that well."

"How about women?" asked Black. "Seen one outside."

"She's leaving. No women till it's over."

Morales chortled. "Deke handles all the women himself. He's our stud hoss."

Vennis's slitted eyes fixed on his Mex lieutenant. "Keep

on running off your fat mouth, Fern, and you'll get that mustache parted with a bullet."

Yaqui Tupelo laughed and gestured at the new recruits. "They all the time horse around prodding each other. It don't mean nothing. I'll show you gents around the layout. Take them bottles and a coupla more with you."

He ushered them out, leaving Vennis pacing the floor while Morales remained sprawling at ease on his blankets.

"They look tough and mean enough." Morales patted his plump belly.

"I wouldn't trust 'em outa gun sight. But they ain't big enough to cross us, Fern."

"Unless they got some friends waiting at the Cimarron."

Vennis spat across the room. "I thought you greasers was s'posed to be cheerful bastards." He turned and stalked back to his own private quarters.

Rammel had brought the girl a bucket of water and blanketed a shed so she could wash and freshen herself. He roped out his own brown mustang and a quiet pony for her, and saddled them up while waiting. He gave her a brush jacket to cover the near-nakedness of her upper body, hoisted her lightly aboard, stepped into his own leather, and they rode out of camp. Vennis had snatched her out of a honkytonk in a tiny settlement called Spooner, and they drifted in that direction.

It was a beautiful day, the sun blazing in a pure blue sky, the heat eased by errant breezes. Dolly had lustrous dark hair, large brown eyes, a lissome curved figure, and a face that was pretty despite the bruised cheek and a sullen hardness. Rammel might have wanted her himself, if she hadn't been with Vennis. It had been a long time since he'd had a woman. But he was gratified just to get out of that bivouac and away from his companions.

Slender and easy in the saddle, Rammel looked nothing like an outlaw. He had fair hair under his tilted flat-crowned hat, clear green eyes, straight pleasant features, and a friendly boy's smile. Clean-shaven, he was immaculate in person and dress, the result of birth and breeding. His looks often got him in trouble with toughs, who thought him a soft touch, but he was fast and sure enough with guns or fists to get him out of such minor saloon jams. His slow soft voice masked natural fighting power and skill.

Virginia-born to a family of high lineage, ruined by the War of the Rebellion, Rammel had been in his first year at Virginia Military Institute when he became entangled with a proud lovely belle from a prominent Richmond family. Ram never considered it his fault. She was a bit older, far wiser and more sophisticated, and she made all the advances and initiated the lovemaking. After she became pregnant, Rammel learned that he was but one in a long line of her VMI conquests, and he turned cool toward her insistence on marriage. He doubted he was responsible for her condition.

Two of her high-headed hot-blooded brothers came after Rammel, and he was forced to shoot them in order to save his own life. One died instantly, the other was badly wounded, and Rammel had to flee from VMI and the state to escape prosecution and certain conviction, even though it had been a fair standup fight with the odds on their side.

Most men on the run then headed for Texas, and Rammel followed the custom. But it was in New Orleans that the notorious Dixie Belle took him under her protection, and it was there that Deke Vennis had saved Ram's life in a gambling casino brawl. He had liked Vennis at first, even though Deke immediately replaced Ram as Dixie Belle's favorite. Vennis had a raw grace and charm, and could be most likable until one discovered what underlay that bright surface, the inherent evil of the man.

So, Rammel had joined the Vennis band and was still with them, although he no longer liked Deke, or any of the other outlaws, since Tallant had died at Salt Creek and Steel Huyett had been killed by Lashtrow. He was sometimes amused by Morales and Tupelo, particularly when they baited Vennis, but Rammel had nothing in common with most of his *companeros,* and was beginning to detest their way of life—and his own.

In recent raids, Rammel had used his weapons only when essential to survival, and in some combats he hadn't fired a shot, or had missed purposely when he did pull the trigger. But it couldn't go on that way. He had to make a clean break and light out on his own. Rammel had no inclination toward the upcoming attack on the Andiron trail herd.

He had finally resolved to make the break, before it was too late.

Today's assignment afforded a perfect chance for escape, and Rammel had secretly packed his warsack, saddlebags and blanket-roll with all the belongings he cared to retain, and all the food, liquor and ammunition he could scrape together. Ram had felt a faint and ridiculous sense of guilt and shame, on leaving the layout, but that had dissipated swiftly on the open trail toward Spooner. He had a sense of freedom and elation.

"Did he abuse you much, Dolly?" he asked the silent apathetic girl.

"No, not much. But the things he wanted—" An expression of ineffable disgust and loathing distorted her even features. "I wouldn't do. I—I couldn't do. So he hit me a couple and threw me out—thank God! That man ain't human. He's a beast!"

Rammel nodded his blond head. "He's filled with some kind of perverse lust."

"If that means crazy, it's got my vote, Mr. —"

"Just call me Ram. The name is Rammel."

She appraised him frankly, her velvety eyes amber in the sunshine. "What's a nice clean boy like you doing in that nest of vipers?"

"I don't know, Dolly. It'd take years to come up with an answer to that one. Have to call it fate or fortune or destiny, some such thing. But I'm leaving the viper's nest, as of now."

Her eyes widened. "You ain't going back? They'll kill you, for sure."

"They aren't going to get the chance. I'm riding up north, Colorado or Wyoming or Montana."

"But what'll you do—Ram?"

"I can always get a riding job, or a gun job. Perhaps even join the Cavalry. A few years ago I was going up to join the Seventh under Custer. Just as well I didn't obey that impulse."

"Oh, yeah, the Little Bighorn." She shuddered and swayed in the saddle.

"You want a drink, Doll?" He was suddenly solicitous.

"Guess maybe it wouldn't harm me none," she said bravely.

They got down in the sparse shade of junipers, and drank whiskey chased with canteen water, walking about to stretch their limbs.

"Why did you leave Spooner and come with Vennis?" asked Rammel.

" 'Cause I'm a goddamn fool, and he's such a good-looking bastard, I s'pose. He ain't as good-looking as you, really, but he's bold and brash and runs right over you. And you, Ram, you're kinda shy and bashful and slow."

Rammel laughed, his green eyes laughing with his mouth. "That's me, Dolly. That's always been my trouble."

"It's not trouble, it's all to your favor, Ram."

"Well, it must have lost me a lot of loving. Not that it matters much."

Dolly flirted her amber-brown eyes at him. "I'll bet you've had your share and more."

Rammel shrugged slim sinewy shoulders. "I don't know. I never really went hunting for it."

"You don't have to, Ram. A man with your looks and manners and all." There was a warm open invitation in her eyes, face and attitude.

Rammel felt a stir of response. It had been a helluva long

while. Perhaps when they got to Spooner, in a private place. . . . "We'd better hit the leather again, Doll."

"I like you to call me Doll." She laughed, as she swung up from his cupped hands. "I like green eyes in a brown face, and how they light up when you smile. Such a sweet smile, Ram."

"Easy, Doll, easy," drawled Rammel. "We got a long ride yet, and it's hotter than hell's lower hinges."

"You're cute when you swear."

"Not when I really *swear*. I can curse with the worst of 'em. Seems that a riding man or a fighting man or a man working cows has to do a lot of swearing, for some reason or other. It just goes with the trade maybe."

"You ain't a real Texan, I bet. From Virginia, huh? That must be a beautiful country up there."

"It was before the War. It still is, but the old way of life is gone, along with the finest people. All of the Old South is gone. Carpetbaggers came down from the North and took over the government, brought corruption and graft and ruin. Where are you from, Doll?"

"Born in Henrietta, Texas. Daddy was a buffalo hunter, we never saw him one year to the next. Ma was a saloon girl—just like me. Never had no chance to be different. . . . Aw, the hell with it. Don't like to think nor talk about it, Ram."

"You're all right, Doll. I can tell you're a good girl." Rammel tried to soothe and console her, but she responded with a string of bordello obscenities. He was sympathetic, sorry for her, but he felt his brief desire waning. Too bad. He'd been looking forward to having this woman, since learning that Vennis hadn't actually possessed her. Well, Ram could wait a while longer. Sex could be drowned out in whiskey. He had managed that often enough, God knows. It had kept him away from Belle's Red Lantern.

As they entered the single street of Spooner, with its scatter of rude outlying houses, mauve and violet dusk softened the false-fronted adobe and frame buildings, and

154

lamps blossomed through the murky haze. A large company of horsemen seemed to fill the street, and Rammel noted with surprise that they were Indians on paint ponies. The sight dried his throat and chilled his spine, despite the quiet patient appearance of the braves.

"My God, where'd all them Injuns come from?" gasped Dolly. "They going to massacree the whole town?"

"I don't think so, Doll," said Rammel, with a calmness he didn't feel. "Looks like Osages and they're fairly peaceful, for the most part. Don't be afraid. They aren't here to make war. See, Doll, there's a white man and a white woman with them."

Even at long range in purple twilight dimness, Rammel recognized the fine graceful figure of Tess Hiller, and knew that these were the Osages who had routed the bandits and rescued Tess and Lashtrow. But the man with her wasn't big enough to be Lashtrow.

Rammel recalled making the torches with Vennis, and riding out to set fire to the dugout roof. All the time he'd been debating whether to light and throw the firebrands, or to shoot Deke Vennis dead. His mind hadn't been made up, when he spotted the Osage charge in its storming dust, but Ram thought he would have killed Vennis and run for it, rather than firing that sod roof. Yes, he was sure of it now. He would have chosen Vennis's death, over that of Tess Hiller and Lashtrow.

For Tess had caught his fancy, Lash had won his admiration and respect, and his hatred for Vennis had been growing daily.

"You want to go to the Silver Horseshoe?" Rammel asked.

"That's where I live," Dolly said tartly.

"Let's go around back then," Rammel said. "Those Osages might remember me. We almost tangled with them a while back."

They turned their horses into an alley on the right, that would lead them to the rear of their destination. The Indians

155

were further up on the left side of the street, near the lesser barrooms. . . .

Since the law forbade Indians entry to saloons, Lashtrow and Bouchard had gone in to make inquiries about the Vennis gang, while Milt Travers waited outside the Tess and the Osages.

Tess had been watching the two riders coming in from the west, a man and woman, and there was something familiar about the man's shape and the way he sat the brown horse, the bronc, too, striking a chord in her memory.

"That's one of them, Milt," she said abruptly. "One of Vennis's riders. I'm almost positive. A nice-looking boy they called Ram. I remember, because he reminded me so much of OK Frellick. I'm sure it's him."

As they both stared intently, the two riders turned off and vanished into an alleyway on the opposite side of the street.

"Yes," Travers said. "Looks like the one who was riding with Vennis to circle behind that dugout. You stay here, Tess. I'll take a quick look over there."

"Wait for Lash," pleaded Tess. "Don't go alone, Milton."

Travers laughed lightly. "There's only one man, Tess."

"The whole crew could be back there," Tess argued, but Milt was already on the move, lance-straight and slim on his coyote dun.

Slanting the dun across the street, he plowed through the shadowy clutter of the nearest alley, but he was too late to intercept his quarry. The dust of their passage hung on the darkening air. Turning left, Travers saw their horses tied at the loading platform behind the Silver Horseshoe.

Milt rode up alongside, vaulted lightly to that back porch lined with barrels and crates, and tried the door there. It was locked tight, the interior of the rear rooms in darkness. Travers knocked, but nobody came. He pondered shortly. No sense breaking in and getting his head shot off. Straddling leather again, he kneed the dun out a driveway to the front of the saloon.

Tess, Fire Hawk, and the other Osages were watching from across the street. There was little traffic at this hour. Travers motioned them to stay put, slipped from the saddle, and strode to the main batwing-doored entrance. His blue gaze swept the smoky barroom, almost empty of clients at this hour. A few nondescript men seated at separate tables. A lithe blond young rider lounging idly at the bar, cigarette in lips, glass in hand. No sign of the woman anywhere. A fat bald bartender mechanically scrubbing the wooden counter.

Travers loosened the Walker Colt in its sheath, swiveled smoothly through the swing-doors and sauntered toward the bar. Rammel set down his glass and turned away from the bar, arms hanging freely at his sides. Travers halted and they stood motionless, twenty feet apart, staring at one another in silence. Men at the tables edged toward far corners. The bartender started a furtive move, but stopped as Milt's blue eyes flicked at him. Ram was trying to decide whether to fight or surrender.

Rammel's right hand twitched toward his gun and froze halfway, as he shook his fair head. He liked the looks of this lean man in buckskins.

"Better keep reaching," Travers advised.

"I don't want to draw on you."

"Looks like you'll have to, or go down empty-handed."

Silence returned and stretched on, slow and agonizing. A strange sort of recognition sprang up between them. Two men of a kind, an aristocrat from Massachusetts facing a cavalier from Virginia, on the razor edge of drawing and shooting. Something told Milt it would be very close, maybe dead even. They might both die here, in this foul dingy frontier saloon.

"You ride with Vennis?" said Milt Travers.

"I did, but not any more. What makes it your business?"

"I'm a Ranger."

157

"Yeah, I remember now," Rammel said. "Brush Creek and Salt Creek. Name of Travers. Mine's Rammel."

"When did you quit Vennis?"

"Today." They had the same bone structure and coloring, thoroughbred lines.

"Why?" They might have been cousins, or even brothers.

Rammel smiled faintly. "Had all I could stand. What Vennis tried on this girl I just brought home was the last straw. Been planning to quit for weeks. Ever since Buford and Salt Creek."

"You don't want your cut of the Amidon herd?"

Solemn and sincere, Rammel fingered the military buckle inscribed VMI.

"No part of it."

"But Vennis is going to hit that herd—soon now?" Travers hooked his thumbs in his gunbelt.

"That's right. This side of the Cimarron." Rammel rolled and lit a cigarette.

"You figure on going straight now, Rammel?"

Ram nodded firmly. "Damned right. I've had it the other way, Trav."

"Maybe we can do business then," Travers said. "You know where Vennis is holed up, Ram."

"I sure do." Rammel's smile flashed, green eyes dancing. "Step up and have a drink."

"Thanks." Travers moved up to the bar, and they leaned elbows on it, side by side. The bartender relaxed with a sigh, and slid another glass across the wood. Rammel poured from his bottle. "Will you tell us where?"

"Better than that, I'll take you there," Rammel said, as they raised their glasses and drank. "Hate to doublecross anybody, even those sonsabitches. But I don't want to see that Amidon crew wiped out. It was bad enough when that bastard Pueblo killed the Amidon girl."

"That's fine, Ram." Travers handed him a cheroot. "Never thought I'd believe a Vennis hand—ex-hand, I should say. But something convinces me you're on the level.''

"I am, at last. And I feel better than I have in years. Even if you have to run me in, Trav.'' Rammel did look happier, his green eyes glowing.

"We don't arrest too many," Travers said. "Either kill them, or lose them. You lead us to Vennis, in time, and you'll never see the inside of a jail. I can guarantee that. And we might keep you on, if you like.''

The batwings squealed to admit Lashtrow, and he walked to the bar, grinning at them. "Quietest gunfight I ever did hear of.''

"Another glass, please," Rammel said. "And bring another bottle with it.''

Milt Travers made the introductions and explanations, and one quick penetrating glance by Lashtrow confirmed that Milt had arrived at the right conclusion about Rammel. The three men seemed to belong together.

The batwings swung inward again, and Rusty Bouchard, broad, solid and red-bearded, ambled bowlegged to the bar. "Since I didn't hear no guns ablasting, I allowed it was safe to come in.''

The barkeeper produced a fresh glass, Rammel filled it to the brim, and Milt Travers said: "Ram, this is Red Bush, in Injun language. Rusty Bouchard, to us White Eyes. Rusty, meet Rammel, a recent defector from the ranks of Deke Vennis.''

Bouchard shook hands with his right, and drank with his left. "Welcome to the side of the righteous. Appears you might fit better here than you did yonder, son.''

"You called it, Red Bush," said Rammel, smiling warmly. "I haven't felt so much at home in many moons.''

"Fine and dandy, Ram," said Bouchard, a grin splitting his beard. "But we oughta get moving, Lash. Them Osages are getting restless out there.''

"That's the ticket," Lashtrow agreed. "Let's ride for the Cimarron.''

"Take those bottles along," Rammel said. "They're paid for and I'll get a couple more. It's all on Deke Vennis, actually. My horse is out back."

Bouchard squinted queryingly at his comrades. Milt Travers said, "Don't worry, Rusty. He's one of us now. Taking us to the Vennis hideout."

They went out the front way, mounted their horses, and waited.

In the back rooms, two bottles under his left arm, Rammel called out up the dark stairs: "Dolly. Where are you? I want to say goodby." There was no reply. Rammel lifted his shoulders, went out the back door, stowed the bottles in his saddlebags, and stepped into the saddle.

Out front he was presented to Tess Hiller and Fire Hawk, doffing his hat to the girl. Then, wheeling his brown bronc, he led the cavalcade westward out of Spooner toward the Cimarron. Rammel regretted not having even kissed Dolly farewell. but perhaps it was just as well. For his own peace of mind, at any rate. "Aubrey," he addressed himself wryly, using the Christian name he detested. "You aren't really much of a ladies' man."

17

Into the Valley of Death

Lashtrow stood on the rimrock of a maroon-and-saffron butte overlooking the firelit basin of the outlaw ecampment. Considerable activity in the sunken bowl indicated that the Vennis band was preparing to move out and strike at the Andiron trail herd. On the plains to the northwest, short of the Cimarron River, blossomed the campfires of the Amidon drovers, shrouded in lowland mist. The night air was damp and cool.

"We're in time," Lashtrow murmured. "Thanks to Rammel. Never would've found them without you, Ram."

"Morales always said Vennis's lust for women would bring them all down," Rammel said modestly. "If it weren't for Dolly, we wouldn't be here."

"Got to get a warning to Anse," said Lashtrow. "And I think Tess'll be safer in there than out here. Can't send her with an Osage detail. They'd be gunned down as hostile Injuns."

Rusty Bouchard shifted his chew. "I'll take her in, and help 'em set up a defense. They won't shoot at a man with red whiskers—will they?"

Lashtrow chewed on his tobacco. "You know what to do, Red Bush. The herd'll stampede when the shooting starts, but the cows'll stop at the river. Make sure the wagons are well out of the way, to the west."

"Yeah, they'll hit the herd first," Bouchard said. "Then

the *remuda* and the wagons. They'll run right into our gunfire.''

Lashtrow nodded. ''You cut 'em up, and we'll hit 'em from the rear.''

''How many you figure, Lone Wolf?'' asked Bouchard.

''There's sixty renegades, maybe more, down there,'' Lashtrow estimated.

Tess Hiller slipped through the ring of men and nestled against Lash's side. ''I'd rather stay and ride with you, honest.''

''No, Tess, you're going with Bouchard,'' said Lashtrow, flatly.

Milt Travers had field-glasses trained on the ranch layout below. ''They're shedding the Apache garb and paint, going in all white. They figure there'll be no survivors, so they won't need any disguises.''

''Good,'' Rammel said. ''This way they won't get mixed up with the Osages.''

Crooked Nose led up the horses, and Bouchard slung and cinched the double-rigged saddles to his satisfaction. Tess Hiller clung fiercely to Lashtrow, but he forced her gently apart. ''We'll be together by daybreak, Tessie,'' he said. ''Tell Anse and Grace we're coming. A little late but still in time. Grace will appreciate your company, baby.''

Lashtrow lifted her onto the buckskin, and Rusty Bouchard mounted his big-shouldered cayuse. ''See you on the shores of the Cimarron,'' he said blithely, and they trotted away toward the down-trail at the rear of the butte. Lash and the others watched until they faded into outer darkness. Then the men, Osages and whites, reverted to cleaning their weapons and checking their ammunition, or mending their gear.

Half an hour later, Small Rib and White Antelope returned from scouting the base of the butte, and reported that the bandits were breaking camp and preparing to hit the trail to the plains. The Osage force erupted into action, with braves gathering arms and equipment and horses being herded in from the picket line. Some of the Indians rode bareback, while others used light rawhide rigs of their own device.

The moon and stars were brilliant overhead, pouring silvery light over the mesa top, but down on the bottomlands mist and fog billowed in from the water course and hovered over the trees, rocks and earth. It would be an unfortunate night for combat down there on the shrouded lowlands.

"Seventy bad White Eyes," Small Rib said. "Too many, too much, no good."

"Caught in a crossfire they won't last long, Small Rib," said Travers.

Lashtrow straightened from inspecting the sorrel's front shoes, and looked at Rammel, tying his blanket-roll on behind the cantle. Travers was spinning the cylinder of a sixgun he had borrowed from Bouchard.

"Ram, you want to go against them?" Lash asked. "You aren't obligated, you know."

"I want to," Rammel said simply. "I've been on the verge of killing Vennis half-a-dozen times."

"You got any friends with 'em?"

Rammel shook his blond head. "Never did have any real friends among them. I liked Tallant and Huyett all right, but they're gone. Beede isn't bad, but no real friend."

"Well, it's up to you, Ram," said Lashtrow.

"I'm riding with you." Rammel smiled through the smoke of his cigarette. "It'll feel good to be fighting on the right side, for a change."

Travers grinned at him. "We're more than pleased to have you."

"Glad to be here, Trav." Rammel threw on his saddlebags and canteen, and settled his carbine in the boot.

They mounted with a creak of leather and jingle of bridles, and Lashtrow led the column out, flanked by Fire Hawk and Milt Travers, with Rammel close behind. It was single file on the narrow switchback down-trail, and Lash was thankful for the sorrel's surefootedness. They seemd to be descending into a white ocean of fog that rolled over the plains.

I got one of them, Steel Huyett, and there's three to go, Lashtrow thought. Vennis and Morales and Tupelo. When they're dead, the gang will be busted apart and scattered to the winds, the mission accomplished. The crux of this one has been a long time coming.

Lash recalled something Rammel had said at the cookfire that evening: "I always had the feeling there was someone higher up giving orders to Deke Vennis, but I can't imagine who the hell it could be."

Lashtrow couldn't conceive of any leader behind the scenes either. He saw Deke Vennis as the kingpin, with a force of sixty-five or more desperados. Lash had twenty-three men behind him, and the Andiron crew numbered about seventeen. The odds against them were higher than three-to-two, but the element of surprise would even the score somewhat. Superior quality would add more balance to the account. The odds weren't too bad.

Down on the bottomland, the mist swirled and shifted, dense and eerie under the moonbeams, dampening faces and hands, leather and clothing, blotting out reality. Occasional rifts in the vapor brought moments of fair visibility. Then it closed in again until nearby riders were mere blurred shadows, scarcely to be seen at fifteen feet. At intervals the vague ruby gleam of Andiron campfires gave them a line of direction. The Osages disliked this night work, but Fire Hawk kept them under control. Us Rangers sure have to count on some strange allies, Lash reflected wryly, as they plodded on through funereal grayness, hoofs chopping and metal clinking.

Ahead, the night stillness was shattered by gunshots and tracered with muzzle flames. Lashtrow threw his sorrel into a gallop, and the others hurtled after him, fanning out on the plain. Then came the rumbling bawling thunder of thousands of cattle panicked into a crazed stampede that made the earth tremble. The long-dreaded raid on the trail herd had begun.

Rusty Bouchard and Tess Hiller had reached the cow camp well in advance of the night marauders. The Amidons had been sitting around the chuckwagon fire with Kloster, Crowleg Dooner, Mule Mundorf, Carlos, Sudalter, Logan, and others. Old Hoss Crull and young Santee were out riding circle on the herd, and Lyle Myatt was with the *remuda*. At the sound of unexpected hoof clops, the men at the fireside had come erect with long or short guns ready.

"Don't shoot!" Bouchard's voice boomed out of the fog. "Friends from Lashtrow. I got a gal named Tess Hiller here with me."

"Come on in—slow," Kloster invited, rifle still at the ready.

"Holy Christ at the crossroads!" Anse Amidon shouted in joyous prayer. "It *is* Tess Hiller. Tessie, my darling girl." His mighty arms lifted her from the buckskin and clasped her tight, until Grace Amidon took her away from him and into her own warm delighted embrace.

"Oh, thank God, Tess, thank God!" Grace cried. "Never expected to see your sweet face again, Tessie. And Lash is all right, too? It's a miracle!"

"Lash and Milt Travers both," Tess said. "They're coming in with an Osage war party."

Rusty Bouchard was talking rapidly to Amidon and the other cowmen. "I'm a friend of Lashtrow and Travers and them Osages they're fetching in. The Vennis bunch is hitting you folks tonight, most any minute now. We ain't got much time to palaver. They'll stampede the herd, figuring 'em to overrun these wagons and camp. Then they'll come in to clean up on what's left. Gotta get them wagons hitched up and moved outa line fast."

"Lash and Milt are both alive and well? Praise Almighty

Jesus for that!'' Amidon said huskily. "Vennis got them Apaches with him?''

"No Apaches. Them was fake Injuns, rigged up to haunt the skyline on you. Just the bandits, white and Mex and mixed breeds. Scum of the earth.''

Logan and Carlos were already harnessing the draft animals picketed nearby, and hauling them toward the wagon tongues. Sudalter said, "I'll go help Lyle with the cavvy,'' and broke into a run, rifle in hand.

"Gotta warn the night riders,'' Bouchard said, gazing around.

Crowleg Dooner nodded toward a pair of ground-tied cow horses. "Me and Mule got the next tour on circle. We'll take you out to the bed ground.''

Kloster, the lank bitter-faced trail boss, had been strangely silent during these preliminaries. He spoke now: "Anse, we'll guard the wagons and the women, with Carlos and Logan.'' He turned to other riders straggling in from outer campfires or bedrolls, latching on gunbelts and carrying carbines.

"There's an attack coming.'' Kloster gestured widely, pointed to the southeast. "You men pick your spots out there, find cover, watch for outlaws coming in. No Injuns, just bandits. You see Injuns later they'll be ours, Osages. Don't fire on 'em. Ramos, you join the boys at the remootha.''

Bouchard swung back into his saddle, as Dooner and Mundorf mounted their broncs, the three of them lining out for the bed ground.

"Where'd you find Lashtrow?'' asked Crowleg Dooner.

"He'd killed Steel Huyett and got to Tess, but Vennis had 'em pinned down in an old dugout,'' Bouchard said. "And Travers, he was riding with the Osages.''

"I'll be goddamned,'' Mule Mundorf said. "We thought they was dead, all three of 'em.''

They reached the near flank of the massed beef, just as Santee and Hoss Crull met there in their two-way circuit, and shooting burst out in the southeast, gunshots flaring and crashing. The cattle started running and soon surged into the full roaring avalanche of a stampede that shook the entire plain. The fog had thinned and lifted a trifle, and it was an awesome sight in the pale spectral moonglow.

"Let 'em go!" Bouchard screamed at Crull and Santee, whose first natural reaction was to run with the herd. "Get the bastards coming in behind 'em. It's Vennis's gang out there, no Apaches with 'em." Crull and Santee were leaning close to hear or read his bearded lips in that deafening noise. "If you see Injuns, don't shoot at 'em. Lash and Trav are bringing in some Osages."

"Lash and Travers?" cried young Santee. "Glory be to God and Heaven!"

Bouchard saw Crowleg Dooner's scarred lips moving: "That goddamn Lashtrow, he's way outa this world. Some kinda man, that Lash."

The cattle were still storming past in a thunderous flood-tide of horned heads and bobbing backs, the dust skewering high into the misted night.

The five riders pulled out their saddle-guns and drifted in the direction of the enemy. Bouchard debated whether they should dismount for accurate shooting, or remain mounted for mobility and speed. He decided on the latter course. Hoss Crull and Crowleg Dooner were both staring at him, as if attempting an identification.

"I know them red whiskers from somewhere," Crull muttered.

"Ellsworth maybe, when it was the railhead," Bouchard suggested.

"Hellfire, yes!" Crull slapped his left thigh. "You was town marshal."

Bouchard nodded, and Dooner said: "That's it, by God. Knew I'd seen you someplace, the minute you rode in."

They shook hands all around, and Santee said: "Never mind the good old days. Here come the bastards now."

They spread out into a skirmish line, advancing toward

the ghostly horsemen coming out of the fog into the skirling dust of the drag.

Deke Vennis had launched a three-pronged assault, the first to hit the herd, second at the cavvy, the third aimed at the wagons. Yaqui Tupelo led the stampeders, expecting to meet no more opposition than a couple of circuit riders. Instead they ran headlong into the concentrated fire from five sharpshooters, Crull and Santee, Dooner and Mundorf and Rusty Bouchard. Outlaw riders were ripped from their saddles, and horses tumbled and rolled in a maelstrom of dirt. The initial enemy rush was checked, turned, and driven back by the five blasting carbines, leaving several men and horses sprawled on the wet buffalo grass.

Heading the wild retreat, Tupelo galloped straight back into the wicked lashing gunfire of Lashtrow, Travers, Rammel and the Osage warriors. His ranks torn and decimated, Tupelo howled, "Holy Mother of Christ, let's get outa here!" and dashed off into the foggy darkness, trailed by frantic survivors furiously spurring their wild-eyed mustangs. Lash and his crew hammered shots after them, but made no pursuit. There were other bandits to be dealt with, closer at hand.

The objective of Fern Morales' detail was the *remuda*, where they anticipated an easy sweep, killing the wrangler and running off the horse herd. But Sudalter and Lyle Myatt were ready and waiting for them, in a brush-screened hollow behind a natural barricade of boulders. Working their carbines with swift precision, the Andiron cowboys cut down a few of the raiders. Gunflames streaked back and forth in a blistering fire fight, as Sudalter and Myatt were pelted with dirt and rock fragments. When riders on either side fo him were blown off their broncs, Morales yelled, "Screw this business!" and wheeled into flight, his followers pounding after him. "That goddamn Rammel must of set us up, Morales thought.

"We sure stopped them sonsabitches!" Sudalter said

exultantly. "We burned them bastards for fair, Lyle. Nice shooting, man!"

There was no response. Sudalter turned in quick alarm, and saw Lyle Myatt slumped face down over his gun barrel, the back of his head a gory misshapen mess. "Oh no, Christ, *no*!" Sudalter gasped, turning away to vomit on the sand. . . .

Deke Vennis himself led the third detachment against the wagons, but it was the same story there. They were rocked, slashed and riddled by heavy and accurate rifle fire from the shelter of the vehicles, as Tess Hiller and Grace Amidon joined in the rapid shooting of the defenders: Anse Amidon and Kloster, Logan and Carlos.

"What in Christ's Name is going on here?" yelled Vennis, as bandits toppled from their saddles around him. "Pull out, pull out!"

They fled southward in a frenzy, forced to veer off westward as Lashtrow and his company, fresh from harassing the Morales party, poured bullets after them in a running dogfight. The rout was completed, a total disaster for the Vennis bunch. The gray-veiled plain was widely strewn with dead and dying outlaws and a few horses. The survivors were gone and the battle was over.

"Perhaps we should have chased them down, Lash," said Milt Travers, as they rode slowly back toward the cow camp, surveying the field for bodies. "They might be crazy enough to regroup and hit us again."

"They won't be back, Milt," said Lashtrow. "They lost too many men. But I s'pose the big ones we wanted got away."

"Haven't found any of them yet," Rammel said, identifying the enemy dead here and there. "Some new ones." He indicated two lifeless forms in a mesquite patch, one wearing a duster, the other a frock coat and crushed derby. "Look like Missourians."

Rusty Bouchard and his comrades from the bed ground joined them, Rusty conferring with Fire Hawk in Osage, while the Andiron riders welcomed Lashtrow and Travers with quiet profane warmth.

"Fire Hawk wants to count coups, which means take scalps," Bouchard said. "Reckons we got no objections?"

Lashtrow gestured in agreement. "They earned 'em. Somebody's got to make a body count. Maybe they'll bury the bastards, too?"

Bouchard inclined his red head. "In one grave. But they won't take no wounded prisoners, Lash."

After somber consideration, Lashtrow nodded. "Well, we've got no time or place for wounded scavengers either." It sickened him to condone such an action, but it was sensible, practical, and no more than the renegades deserved.

"I'll go along and check ahead of 'em," Rammel said, with a wan tightening of lips. "See if I can find Deke or Fern or Yaqui—which I doubt."

"Good boy, Ram." Smiling at him, Lash rode on toward the wagons, where there seemed to be no casualties.

But they found young Lyle Myatt dead at the cavvy, with Sudalter still sitting in shock nearby. And the bullet-torn body of Ramos, halfway between the *remuda* and the wagons.

"I'll take care of this one myself." Big Mule Mundorf swallowed convulsively and got down beside the Mex boy who had worked the drag with him all those hundreds of miles.

Anson and Grace Amidon greeted Lash and Travers like long-lost sons, and even the saturnine Kloster seemed happy to see them back. Tess Hiller's powder-streaked face and violet eyes lighted up at the sight of them and Bouchard, along the Hoss Crull, Santee and Dooner. But someone was missing, and anxiety shadowed her features.

"Where's Rammel—and Mule?" she asked, fearfully.

"They're all right," Lashtrow told her, and looked at Amidon. "But you lost two men, Anse, I'm sorry to say. Myatt and Ramos."

"Jesus!" groaned Anse. "Two more men, two kids.

170

Damn good ones, both of 'em. Goddamn that Vennis to hell eternal!'' He shook his gray head and drank deeply from a bottle of whiskey. "That smirking curly-haired little sonofabitch! . . . But I reckon we're lucky as hell to lose only two, when you stop to think of it. We'd all be laying dead here, for chrisake, if you boys hadn't showed with them Injuns.''

"Yes, Anse, we have to count our blessings," Grace Amidon said. "My heart bleeds for them two boys, Lyle and Ramos, but it could've been an awful lot worse.''

"We got that herd to round up again, too," Kloster remarked gloomily. "And we're really shorthanded now.''

Lashtrow glanced at him with slitted gray eyes. "Shorthanded, hell! "We got twenty Osages to help with the gather, Klos. The cattle won't stray from the water. It oughta be an easy chore, rounding 'em up and pushing them across the Cimarron.''

"After the crossing we'll be left damn short of men,'' Kloster persisted.

"Maybe not," Rusty Bouchard said, wiping his bearded mouth after a copious drink. "I might sign on for the rest of the drive, if you want me. Reckon Rammel might join up, too. We got nothing better to do.''

"You mean that, Red?" Amidon was plainly gratified and relieved. "We could swing it, with you two.''

"They had any experience working cows?" Kloster demanded dourly.

Amidon glared at him. "What the hell's eating you, for chrisake? How much training does a riding man need to wrangle a cavvy or push the drag?''

"All right, Anse, all right," Kloster said wearily. "I ain't saying no more. But they could hit us again, you know. Deke Vennis ain't a man to give up easy.''

Lashtrow was still watching Kloster narrowly, and Milt Travers said: "We killed about twenty of them. You think that crew's going to try it again?''

"Forget it, for chrisake." Kloster turned sullenly away to fuss around the tailgate of the bed wagon.

They were all drinking coffee and whiskey around a new fire, when Rammel rode in with Fire Hawk and the Osages.

"Counted seventeen dead and they may have dragged off some more," Rammel reported, swinging down and pulling a whiskey bottle from his saddlebags. "If I ever needed a drink it's right about now."

Kloster had returned and stood, hands on hips, staring with fixed coldness at the slender fair-haired Rammel.

Rusty Bouchard said: "Amidon needs a coupla riders, Ram. You want to work the rest of this trail drive with me?"

"Sure, Red Bush." Rammel casually tipped up the bottle once more.

Lashtrow arose with reluctance from the fireside. "Well, Milt, we've still got some work of our own to do."

"Right you are, Lash." Travers straightened off the wagon wheel he'd been lounging against. "No rest for the wicked, it has been said—often."

Milt was feeling better, having retrieved his own belted twin Colts and Winchester from the supply wagon, discarding the old Walker and Spencer.

Rammel moved in close to them and spoke softly: "I'd like to go with you."

Lashtrow shook his bronze head. "Like to have you, Ram. But this is Ranger work."

"Couldn't you deputize me?"

"No." Lash's smile was slow and friendly. "But we'll give you a permanent job, when you get back from Abilene." Bouchard had joined them now, in a private foursome, and Lashtrow went on: "Keep an eye on Kloster, and don't turn your backs to him too often. I still can't figure that man."

"If you won't take me along," Rammel said, "take this tip, at least. Most of that gang will scatter and disappear, but Vennis and Morales and Tupelo will go back to that

172

abandoned ranch house. They must have left most of their stolen treasure hoard buried there."

Lashtrow nodded gravely. "I think you've called it right, Ram. That'll be our first stop. We don't catch 'em there, we'll try Dexter."

"If I was with you, it would even the odds," Rammel said wistfully.

Milt Travers laughed and clapped him on the back. "Three-to-two is even enough for us daring Rangers, Ram. We need you and Rusty here to take care of Tess and the Amidons."

"And to watch that sour-faced bastard Kloster," added Lashtrow. *"Adios, amigos."*

"Yeah, *vaya con Dios, compadres,"* Bouchard said gruffly.

Everyone about the campfire watched and waved, as Lashtrow and Travers mounted and rode out into the fog-bound night.

Rammel found Tess Hiller at his side, her eyes and face alight, and a glowing sensation rose in him. She said, "I'm glad you made it. We owe you an awful lot, Ram."

"Thank you, Tess," said Rammel. "You know I had to see you again."

18

Destiny in Dexter

Dixie Belle was an incongruous, almost ridiculous sobriquet for the young madame of the Red Lantern in the outlaw capital of Dexter. It conjured images of a frivolous shallow lady of pleasure, whereas in actuality she was a woman of sinister beauty and mysterious depth, marked by a nearly cruel sexuality of face and figure. Dark and tall and fla- grantly feminine, she had the air of ancient Egyptian queens, Assyrian princesses or Aztec high priestesses, and she inspired more fear than desire in most men. They fan- tasized about raping her, rather than seducing her.

Her room was an incompatible as her nickname, all pink and gold, silk and satin, with lavish fittings she had brought into the wilderness from New Orleans. She sat at her dress- ing table, aglitter with delicate bottles and jeweled cases, backed by a gold-framed mirror in which she was watching Deke Vennis pace the pile-carpeted floor. Booted and spurred, battle-grimmed trail-dusted and gunhung, he was drastically misplaced in that dainty perfumed setting.

"Men have been beaten before," Belle said coldly. "You are not unique. "It isn't fatal, if you survive."

"*I* never have, goddamn it," Vennis rasped. "How could it happen? They were all set and waiting for us. They shot us down like buffalo. Musta killed half of our men."

"You aren't mourning the men. They never meant that

much. Your pride is hurt, Deke. Quit crying like a baby, and take it like a man."

He went on pacing and swearing, shaking his curly head and snarling, gesturing with large dirty hands.

"Go get a bottle and a bath and a change of clothes," Belle advised. "It's not the end of the world. Where's the rest of your crew?"

"Scattered from here to hell and the Gulf of Mexico by now."

"They'll be back to collect their wages."

"Mosta them was paid in advance. They won't be back. They'd never ride with me again."

"What about Morales and Tupelo? Are they dead, too?"

"I dunno. Most likely. I don't give a goddamn. They was getting on my nerves lately."

"Well, you've got a small fortune cached with King Fischer. It's all yours now, if they're gone. Think of that, Deke."

"I can't think of nothing but them christly guns blazing and flaming at us from everywhere. Jesus, it was terrible, a frigging nightmare."

Belle motioned at the short service bar with its sparkling array of bottles and glasses. "Have a drink, for godsake."

"I don't even feel like drinking."

"You *must* be sick, boy." Belle rose with stately grace. "I've listened to you rant and rave for half an hour. That's enough. Go and get yourself together and cleaned up. You look and smell like a Mexican bandit."

Deke Vennis whirled on her, hand flicking to his bone-handled .44. "Don't you turn on me, too!"

Belle laughed. "You going to shoot me, Deke? Because you couldn't hit anybody else the other night. You—" A rap on the door interrupted her, and she said: "Who is it?"

"Me, Morales. I gotta see Deke."

Vennis grimaced as Belle went to unlock the door. Morales entered with his half-sneering grin. He had bathed and

175

shaved and donned clean clothing. His blue-black hair gleamed and his mustache was neatly waxed.

"That was quite a jackpot we run into, Deke. I thought maybe you was dead, till the King told us you was here."

"Yaqui's all right then?"

"Except for a few bullet burns and being madder'n a horned toad."

"Anybody else with you?"

"Naw, they're all gone, far and wide," Morales said. "Them that lived through it. Which was no large army."

Belle was at the bar pouring drinks. Morales accepted his, and the brocaded chair she offered. "*Gracias.*" Vennis ignored both his drink and the straight wooden chair Belle indicated for him to occupy. Belle said: "He's been tromping that rug with his filthy boots ever since he got in, Fernando."

"Well, it don't make a man happy to have twenty-thirty men shot out under him, Belle." Morales saluted her and sipped his drink.

Vennis glared at him. "You ain't taking it too hard, Fern."

"What can you do?" Morales shrugged heavily. "It happened, it's over."

Deke Vennis bared white teeth. "*Why* did it happen? *How* did it happen?"

"*Quien sabe?* Nobody knows for sure. But it ain't hard to figure out. Young Rammel never come back, did he? He musta run into Lashtrow and them Osages, and tipped them off. They got word to Amidon in time, and them drovers was waiting with cocked guns."

"So you and Yaqui got it all figured out," Vennis said. "That sonofabitch Rammel! I shoulda let him die in New Orleans that night. He never did fit in."

"You're right, there," Belle agreed. "Rammel's a gentleman."

"Why didn't you stick to him, then, goddamn it?"

Belle laughed lightly. "He didn't really want *me*. Now

boys, you'll have to excuse me. I want to freshen up. Go on down to the bar, please. The drinks are on the house."

Downstairs at the bar, Vennis decided to end the drought and threw down three quick drinks while Morales was nursing one.

"So it was all my fault, as usual?" Deke Vennis said, expecting a denial.

"Yeah, it was, Deke," admitted Morales calmly. "Women, women, like we always told you. If you hadn't dragged that girl Dolly along out Spooner, Rammel wouldn't had to take her back home. And we'd been herding three thousand cattle insteada hiding out in this stinking hellhole of a ghost town."

Vennis eyed him with hatred, but kept control. "What you planning on next, Fern?"

"Splitting the money King's holding and taking off. This country ain't going to be healthy for us for quite a spell. You think them Rangers ain't on our tracks right now?"

Vennis laughed, in contempt. "There's only two of 'em, for chrisake!"

"Plenty more where they come from."

"We could recruit another bunch and hit the trail herd again."

Morales shook his shiny black head. "We couldn't recruit horseshit after that mess on the Cimarron. Even if we could, it wouldn't do no good. Nobody's going to hit that herd the resta the way. They'll have newspapermen and photographers and probably a company of U.S. Cavalry with 'em from here on in."

"We could burn down Yaqui and split the boodle two ways." Vennis suggested. "That crazy breed don't know what to do with that much money. It'd be wasted on him. And don't forget, if his goddamn faking Apaches had showed, like he promised, we'd of been home safe anyhow. It's Yaqui's fault more'n mine, Fern."

Morales regarded him almost sadly. "You're a bad bastard. I never rode with worse."

177

Vennis was standing on the left. He raised his glass in his left hand, and smiled. "Cheer up, Fern. You ain't riding with me no more."

Fern Morales saw the glint of madness in those mocking eyes, pushed his squat bulk off the wood and reached for his holster—too late. Deke Vennis had drawn right-handed, his gun already aflame as he shot Morales twice through the body, jolting him back along the bar. Morales's pistol exploded into the floor as he fell forward, kicking over a spittoon and landing face down in the dirty sawdust.

Vennis's mad gaze swept the room, but nobody was stirring, stunned and frozen by the shocking suddenness of the gunshots. "Hold right still," Vennis ordered. "Nobody moves, nobody dies." Gun ready in hand, he swaggered across the floor and out through the ornate batwing doors into the darkening street.

All he had to do now was find Yaqui Tupelo, and it would be a one-way split, winner take all.

Having found no one at the old ranch in the hidden basin, Lashtrow and Travers, saddle-worn and combat-weary as they were, pressed on south toward Dexter.

The outlaw rendezvous was off-limits for all law men, but they had to go in there after the three bandit leaders. Unshaven, sooted black with gunpowder and trail dirt, they might pass unrecognized long enough to apprehend their quarry, but they'd have to get in and out very fast. Lashtrow, more apt to be identified because of his six-two height and the sorrel, was to circle around and come in the back way. Travers would ride straight in, and hope for the best.

They were arriving at a good time for a secret entry. Darkness was coming, and most of the inhabitants would be at supper, either in King Fischer's main mess hall or in private quarters. Those not interested in food were likely to be drinking or gambling in the Palace, or drinking and consorting with the girls at the Red Lantern. The settlement looked desolate and forsaken, with only a few faint lights showing through the gloom. It had the decrepit appearance of a true ghost town, yet there were hundreds on hundreds of fugitives living there or coming and going. Outlaws and killers, drifters and vagabonds, exiles and derelicts of all creeds, colors and races. Dexter, sinkhole of sin and evil, sanctuary for the wicked and lawless, ruled by King Fischer and Dixie Belle and Doctor Merriwether.

Milt Travers, slack in the leather, painfully aware of the foul odor of his own unwashed body and buckskins, drifted his coyote dun in through the deepening shadows past sagging hitch-racks and caved-in structures of wooden planks or adobe bricks. He was chewing tobacco to ease mouth-and-throat dryness. His beard bristles itched, even more than his crotch, and his over-long hair fretted his ears and neck. He laughed at what the Back Bay Brahmins would think if they could see him at this moment. He yearned for a tall iced drink, a long hot bath, and clean crisp clothes.

The street seemed absolutely empty, except for a few racked horses. In occasional ruined buildings, a dim flicker of candle- or lantern-light pricked the blackness. Merriwether's entrance was well-lighted, and beyond dull luminous glows marked the Palace and the Red Lantern. But nothing moved in the street, until he glimpsed a horseman approaching from the far end. Eyes squinted, Travers fixed them on the shadowy rider.

Earlier, while Deke Vennis made directly for Dixie Belle, and Fern Morales sought the baths at the barbershop, Yaqui Tupelo had remained on the alert, riding a circuit of the settlement to watch for the Rangers he knew would be coming. He could have appealed for security from King Fischer, but Tupelo was too much a fighting man to stoop that low. He privately believed he had more guts than Vennis and Morales combined.

Tupelo spotted the lone rider coming up the street, grabbed at his carbine, and then decided he could handle a pistol better on horseback. Recognition was almost simultaneous and mutual. Tupelo identified the *bayo coyote* first, the man second. Travers recognized the vulpine head and shape of Tupelo on a spotted mustang, and pulled his right-hand Colt. As they moved toward one another slowly, warily, the range still long for handguns, gunfire broke out in the Red Lantern some distance behind Tupelo, three quick shots blending into an echoing concussion.

Travers and Tupelo opened up then, gunflames streaking the darkness, and Milt drove his dun forward into full stride. Startled and amazed by this abrupt reckless charge, Tupelo let go a couple more shots and threw his bronc toward the shelter of the nearest alleyway, with bullets searing the air about him. Low on his horse's neck, Travers returned the fire and felt the hot breath of slugs zinging past him, but maintained his rocketing rush, veering toward the alley mouth into which Tupelo had vanished.

Rubbish, bottles and tin cans jangled under hoofs, as Travers drove into the narrow passage. Tupelo was silhouetted vaguely at the rear end, and Milt had a bead on the man's wiry back when Yaqui disappeared from the saddle, caught across the chest by a strung rope or wire, swept back and down at the spotted horse fled onward into the night.

Travers reined up hard and tight, bringing the dun to a skidding rearing halt, as flame leaped up at them from the ground. Milt kicked free of the stirrups and slid back over the upreared dun's rump, landing on his feet and lashing shots at the fallen outlaw. Tupelo triggered once more as Milt's slugs hammered into him, jerked and rolled and lay still in the rubble. Making certain he was dead, Milt Travers caught the dun's reins and led him back to the street, aware that his right-hand gun was emptied. He holstered it and was reaching for the left-side sheath, when he saw Deke Vennis, wild-eyed and tousle-haired, facing him over a leveled gun barrel in a spread-legged stance.

"Hold it, Travers, or you're dogmeat!" Vennis barked.

"You got the drop all right."

"Did you kill Tupelo?"

Travers nodded, praying silently for Lashtrow to appear.

Vennis laughed. "Saved me the trouble, huh? I oughta let you go for downing Yaqui. But I ain't going to. You bastards caused me too much trouble."

"Give me a fair shake," Travers said. "Start even, Deke. You're faster than I am, and I'll have to pull left-handed."

"Fair shake, hell! I'll give you three in the gut, you sonofabitch! I'll blow—"

"Over here first, Deke," said Lashtrow clearly, from in back of Vennis.

Deke Vennis spun and fired instantly, .44 jetting orange, but Lash had already lined home a slug that shattered Vennis's right shoulder. Snake-quick, Vennis's left hand snapped to the other gun butt, only to go reeling backward as gunflame stabbed from Lashtrow into his left side. Vennis was falling when Travers caught him under the arms, and flipped aside both his weapons.

"Throw him over your pommel, Milt," said Lashtrow, whistling for his sorrel. "We gotta clear town before the King's clan gets moving."

Travers hoisted the half-conscious Vennis over the dun's back, and climbed into the saddle behind him. The sorrel came on the run, and Lash caught the horn and swung up in a flying mount. They raced down the street, turned into another alley, and were out of sight before men came tearing out of the Palace and the Red Lantern to fill the street and queery one another: "What the hell's going on?" "For chrisake, what happened?" "Who the hell was it?" "Where'd the sonsabitches go?"

After several minutes of confusion and disorder, it was ascertained that Fernando Morales was dead in the Red Lantern, shot by Deke Vennis, and Yaqui Tupelo was dead in an alley, shot by persons unknown. Deke Vennis, alive or dead, was gone from Dexter, in the hands of some strange riders, who had come and left like flashes of lightning out of a clear night sky.

"I swear I seen Lashtrow," declared an old-timer. "It hadda be Lashtrow. Nobody else moves that fast. . . ."

No one, including King Fischer and Dixie Belle, cared enough about the fate of Deke Vennis, or the death of Morales and Tupelo, to organize any kind of pursuit. Life was cheap in Dexter, and King Fischer was thinking smugly of the money he had just inherited, suddenly and unexpectedly. A legacy large enough to allow him to reitre from this bloody business, and go live like a real monarch in Chicago or New York City—or maybe even abroad in London or Paris, if he chose.

Well away from town, with no posse materializing behind them, Lashtrow and Travers stopped to dismount and lay Deke Vennis on the prairie grass. He was obviously dying, but somehow still conscious and more or less rational, cursing them with slow panted breath.

"Well, Lash, this ought to wind it up," Milt Travers said. "If Deke got Morales."

"He got him all right. I took a peek and saw Morales on the floor."

"Thank God it's over, Lash."

They were startled when Vennis broke into a painful strangled laugh. "What's over? . . . Poor—goddamn—fools. Kloster started—whole thing. He'll have—that herd. 'Fore they—ever reach—Abilene." He choked off, gasping and groaning, lips twisted into a ghastly grin as he died, mocking even in death.

Staring blankly at one another, Lashtrow and Travers shook their heads.

"The only way he could do it is to murder the Amidons," said Lashtrow, after a prolonged and thoughtful silence.

"He can't get away with that," Travers protested. "Red Bush and Rammel will be watching him. Crull, Dooner, Santee, Mundorf and the rest are loyal to Anse and Grace."

"But Anse trusts Kloster. There's some danger, Milt.

182

Klos would make it look accidental, of course. Anything can happen on a trail drive.''

''That sour sonofabitch,'' Travers murmured bitterly. ''All those years he's been with Anse. Must be envy, jealousy, greed, eating inside Kloster, building up day by day.''

''Kloster hired Pueblo and Tench, both Vennis men. He hired Santee too, but that boy's straight. Musta persuaded Anse to give Vennis a job. Set up the whole rotten deal . . . . Well, Milt, we got some hard riding to do.''

Travers nodded gravely and looked down at Deke Vennis's body. ''Can't spare the time to bury you. Let your real friends take care of you. The coyotes and vultures.''

''Christ, I hate to punish these horses.'' Lashtrow bit off a chew. ''But there's no way out of it.''

''They must know we wouldn't do it if it weren't absolutely necessary,'' Milt Travers said.

''Well, I sure hope so,'' Lashtrow drawled, as they stepped up into their saddles.

A few miles later, Lash glanced at his partner. ''Anything left in that magic flask, Milton?''

''I thought you'd never get around to asking,'' Travers said, with a sigh of relief, reaching for the pocket in the leather.

They drank in turn, twice around, and went rocking onward in the moonlight, racked with aching weariness themselves but feeling for the horses in under them, pushed beyond all normal limits of endurance.

19

Kloster

Kloster had seen his dream of an empire fade and die in the crash and flickerflare of gunshots, as the outlaw raiders of Deke Vennis were shattered and routed. He would never be a cattle baron now. Everything had gone wrong. Pueblo and Tench had failed him, Santee had switched sides, Vennis and Morales and Tupelo had failed. But mostly it was that goddamn Lashtrow who had beaten him. Hatred welled up like acid in Kloster's mouth, as he ducked under sprayed dirt and wood splinters to reload.

At one time during the defense of the wagons, Kloster had found himself hunched behind a wheel and close beside Tess Hiller. Even under gunfire, working their carbines at full speed, Kloster had felt a quickening burn of desire in his loins. The powerful sex drive in Kloster was something men were unaware of, but women often sensed it and some were stirred to a primitive response. He was an ugly man, but women were sometimes attracted to male ugliness. Tess felt it and glanced at the gaunt hatchet-faced man in astonished wonder, as bullets shredded canvas above them or showered them with dust. Kloster, not looking her way, went on firing steadily, wasting cartridges as he purposely missed, high or low.

Kloster was a human paradox, a dark enigma, a lank tower of contradictions. He did not drink alcohol or use tobacco in any form, yet his lust for female flesh was obsessive and insatiable. When women were unavailable, he had vented his blinding passion on heifers or sheep. He could be a lion or a jackal; brave or cowardly; kind or cruel; gentle or brutal; strong or weak; smart or stupid; generous or selfish; proud or humble; sensitive or callous; noble or evil. Frequently he could not understand his own actions or motives.

Years ago, when Kloster was convalescing from a wound in the Andiron ranch house and Anse was away on the spring roundup, he had made advances to Grace Amidon, and been rejected firmly but without humiliation. They had parted amicably when Kloster was well enough to ride again, and Grace had never told Anse about the incident, knowing that if she did Anse would go for Klos with a gun—and one of them would die.

The matter was apparently forgotten, buried in the past, and a daughter was born to the Amidons. Kloster seemed to adore little Kate, almost as much as Grace and Anse did, and nobody could have treated a child with more devotion and tenderness. Until Kate was twelve years old, and Kloster took his revenge for the rejection he had suffered at Grace's hands. He seduced the budding young girl and aroused in her a sexuality akin to his own, which later sent her burning from one man to another and ended only with her premature death this summer at twenty-two, when she caught the bullet Pueblo had meant for Anse Amidon.

Then Tess Hiller joined the drive with Lashtrow and Travers, Kloster had set his sights on her, inevitably, but he was extremely careful to conceal his hunger. In fact, he never looked at or spoke to her, unless chance made it unavoidable, and Tess had no inkling of his interest in her, until that night behind the wagon wheel in the midst of combat.

Now, in the absence of Lashtrow and Travers, Kloster decided to start his subtle approach to Tess Hiller, only to discover that the girl shrank from the slightest contact with him. And with the coming of young Rammel, it was soon obvious to everyone that Tess had eyes only for him.

One of those instantaneous things, sparked to life the moment they met in Spooner. Natural, inexplicable, ordained by fate, they looked at one another, felt the electric current between them, and knew at once they were destined to meet and love and merge, meant for each other from the beginning. Neither had experienced anything like it before, but they *knew* and understood at once, took deep delight in it, felt their lives were just starting.

"I feel guilty about Lash," Tess told Grace. "Even though I know Lash didn't want to marry me—or anyone else. Not for a long time anyway. But even if he did, I couldn't help this. . . ."

"Love at first sight," Grace Amidon said. "I've read about it and heard about it, but never seen it happen before my very eyes. Has he got a first name, this young man?"

Tess laughed. "Of course, but he's like OK Frellick, who wouldn't use his Christian name, Orlando. Ram doesn't like his given name either. It's Aubrey."

"Well, I don't know as I blame him, Tess. Sounds too much like a girl."

"Grace, we want to get married. Right away."

"You're plumb dead sure, are you?" Grace wrinkled her forehead. "There's a town ahead named Winfield, on the Walnut River, I noticed on Anse's map. Oughta be a parson there."

The drive was in Kansas at last, the Cherokee Strip behind them, with Abilene some 150 miles to the north. They were joined by two U. S. Marshals, who informed Anse that a platoon of cavalry from Fort Hays was en route to escort them the remainder of the journey.

Kloster was disgusted. "We don't need no goddamn cavalry now! Coulda used 'em back on the Cimarron maybe, but even there we fought our own way out."

"Well, you're getting 'em whether you need 'em or not,"

one of the officers said, with flat finality. "And you're getting us, too."

That does it! Kloster thought bitterly. The last goddamn straw. Only chance I had left was to get rid of Anse, make it look like an accident. But hell, I couldn't done that neither. I'm licked. I been licked all my christly misbegotten goddamn life.

Soon thereafter they were joined by a Concord coach loaded with newspaper reporters, camera men and meat-packing officials from Chicago, and somewhat later a smaller coach arrived carrying the famous Ned Buntline and his entourage.

"This trail drive's being turned into a three-ring circus, for chrisake!" Kloster complained. "Pay me off, Anse. I'm quitting this goddamn sideshow."

"You'll get paid off in Abilene, like everybody else," Amidon said. "Don't you wanta get your name and picture in the papers, Kloster?"

"Piss on the papers!" Kloster said, wheeling his bronc away in fury. A pertinent fact pierced his hate-clouded brain: If Lashtrow and Travers took any of them outlaw leaders alive, they'd talk for sure, and the Rangers would be coming back after him. Pay or no pay, it behooved him to light a shuck before Lash and Trav returned.

At the chuckwagon fire that evening, Tess Hiller and Rammel were missing. In response to queries, Grace Amidon said: "Them two lovebirds couldn't wait no more. They went to Winfield to find 'em a preacher."

Old Hoss Crull shook his gray head in sorrow. "Never figured that Tess Hiller to be flighty-headed and scatter-brained. But hell, she's in love, and I think it's the real thing, for both of 'em."

"Well, that Rammel's a nice boy," Crowleg Dooner admitted. "But he don't stack up against a man like Lash-trow."

"Lash ain't about to marry anybody," Grace said. "We

all know that. A gal like Tess can't waste her whole life awaiting.''

"Lash and Milt oughta be getting back before long," Rusty Bouchard said.

"Sure." Santee laughed boyishly. "I'll lay ten-to-one they took them three renegades, Vennis and Tupelo and Morales. If they could find 'em.''

"They'll find 'em and take 'em," Anse Amidon said, with conviction. "But if Lash sees Ned Buntline here, he might head home for Austin.''

"Wonder how Lash'll take it—about Tess Hiller?" Mule Mundorf asked.

"In stride," Bouchard said. "He likes that Rammel kid.''

"Where the hell's Kloster?" asked Santee, searching the firelit faces scattered unevenly about the campsite.

"Sonofabitch's sulking again," Hoss Crull answered. "Grabbed a plate and cup and went off by himself. More'n half-crazy, that man is."

"Klos is all tore up over the news hawks and big moguls and the cavalry coming," Crowleg Dooner offered. "Amongst a few hundred other things."

"I noticed the looks he was giving Rammel," said Santee. "That kid'd better watch his back.''

"Aw, the miserable bastard hates everybody," Hoss Crull said. "Himself worst of all.''

"He ain't bad with a gun," Crowleg Dooner said. "When he feels like fighting.''

"He's damn good when he's right," Santee said. "I seen Klos face down some tough customers, and I seen him back down himself. Hard to figure."

"Ned Buntline wants to write a book about you and me, Hoss," said Dooner.

Crull grinned. "It's about time somebody did. I can top any lies you tell him, Crow."

The next morning at breakfast, Kloster made no appearance, and an inspection of the supply wagon revealed that all his gear was gone.

Santee shook his lean head and hitched at his gunbelt. "I'll bet that sonofabitch's gone to Winfield to bust up that wedding."

"Naw, he wanted to quit yesterday when he heard about the cavalry," Anse Amidon said. "He'll show up in Abilene to collect his wages, don't worry."

Sudalter, the wrangler, sunken-eyed and hollow-cheeked from lack of sleep, was the only one who had witnessed, Kloster's midnight departure.

"He come out to the cavvy, hauling all this extra equipment, and had me cut out his black stud and that strawberry roan from his string. He didn't wanta see nobody nor talk to nobody. He did talk a little to me. I asked where was he going, and Klos said: 'This goddamn drive has been frigged-up from the start, and now they're turning it into a comic opera. I can't stand any more of this cheap shit.' He saddled the stallion, packed gear on the roan, and rode out to the south." Sundalter gulped hot coffee.

"He ain't headed south though," Santee said. "I'll bet my bonus money he circled to the north, soon as he was out of sight."

"Klos was acting kinda loco, so I kept watch of him. He swung back once, within rifle range, and I saw he had his rifle out. There was still a few around the campfire, Anse and a coupla other boys, waiting their shift to ride circle, I reckon. Klos threw up his rifle and drew a bead on somebody at the fire, and I cut out that way with my carbine cocked. But I was still far off when he shook his head, stuck the rifle in the boot, and rode on out. Last I saw of him." Sudalter poured another coffee.

"The bastard *is* crazy," Anse Amidon said. "It hadda be me he had in his sights. He was thinking of killing *me*, the best goddamn friend the sourlipped sonofabitch ever had in this world. How do you like that?"

"I don't like it," Santee said, finishing his coffee and

twisting up a cigarette. "And I don't like the idea of Kloster sneaking into Winfield and shooting down that Rammel boy. And breaking Tess Hiller's heart. Lemme go after him, Anse."

"Don't wait too long, Anse," warned Santee. "That bastard Kloster is aching to kill somebody, and that's for goddamn sure."

20

Wedding in Winfield

Light from a great golden moon flooded the plains of Kansas, as Lashtrow and Travers, on thoroughly jaded horses, reached the Chisholm Trail a little way north of the trail herd. They were about to turn south to the cow camp, when they glimpsed a pair of riders in the distance, moving slowly northward. They rode close together, and at times seemed to be swinging clasped hands between their mounts. There was something familiar about the horses and the figures on their backs, and Lashtrow delved into his saddlebags for the fieldglasses.

"Very romantic," Milt Travers remarked. "A night made for love."

"Yeah." Lashtrow was busy focussing the glasses. Sure enough, it was Tess Hiller on her buckskin and Rammel on his brown bronco. "Well, I'll be goddamned," he murmured, wonderingly, and handed the binoculars to Travers.

Milt adjusted them, took his long look, and said softly: "Likewise, Lash. I thought Tess was rather interested in Ram, but I had no idea. . . ."

Lashtrow's laugh was a trifle forced. "They're in love all right. It shines all around them, even at this range."

They were plainly enrapt in one another, oblivious to the rest of the night world.

"Well, there's good breeding and blood in that boy," Travers said. "I don't know how he got to be an outlaw, especially with a gang like Deke's, but I think he's all right now, Lash.''

"I just hope he's as good as we think he is, Milt.''

"Yeah, let's drink to that.'' Travers produced his silver flask, and they silently toasted the faraway couple. "What do we do now?''

Lashtrow contemplated briefly. "Reckon we split here. You go on in to camp and report to Anse, see what's going on there. Watch Kloster, but don't take him, unless he forces it. I kinda want that sonofabitch myself. It looks like Tess and Ram must be heading for Winfield up there, by my calculations. I'll just follow them in and make sure everything's all right.''

"Ram can handle a gun and I have an idea he's fast,'' Travers said. "He stood up to me in Spooner like a real gunfighter. Not that I'm worried about you, but don't get careless, Lash.''

Lashtrow smiled bleakly. "I'm not going to fight a duel with him, Milt. Tess knew there was no future in me. Hell, I'm already too old for her. I just wanta talk to them, that's all.''

"Okay, pardner.''

"Maybe I can get a bath and shave, haircut and new clothes in there.''

Travers laughed. "That's what I crave most of all.''

"You've got the tough assignment. Kloster's unpredictable and dangerous as hell.''

"Well, I've got a lot of help in there—which I won't need.''

They smiled, raised their left hands, and rode off in opposite directions. Lashtrow felt it was like letting half of himself go, and he knew Travers must share that emotion. Seeing Tess Hiller like that with Rammel had hit Lash harder than he'd ever admit. He knew it was bound to happen eventually. Hell, he was going to insist on it himself. But he hadn't expected it this soon. It shook him considerable, left him empty and desolate.

But if Ram's the man we think he is, it's the best thing that could happen to Tess.

"I'm getting to be a selfish old rascal, Mate," he confided to the tired sorrel. "Wanta eat my cake and have it too, as they say. Cheer up, Soldier. Only a few more miles and this ungodly long march'll be ended."

I ought to be relieved, Lashtrow mused. Couldn't figure any nice decent way to break off with Tess, and now she's made the break herself. I *am* relieved and grateful, yet I'm hurt at the same time. My ego and pride is hurt, I suppose. Ah, the foolish vanity of man! . . . What the hell do I expect? Want all the women to love me, but don't want to have to marry any of them? Well, I been lucky so far. Escaped without making them hate me too much. Lucky here again, and don't know enough to appreciate it. Mewling and pewling around like a schoolboy who's lost his first gal, for chrisake. What the hell ails me? Don't a man ever grow up?

Plodding along, Lashtrow started singing in a low plaintive voice, irrelevantly and almost unconsciously:

"I ain't got no use for the women,
  A true one ain't never been found;
They'll use a man for his money,
  When it's gone, they'll turn him down.

They're all alike at the bottom,
  Selfish and grasping for all;
They'll stick by your side when you're winning,
  And laugh in your teeth at your fall.

My pard was an honest young puncher,
  Upright, straightforward and square;
But he turned to a gunman and gambler,
  And a woman put him there.

All night long we trailed him,
  Through mesquite and chapparral;
And I couldn't help think of that woman,
  As we saw him pitch and fall. . . ."

Laughing at himself, Lashtrow drank water from his canteen, bit off a fresh chew of tobacco, and went dragging on, half-dead from exhaustion on his worn-out sorrel, weird unrelated images flashing through his mind. Tonk Hiller dead in the dirt at Salt Creek . . . Tess as a little girl on his knee . . . Kate Amidon in a hotel room at Fort Worth . . . Deke Vennis laughing through gunsmoke . . . Hoss Crull with blood running down his scarred leather cheeks . . . Anse Amidon holding his dying daughter Kate . . . . Tess Hiller, a fullgrown woman in his arms, her violet eyes shining up at him . . . Kloster, with his beaked nose and down-slashed mouth . . . Travers in Osage buckskins and a Confederate cap, elegant despite powder grime and trail dust . . . Grace Amidon, beaming and motherly over the cookfire . . . . Bouchard chortling through his red beard . . . . Rammel's proud blond head and clean profile, his gay boyish smile . . . . Tess, flushed and laughing in firelight, her golden hair glimmering . . . Steel Huyett grinning over his big bowie knife . . . Tess Hiller crouched at a rifle slit in a mouldering dugout . . . Santee, dashing and devil-may-care at the point of the herd . . . Lyle Myatt, the kid wrangler who wanted action, lying in a bouldered pit with the back off his head blown off . . . Rammel, gracious and graceful, pouring whiskey from a bottle . . . The look and feel of Tess Hiller, the sweet fire of her lips and body.

It was gray morning when Lashtrow walked the sorrel into Winfield, and straight to the livery barn, where he unsaddled and left explicit orders with the hostler for rubbing down, graining and caring for the horse. The town was awakening, business places open, storekeepers sweeping off front steps and galleries, a scatter of saddled horses already at the racks.

Lashtrow had to find a bed before he fell on his face, but first he wanted to get clean. His sweat-soaked dirt-drenched clothes felt like a filthy crust of outer skin and smelled worse. Fortunately the barbershop was open, and there was a dry-goods store where Lash purchased underwear, stockings, shirt and pants. The barber conducted him to a back room equipped with three large barrel bathtubs, and a Negro assistant started filling the one Lash indicated with hot water from a huge stove.

Lashtrow had selected a tub near the wall and shelf, where he could lay a Colt .44. It was always essential to have a gun at hand, the way Lash lived. Every door that opened, every corner turned, might bring some enemy who wanted him dead. Being a Ranger of his status was as bad as being a hunted fugitive. There were men on both sides of the law, who would turn bounty-hunters at the sight of Lashtrow. He had chosen a helluva way to make a living, but it paid a lot better than punching cows.

With vast thankful relief, Lashtrow peeled off the foul clothing and sank into the steaming cask of water. Nothing had ever felt better, not even the ultimate pleasure of sex. After soaking awhile, he stood up to soap himself all over, and then slid blissfully back into the soothing warm depths. He dozed off soon after, unable to keep his eyes open a minute longer.

Lash had no idea of how long he slept, but when he awoke the water was cooling. And Rammel stood before him, smiling and easy but alert, hand casually on his sheathed gun. Lashtrow made no motion toward his own weapon on the shelf.

"You won't need that, Ram," he said, nodding at the holster, and Rammel let his hand drop away.

"I thought perhaps you'd come after us," Rammel said, in quiet cultured tones.

"Well, I did, in a way," Lashtrow confessed. "But just to talk you, no more. Where's Tess?"

"Sleeping in her room at the hotel. We had separate rooms, of course, but I felt too dirty to sleep in a clean bed. Tess got her bath there, but I had to come over here. Did you get the men you went after, Lash?"

Lashtrow nodded. "In Dexter. Vennis killed Morales before we got to him."

"I knew he'd do it, sooner or later. Is Trav all right?"

"He's fine. Went on to camp while I came here. He took Tupelo, and I got Vennis. Deke didn't die right away. We carried him outa town—but he didn't last long."

Rammel looked almost incredulous. "How the hell did you do it? Get into that town, nail the men you wanted, and make it out again. I didn't think it could be done—in Dexter."

"We were lucky, Ram. We were damn lucky."

"You must have been. Damn good and damn lucky, both. Well, that cleans the slate, I guess."

Lashtrow shook his damp bronze head. "Not quite. Vennis talked a little, just before he died. Your hunch about a higher-up was right, Ram. Deke said Kloster set up the whole thing."

"Kloster? Amidon's own foreman all those years? Well, he looks capable of it. And he's been dead-eyeing me ever since I got there. Did you know Kloster was a great womanizer, Lash?"

"No, I never even considered such a thing," Lashtrow said. "He didn't seem any more interested in women than he was in drinking and smoking."

"He kept it well covered up, but one of the old-timers told me he was woman-crazy, practically a sex maniac. Started Kate Amidon off when she was a little girl twelve years old."

"Why, that rotten sonofabitch." Lashtrow sloshed around in his barrel, rose and signaled to the colored boy, who came to douse a bucket of cold water over his head and hand him a towel. "Why don't you take your bath, Ram, while I'm getting barbered up? My hair and whiskers haven't been this long in some time."

"Good idea." Rammel unstrapped his gun belt and started to undress, while the attendant filled another tub with steaming water, and Lashtrow toweled himself roughly dry and got into the crisp new garments.

After the haircut and shave, Lashtrow felt like a wholly new man, fresh and glowing and scarcely sleepy anymore. He sat down to read an old newspaper and wait for Rammel. The barber brought him a mug of coffee, and said, "Recognize you now with that hair off your face. Ranger Lashtrow! Been reading about you in all them papers. Some battle you had down there on the Cimarron, huh?" He held out his hand and Lash shook it.

"It wasn't quite as bloody or heroic as this makes it sound, but it was a pretty fair fight." Lashtrow was reading a lurid account of the outlaw attack on the Amidon trail herd. There were "Wanted" poster sketches of Vennis, Tupelo and Morales, along with official Ranger photographs of Lashtrow and Travers, and an old Matthew Brady picture of Anse Amidon.

Rammel came out of the back room, looking so fresh, young and handsome it made Lash wince inwardly. The barber didn't want to take any money, saying it was a great honor and privilege to serve Ranger Lashtrow and his friend, but Lash insisted on paying for everything.

"It's outlaw money anyway," he explained. "We got a lot of it, so you might as well have some, rightly earned. Here's a buck for the boy, too."

Rammel had shaved in his room previously, so they were ready to leave. The barber recommended an eating place nearby, and they went in there and ordered breakfast. Since his bath, Lashtrow was more hungry than sleepy, but he'd have to spend a few hours in bed before long, he realized.

"I don't know how or why it happened, Lash," said Rammel. "But it just did. We looked at each other and knew it was there, true and real and perfect. I love that girl, and—and I guess she loves me."

"Things happen like that sometimes, I reckon. What are you going to do?"

"We're getting married this afternoon," Rammel said simply.

"That's good. If you're both certain it's what you want."

"No doubt about it, Lash. I know it must look as if we were pulling out before you got back, but it wasn't actually that at all. We couldn't wait. We had to have one another, and I wanted to do it properly."

Which is more than I can say for myself, Lashtrow thought, with irony. We said: "Then I'll stand up with you, or give the bride away, or whatever is done in such a matter. That is if you want me, of course."

"*Want you?*" Rammel thrust his hand across the table, with a smile so radiant that Lash felt dazzled. "We've both been sick over what you might think or feel or do. This makes me happy and proud, Lash, more so than I can say. It'll make Tess happy, too."

"I hope so. Her happiness is my prime concern, Ram. Her dad was one of my best friends."

"I know, Lash, I know. Tess has told me everything."

Everything? Lashtrow thought, with mild horror. Not quite, I hope, not every damn thing . . . . He said, "Let's eat. First real meal I've had in days, or maybe weeks."

They devoured the ham and eggs, potato and biscuits, and called for more coffee. Rammel had a pack of thin cigars, and the tobacco tasted delightful after a good breakfast.

"I've got to catch some sleep," Lashtrow said. "Can't remember when I last had a full night's sleep."

"There are rooms in the Royal Kansas," said Rammel. "That's our hotel, but doesn't exactly live up to its name. However, it's neat and clean. The wedding's at three o'clock, in that little white church down the street. Do you want me to wake Tess?"

"No, let her sleep as long as she can, Ram. You better call me about two, unless you need me earlier."

"You might as well use my room, Lash, the bed's unslept in. I'm so wide awake now I think I'll stay up. I had a

198

notion Kloster might follow us in here, try to break up the marriage or something. There's murder in his eyes every time he looks at me, for some reason.''

"Does he know you rode with Vennis's bunch?''

Rammel shook his fair head. "Don't see how he could know. We never saw him, and as far as I know he never saw us. Only ones he knew were Deke and Fern and Yaqui. Can't understand why he hates me so much.''

Lashtrow laughed quietly. "Kloster hates most everybody. You keep a sharp lookout. He's a sly treacherous bastard. Wouldn't surprise me if he carried a hideout gun, derringer on some kinda small pistol. He's made men think he was giving up, dropped his belt, and then killed 'em with a sleeve-gun.''

"I'll watch him like a hawk, if he does come in.''

"You better call me if you see him, Ram, no matter what time,'' Lashtrow suggested. "My job now is to take Kloster, and I want him.''

Rammel sighed, in regret. "All right, Lash, if you say so. Even though I'd like to take the sonofabitch myself.''

They were strolling leisurely toward the Royal Kansas Hotel, smoking their cigars and talking, with eyes ever watchful. Rammel showed Lashtrow up to his room, and left him there. Lash locked the door, took a drink from the bottle Ram had on the table, stripped off his new clothes and tumbled into the nice white bed, after closing the shades.

He had grown drowsy again, after eating, and he sank almost instantly into deep slumber.

Lashtrow awoke to a rapping at the door, and a room filled with afternoon heat. He went to the door, sweating lightly. "Ram? Are you alone?''

"Right. Tess is waiting in her room.''

Lashtrow unlocked the door and Rammel walked in, asking: "Did you sleep well?''

"Like the dead. Did you see Kloster?" Lashtrow started washing up at the basin of water.

"No. Thought I saw him once, way down the street, but couldn't find him when I got there." Rammel poured whiskey into two glasses.

"He rides a big black stallion." Lashtrow dried his face and hands, and began dressing.

"Yeah, I know. Couldn't find the stud horse either." Rammel tossed off his drink, and refilled the glass. "You know, I'm nervous. Didn't think I would be."

"A man's bound to be, Ram." Lashtrow hand-brushed his tawny shortcut hair. "I doubt if I could stand it." He picked up his glass and clicked rims with Rammel's. "To the bride and groom."

Rammel poured another round. "To the best man."

"The best man never gets the girl," Lashtrow said dryly. "Now why is that, I'd like to know?"

Rammel laughed. "The best man doesn't need a girl perhaps."

"I don't know, Ram." The new clothes felt good on his clean body. He buckled on his guns and tied down the sheaths. He actually hated wearing two guns, but in his case it was imperative. "Is Tessie ready?"

"She's eager. And so goddamn lovely it takes your breath away. She's anxious to see you, Lash. I'll show you her room, and then come back and wait here. You should be alone together."

Lashtrow saluted him with the glass and drained it. "That's damn decent of you, Ram. Very thoughtful and considerate."

"Thank you." Rammel smiled warmly. "Another drink?"

"When we come back."

They sauntered along the corridor to a certain door. Rammel pointed and turned back. Lashtrow felt nervous too, drawn tense and tight. He tapped on the panel. The door swung inward and Tess Hiller stood there, slender and graceful in a white dress trimmed with gold, sparkling like a diamond. He stepped inside, a strange ache in his throat and chest. Tess shut the door and came at once into his arms. He held her firmly, tenderly, his mouth against the soft fragrance of her golden hair, his throat too full to speak. He steeled himself against the warm curved depth of her body.

"Oh, Lash, I'm glad you're here," she said. "I was afraid to face you, but I'm glad you came—in time."

"Why were you afraid, Tess?"

"It—it happened so fast, like magic. Too soon. It made me look like a silly fool of a girl. I was afraid and ashamed, but I couldn't help it. It was there, for both of us, struck by lightning, lost in a storm. Nothing else mattered. Just we two. Oh, Lash—"

"It's all right, baby." He gently stroked her shining head and patted her satiny strong shoulder. "Everything's all right. Ram's a fine boy, you're a lovely girl, and I'm happy for both of you."

"Are you, Lash? Are you really? Oh, I'm so relieved, so thankful, to hear that. And to have you here with me—with us." She looked up at him for the first time, her violet eyes brilliant but brimming wetly. "My friend forever, Lash?"

"Forever and ever," Lashtrow drawled. "You oughta know that, without asking."

"We're so in love, Lash. It's like a miracle. It doesn't seem possible—or quite real. But it is, it *is*!"

"You won't always be this high, Tess," he said gravely. "You're at the peak now, the top of the world, but there'll be valleys, lowlands and swamps along the way."

"I know that, Lash. We know it. But we can take whatever comes, high or low or in between."

"I sure hope so, and I think you will. You'll make it." It was too painful to go on holding her this close. It wasn't easy to curb a desire he didn't want to feel. She was too beautiful in face and form, too lushly feminine and sweet. He moved her lightly away, and said: "Let's go have a drink with the groom. He's too nerved up to be left alone with that whiskey bottle."

They found Rammel pacing the floor, and Tess went quickly to his embrace, her face uplifted. But Rammel restrained himself from kissing her, and Lashtrow's respect for him grew. They fitted well together, a strikingly handsome couple indeed.

Lash smiled fondly at them, and reached for the bottle.

At three o'clock they stood before the altar in the plain white spired colonial church that some transplanted New Englander must have built in in this raw Kansas town. The Reverend Whitmarsh, small, prim and bespectacled, regarded them severely.

"Is it necessary for you men to wear those guns?"

"Yes, it is, Reverend," said Lashtrow. "I'm a Ranger and this boy works for me. There are men out there who'd shoot us down the minute they caught us without guns."

"But certainly they would not desecrate the church of God."

"You don't know those men, Reverend," said Lashtrow. "They'd desecrate heaven itself, if it served then."

It was blessedly brief, and they didn't pay much attention to the words, but in a few minutes it was over, and Aubrey Rammel and Teresa Hiller were man and wife. . . . "Let no one part asunder."

At the front of the church, Lashtrow stepped aside to peer out a narrow mullioned window. "Can't see him, but I got a feeling he's out there."

"We better leave Tess in here," Rammel said.

Lashtrow shook his sandy head, his gray eyes turning emerald-green. "No, you walk out together, natural and easy, Tess on your left arm. I'll cover you. He'll never get off a shot at you, but he might at me. If he does, it'll be too late." Lash eased his right-hand gun in the leather.

Rammel was hesitant about taking Tess out there, but he finally extended his left elbow for her to grasp, and they went out the front entrance and down three steps to the gravel path, with Lashtrow poised watchfully behind the nearly closed oak door.

As they walked toward the street, Kloster appeared suddenly from a little cluster of walnut trees, pistol already drawn, hanging in his large bony right hand. He moved in their direction, a lanky high-shouldered shape, his beaked face distorted, slitted eyes burning blackly, lipless mouth curving down, cruel as the blade of a scimitar.

"So you're married, Rammel? And you're also dead. All in the same day," Kloster said, gloatingly.

"Brave man with a drawn gun," Rammel said, in contempt. "Holster it, you bastard. Give a man an even chance, if you've got the heart."

"I'll give you nothing but a bellyful a lead, pretty boy!" Kloster snarled, teeth showing like a wolf's. "Shove the girl aside. I got better plans for using her."

Rammel pushed Tess gently away to the left, and wondered how long Lash was going to wait. Kloster started bringing up his barrel, and Lashtrow emerged and spoke clearly from the church steps: "Who you going to shoot first, Kloster?"

The unexpected sight of Lashtrow seemed to freeze Kloster momentarily. In that split-second interval, both Rammel and Lashtrow went for their guns with smooth fluid swiftness. Kloster swerved his barrel toward Lashtrow, too late. Lash could have drilled him, but Rammel's Colt was already blasting and flaming, the muzzle flashes pale in the sunshine. Kloster jerked and shuddered backward under the ripping impacts, and his shot went high over Lash's head and splintered the church facade.

Lashtrow still held his fire, letting Rammel have his well-earned victory and finish the job. Kloster was breaking apart, still upright somehow but sagging and floundering about, his unaimed shots tearing up turf and gravel. Rammel sent another slug streaking into that disjointed hulk, jolting Kloster into a slow-spinning fall and loose roll, the dust smoking up around his bloodied body. It was all over now, beyond any doubt. The end of another long intricate and perilous mission.

Tess rushed to the protective comfort of Rammel's left arm, and Lashtrow walked forward with a slow smile, sheathing his unfired .44.

"Nice work, Ram," said Lashtrow.

"Hell, the sight of you paralyzed him, Lash," said Rammel. "Nothing to it after that."

"I never had to fire a shot. Don't think that ever happned before. Told you the Rangers could use a man like you, Ram." Lash smiled at him.

A crowd had gathered about the body of Kloster, and was spilling over in their direction. The town marshal and two deputies came striding up, their curled-brim hats cocked and badges gleaming in the sunlight. Lashtrow thumbed his silver-encircled Ranger's star out of a vest pocket and showed it to them, describing the case with concise brevity.

Some of the onlookers had already identified Lashtrow, and his name circulated through the growing ranks of curious humanity.

"I didn't have to do a damn thing here," Lashtrow informed the law officers and spectators. "My assistant here, Aubrey Rammel, shot the hell outa that ugly bastard. And now, if you'll kindly excuse us, we've got a little wedding party to celebrate."

All eyes were on them as they walked toward the Royal Kasnas Hotel, and tongues were wagging at a furious rate. "Jesus!" a man said. "That Rammel boy must be as good as Lashtrow himself."

"Nobody's that good," an old-timer declared. "Never was, never will be. "I've knowed Lashtrow from way back, and there's only one like him."

No stranger to gunplay and violent death, Tess was nonetheless sickened and shocked, the beauty of her day despoiled and blackened.

The burly broad-beamed marshal and his two scrawny

deputies, overtook them in the hotel lobby. "You know you Rangers got no authority up here in Kansas?"

"Naturally I know it," Lashtrow said. "I told you I had nothing to do with that shooting, and it was pure self-defense for Rammel. That Kloster came at him with a drawn gun."

"And he still put three bullets in Kloster, and got nary a scratch?"

"That's right. I didn't fire a shot. You wanta sniff my gun muzzle?"

"You musta done *something*, Lashtrow."

Lash smiled. "Well, I did ask Kloster which one of us he was going to shoot first." The marshal snorted, and Lash went on: "Rammel just got married. You think he came out of that church looking for a gunfight? Use a little commonsense, Marshal."

"Okay, okay, you're clear and free," grumbled the marshal, and led his deputies out into the street.

The hotel manager approached with an ingratiating smile. "There's a small patio out back where you folks could sit in the shade and have some cold drinks. We've even got some ice today."

They sat at a table in the shade of a great cottonwood, drinking, talking and smoking in private solitude. It was very pleasant, but Lashtrow knew he must get going, and Tess and Ram wanted to be alone.

"Well, back to the trail herd for me," he said.

"You won't like it, Lash," said Rammel. "Ned Buntline and the newspapermen and the packing-house executives are out there."

"I'll get rid of 'em easy." Lashtrow laughed merrily. "I'll send 'em in here to interview you, Ram."

Tess looked horrified. "You wouldn't do a thing like that!" She broke into laughter with the two men. "Of course you wouldn't. I'm still taken in very easily."

"It's true though," Lashtrow said. "The big star in this show only came on in the last act. And he got the girl, too. . . . Well, Milt and I'll be heading home soon. The drive'll be a breeze the rest of the way. When it's over, Ram, I hope you and Rusty Bouchard will come back down and join the Rangers.''

"I think we will, Lash. If Tess can stand being married to a Ranger.''

Tess laughed, with a sound like music. "I'm practically a Ranger myself, Aubrey. I rode and fought with Lash and Milt. I won't like all that roving around you'll have to do, but I can stand it.''

"You'll have to stop using that name Aubrey, or this marriage'll get nowhere,'' Rammel warned with mock severity.

"Sorry, sweet, it just slipped out,'' Tess said coyly.

"Well, we'll see you back in Austin then.'' Lashtrow downed his drink, kissed Tess on the brow, shook hands with Rammel, and left the walled-in patio with his free easy stride. They watched him go, but Lash didn't look back. Their mutual happiness filled him with mingled emotions, ranging from sheer joy to lonely despair.

"There goes some man,'' Rammel said, with a catch in his voice.

"The greatest,'' Tess agreed, with feeling. "Present company excepted.''

"Present company, hell!'' Rammel said. "I know I'm good, Tess. No false modesty here. But that Lashtrow is something else. There'll never be another.''

"Dad always said he was the best.''

Rammel twirled his glass. "You know, he could have taken Kloster himself.''

"Why didn't he then?''

"I don't know. I think he saw I had Kloster beaten, so he let me have him.''

"He took a chance on your life, if that's so.''

"No, he took a chance on his own life. Kloster was going for him, not me.''

206

Tess frowned at her drink. "Maybe he was testing you, Ram."

"Maybe. I don't know."

"You—you've killed before?"

Rammel smiled thinly. "If I hadn't, I wouldn't be here."

"I know, darling." Tess sighed. "A man has to, in this country. But why does it have to be that way?"

"It's new and raw and wild, I guess. If you want to stay alive, you have to kill."

"But what—after—how—?"

"How do I feel?" Rammel finished for her. "I don't feel good. I don't like it. But it's better than being dead. And I don't like to talk about it either."

"I'm sorry, sweetie. We won't talk about it."

"Are you happy?"

"I was—until that happened."

"We're going to forget that, baby." Rammel grasped a bottle of brandy and two glasses. "It must be around siesta time, my lovely. Let's go to bed."

"I wondered what the hell you were waiting for," Teresa Hiller Rammel said, with a gay lilt in her voice.